Zayden's eyes bulged with fear

"Wait!" The desperate man leaned toward Mack Bolan as he spoke. "I'm serious. Rabin's death was a contract killing. I was the one who delivered the request. I was the courier who delivered the up-front payment, the guns, all those things."

"Nice coincidence for Kassem," Bolan said, "someone else wanting the same guy dead. And willing to pay for it, too."

"Just because someone else footed the bill doesn't mean Kassem wasn't happy about it."

Bolan considered that. Once it had become clear that the Libyans had made the kill, the big American had assumed Kassem had done the deed to get even. "Fair enough. Lots of people wanted Rabin dead. So who hired him?"

Bolan unleathered the Beretta.

"And don't tell me the intel is above your pay grade."

Don Pendleton's Mack Bolan®

Illicit Supply

BLOOD MONEY

BOOK 1

A GOLD EAGLE BOOK FROM

WORLDWIDE®

TORONTO • NEW YORK • LONDON
AMSTERDAM • PARIS • SYDNEY • HAMBURG
STOCKHOLM • ATHENS • TOKYO • MILAN
MADRID • WARSAW • BUDAPEST • AUCKLAND

Recycling programs
for this product may
not exist in your area.

First edition September 2013

ISBN-13: 978-0-373-61563-6

Special thanks and acknowledgment to
Douglas P. Wojtowicz for his contribution to this work.

ILLICIT SUPPLY

Printed in U.S.A.

War is an ugly thing, but not the ugliest of things. The decayed and degraded state of moral and patriotic feeling which thinks that nothing is worth war is much worse. The person who has nothing for which he is willing to fight, nothing which is more important than his own personal safety, is a miserable creature and has no chance of being free unless made and kept so by the exertions of better men than himself.

—John Stuart Mill
1806–1873

My war includes trying to save the world from its savages, but it seems, sometimes, that I'm one man fighting a brush fire. Stamp one spark into oblivion, and another flicker of flame rises elsewhere. I'll continue the good fight until my last breath, because I am a person who has something to fight for.

—Mack Bolan

CHAPTER ONE

Zachary Winslow double-checked his gear. Actually, this was the fifth time he'd gone over it. He was getting tired of waiting. Medellín wasn't one of his most favorite cities in the world. Sure, things had quieted some since the eighties when it had been called the most violent city in the world, when there was open warfare and brutal bloodshed between the cartels. Medellín was still dangerous, still too hot, still too damned alien to him. Winslow hated himself for giving in to prejudices, but sometimes stereotypes didn't disappear when encountering people who were on the wrong side of the law. Sometimes they were reinforced.

Winslow was in Colombia with a detachment of the United States Secret Service, and the mission wasn't in Medellín itself. They were heading outside the city. Winslow forced himself to stop double-checking the magazines of 5.56 mm NATO ammunition for his SR-16 rifle, stop making certain every snap and strap on his load-bearing harness was drawn and tight. It was the wait, the predeployment jitters.

His Secret Service team was coordinating the mission with a group of locals who had no compunctions about smoking cigarettes. Winslow remembered the trouble, the struggle he'd gone through trying to break that damned habit. The nicotine hanging in the air begged for his attention. He had to keep from inhaling deeply. Back in the U.S., he wouldn't have been exposed to this much secondhand smoke, mostly due to health regulations.

Here, it was like being a diabetic in a candy store. So much good, so much wrong, so much temptation.

Winslow fought off the urge to succumb to his baser desires. He felt that grabbing a cancer stick and sucking it like a baby with his bottle would be an even worse betrayal of himself. He grumbled.

The locals looked at him. They'd seen the way Winslow had looked at their cigarettes, and had made offers of coffin nails. He'd have loved one—they could probably see the way he paled, yearning for a shot of nicotine—but he refused.

"Keep denying yourself the pleasures in life, and you'll end up regretting your old age," Miguel Villanueva told him. Villanueva was one of the old guard of the local law enforcement, and as such, he was allowed some eccentricities. He wore his silver hair under a black fedora that he was never without. Winslow could not make out the age of the man, because he had a sort of youthful cast to his features, but obviously he had been around.

Villanueva was a legend in Colombian law enforcement, and there was a bounty out on his head, one that had not been collected, but not for lack of trying. Because of his status, Villanueva was given some leeway in his choices of appearance, his personal gear and who he wished to work with. Previously, he had been part of the JUNGLA, the Colombian National Police's elite anti-narcotics strike force, which penetrated the rain forest in order to combat the flow of cocaine that fed the cartels.

Later, he became one of the key members of Search Bloc, the elite organization which, allied with the U.S. intelligence and special forces assets, had taken down Pablo Escobar, dismantled the Medellín Cartel and then moved on to Cali, finishing off those two powerhouse cocaine organizations in the nineties. His most recent work had been against the North Valley Cartel, which had been working south of Medellín, but now they were expanding northward from Cali.

Search Bloc had asked the Secret Service to send in a group because they had been encountering more and more counterfeit bills, both Colombian pesos and U.S. dollars. The money was of extremely good quality, recognized as being fake only by the fact that several pages had not been cut, and the serial numbers were all wrong. With a counterfeiting operation involved, Winslow and his partners were on their way to Medellín.

Winslow looked at Villanueva. The man didn't smoke himself, anymore, but he placed a pack on the table next to Winslow.

"Miguel, man," Winslow began.

Villanueva shook his head. "We've got a few more minutes before we take off. Instead of trying to calm jittery nerves with busywork, why not take a puff or two. Living forever is overrated."

Villanueva took off his black fedora, folding it tenderly, and placing it under his body armor next to his heart. He turned and walked out of the ready room.

Winslow's gaze was locked on to the pack of cigarettes. His nose wrinkled as he looked it over.

He was wearing body armor, and was armed to the teeth with a .357 SIG-Sauer pistol and a special-purpose version of the U.S. military's M-4 carbine. Trauma plates covered his vital organs, and in a few minutes, he'd tug down a Kevlar pot over his skull to keep a bullet out of his brain. With everything he had, Winslow still knew that such armor and protection was scarcely enough to ward off death. There was armor-piercing ammunition, fragmentation grenades, rocket launchers and all other manner of mayhem that could be unleashed.

He would be facing down bullets and bombs, and yet he was afraid of one more dose of nicotine, arsenic, ammonia and a cocktail of other poisons and carcino-gens that would take years to kill him. Winslow picked up the pack. It was new, the foil still unwrinkled from where one cigarette had been taken.

Unsmoked cigarettes had that smell, a delicious, wonderful scent that was even sweeter than the rush through his lungs. Winslow thumbed open the flap, and the aroma wafted up seductively, the evils in Pandora's box beckoning to him.

Winslow shook his head. "You little fuckers are going to kill me."

He tapped the pack. One of the cigarettes presented itself, jutting upward. The next thing he knew, the lighter flared, its hot sizzle hissing as he lit one end of the cigarette. One deep breath, the burn entering his lungs, and he pushed the smoke through his nostrils after cycling it down through his lungs.

"Damn, I missed you bitches," Winslow muttered.

"Zack!"

Winslow was roused from his nicotine trip. It was Bradshaw, his helmet tugged on, goggles obscuring his eyes. Winslow felt almost drunk with embarrassment. "What?"

"The engines are all starting. Grab your shit and let's go!"

Bradshaw left the doorway, and Winslow turned, scooping up his helmet. His fingers brushed the sling of his rifle when the floor shook beneath his feet, a sudden harsh breeze whipping through the doorway from the outside. Winslow turned, insensate, the cigarette dangling between his lips. A cloud of dust rushed in, scouring past his face, chips of stone and splinters of wood peppering his bare cheeks as he blinked against the sudden gust.

With the flow of wind came a thunderous roar. Later, he would realize that vibrations traveled through solid matter faster than they would air, so when the high explosive rocket hit, the tremor ran through the ground, beating the crack of thunder in the air by a millisecond. The next thing that Winslow knew, he was being tackled to the ground, his shoulder smashing hard against the concrete as he was pinned down.

The thunder had trailed off into staccato pops of gunfire, especially deep and throaty and extended. It was heavier than the sound of Secret Service SR-16s and Colombia National Police-issued 5.56 mm Tavor-21 rifles. Winslow remembered the noise, though, from his time in Iraq. That constant rumble was the all-too-familiar growl of an M240 light machine gun, the big Thirty that he and his fellow marines used to make the insurgents cower in terror. The M240 punched through brick and automobiles and chewed up whatever human was on the other side.

The only thing better than having an M240 on your side in a firefight was getting an M-2 Browning, which took rolled steel armor plating and turned it into Swiss cheese, but there weren't any men who could carry such a beast on a sling or fire it from the hip, let alone the shoulder like an M240.

Winslow hoped that the CNP had one of those weapons firing on whomever launched the rocket that struck the building. If not, he knew he was going to be in for a bad day, because being on the receiving end of such firepower was going to be brutal.

Winslow pushed aside the man who had tackled him. Only with a side glance had he seen it was Villanueva, stunned and dazed from a chunk of the ceiling falling onto him. He reached the doorway, then watched the wall opposite his doorjamb suddenly vomit out divots of smashed brick and plaster, ultimately exploding and crumbling in an avalanche to the floor. Just like he'd seen after battles in Iraq when one of his Automatic Gunner squad mates had cut loose on a house full of bad guys.

Winslow couldn't find his rifle, but he tore his SIG-Sauer P229 pistol out of its holster. He had three spare magazines for the weapon, and hoped that forty-nine rounds would be enough to contribute to the fight going on outside. Up until now, his general opinion had been that if he couldn't solve a problem with just a 12-round magazine and one up the pipe, that payload adding up to a grand total of three and a half tons of muzzle energy, then he shouldn't have gone pissing off Tyrannosaurs in Jurassic Park.

Being on the receiving end of a light machine gun had changed that thought quickly enough.

Something struck him like a hammer. Once more, Winslow bounced to the floor, hurled down by the impact. Once more, his sore shoulder met the concrete with agonizing force. He rolled onto his back, struggling to breathe.

The only thing that had saved the man from being cored like an apple by a round from the M240 had been the thickness of two brick walls and the ceramic plate of his body armor. Had he shifted his position by an inch, that slug might have found only layers of Kevlar to punch clean through.

Out of breath and hurting like hell, Winslow rolled. Villanueva struggled to his hands and knees. His silvery hair was matted down, streaked with blood from where a chunk of ceiling had split his scalp. His eyes were unfocused, the only time Winslow had ever seen the man without his wits about him, always searching his surroundings with a trained investigator's eye. Another shock wave rolled through the ground under Winslow's back, and Villanueva toppled onto his face, thrown off balance by the blast.

The Secret Service agent grimaced as he tried to sit up, but Villanueva shouted something. Later on, his conscious mind would make out the Spanish for "Get down!"

Even so, his unconscious mind translated, and he went flat. More bullets tore through the wall, missing him, their passage whipping his hair off his forehead. Winslow clenched his eyes shut and winced.

He was helpless. Any effort to try to fight back would end in only one way.

He'd be sawed in two.

Hating himself, he played dead as bullets tore apart the ready room and explosions shook the floors above.

MACK BOLAN HATED to watch these videos. It was never pleasant in any instance, but as he sat, thousands of miles away from Kuala Lumpur, days after the event, he could only note the utter impotence at seeing suffering that he could do nothing to alleviate. Three days ago, he thought. He'd just been in Florida, putting down another coalition of drug dealers and murderous psychopaths.

The Executioner tried to save the world from its savages, but he was one man fighting a brushfire war. Tamp down one spark, stomp it into oblivion, and another wisp of smoke, another flicker of flame, rises elsewhere. And while Bolan knew he couldn't be everywhere at once, he loathed the gruesome reminder of that truth. A gruesome reminder that was written in shrapnel-ripped faces, torn and bloody clothing and crying, frightened people clutching friends or loved ones as sirens wailed and news reporters stood outside a perimeter.

"I'm sorry, Striker," Brognola said as he fidgeted with the remote control.

"It's a necessary evil," Bolan answered, studying the screen. "Has Gary seen this?"

Bolan referred to Gary Manning, one of the many genius-level members of Phoenix Force. Prior to joining the free world's most elite and secret strike force, Manning had been both a demolitions expert, utilizing high explosives on a daily basis, and he had also been a counterterrorism agent for the Royal Canadian Mounted Police.

The big Canadian had set up demolitions while on missions for Stony Man Farm, and had been present on other occasions to see the horrible aftermath of terrorist acts where explosives had been used against innocent people.

"He has," Brognola returned. "I just wanted to see if you came to the same conclusion."

Bolan nodded for Brognola to pause the video, then motioned for the remote control.

He rewound the footage until the television cameras had a good image of the side of the American embassy in Malaysia. Bolan was slightly surprised with himself at how easily he could compartmentalize the concern and worry for dozens of State Department workers, both American and local Malaysian, who were wounded or killed by this attack. He needed emotional control, however. This footage looked like a terrorist attack. The placement of the blast craters in the side of the building, each of them vomiting smoke, flickers of orange flame frozen on the high-definition monitor on the wall, had indicated that someone had used precision rockets with deadly effect.

Bolan had swallowed his anger at this attack on sovereign American soil and noncombatants. Those wounded would heal. Those murdered would be avenged. That was the one thing that the Executioner could make sure of.

"From the state of the damage incurred, we're looking at thermobaric warheads from a shoulder-mounted system," Bolan stated. He traced several of the craters, showing how the walls seemed to have been punched in, the building dented by the fist of an invisible giant. "While there is significant damage, you can see where the rooms shot seemed to have imploded."

"Part of why they call the damned things 'vacuum bombs,'" Brognola said. "The explosion produces so much heat and force that ground zero of the explosion actually has most of the air pushed away."

"Air pressure drops so sharply, the resultant partial vacuum actually causes an implosion in the room where the warhead detonates," Bolan said. "You get that kind of damage from some of the more advanced RPG-7 compatible rocket grenades, but U.S. embassy protection wouldn't have let one man, let alone three or four, within the two hundred meters necessary to produce a one-in-two chance of hitting even a building."

"What makes you think that their shots were so precise?" Brognola asked.

Bolan rewound to a point where they could see the whole face of the stricken embassy. "Nine hits. All on windows, not on walls."

"The importance?" Brognola asked.

"Glass doesn't necessarily provide the proper surface to set off an impact fuse for a shaped charge," Bolan said. "You get an explosion, but these warheads are meant to breach targets as thick as six inches of concrete, and they detonate with a shaped charge effect spearing into the room beyond the wall. A thermobaric explosion, on the other hand, is meant to go through gaps and detonate at the proper range to create the overpressure inside of the structure it wants to hit. The shooters knew to aim for the windows, as opposed to just lobbing standard RPG shells at any target of opportunity. They wanted to hit the rooms and offices that they were aiming at, not send missiles deeper into the core of the building."

Brognola nodded. "That's what Gary thought, as well."

Bolan didn't relish that kind of an intellectual victory. "As the embassy is built to withstand attacks, especially against RPG shells, the walls shouldn't have collapsed so easily. That means we're looking at something with greater range, and precision at that range, and a greater explosive capacity than usual."

Brognola tilted his head.

Bolan frowned. "We're looking at either an Israeli Shipon or a U.S. Military Shoulder-Launched Multipurpose Assault Weapon. And the warheads are specifically SMAW-NE, Novel Explosive, which our soldiers in Iraq have been using to great effect in urban operations. That can explain the collapse of the walls, and five hundred meters is the limit for most soldiers to get a hit on something as large as a building."

"How long is your best recorded shot?" Brognola asked.

Bolan shrugged. "Seven hundred, but I'm used to wind drift and bullet drop."

Brognola nodded.

"So who was visiting the embassy on that day?" Bolan asked.

The big Fed frowned. "You know that it was someone specifically targeted."

"They were aiming at offices. One was the intended target, the others were collateral damage to obfuscate investigations," Bolan returned.

Brognola drew out a clear plastic evidence bag with burned papers within. "The People's Republic of China sent a special activities division operative to our embassy with samples. Those were all that was recovered."

Bolan picked up the bag, but even before touching the evidence, he could see the familiar patterns of a U.S. one-hundred dollar bill, and its yuan equivalent, damaged by fire and blast, but still recognizable. "All that was recovered?"

Brognola nodded. "They were good shots. The overpressure and the heat of the thermobaric explosion all but made sure that any paper within the offices hit was incinerated. Blast pressure was the only thing that threw these things outward."

"Counterfeit money," Bolan said.

"We had our Secret Service technicians take a close look at that, and it was confirmed," Brognola said.

"Chinese yuan," Bolan mused. "Any other country's denominations?"

Brognola nodded. "We've also had an incident, earlier this morning. We had a Secret Service team in Medellín, Colombia. Colombian pesos and American money was picked up by the CNP, and that prompted Homeland Security to assign a squad to go there. They were going to accompany a Search Bloc team to a suspected printing press. Everyone was armored up, armed to the teeth...."

"What happened at the incident?" Bolan asked.

"As the task force was getting ready to leave the station, they were cut down by light machine guns and more rockets," Brognola said. "The survivors recognized the guns as M240s. The American survivor was able to place the sound of the rocket as a SMAW-NE. He'd been in action in Iraq, and used more than a couple to knock down buildings where insurgents were dug in."

Bolan looked at the screen. "Casualties?"

"Thirteen killed, dead right there. Five wounded, but they're so bad, it's not likely that they'll survive. There were two who suffered minor injuries, and that's just from the combined strike force. There's another dozen who were hurt just because they were in the building," Brognola replied. "Ironic little twist. The one American survivor stopped to have his first smoke in five years."

Bolan frowned. "Usually they say those things could kill you."

"I know you've stopped," Brognola returned.

Bolan managed a weak half smile. "In this case, it was a lifesaver."

The big Fed sighed. "In this case, nicotine flavored."

"Who was the other person who suffered minor injuries?" Bolan asked.

Brognola tapped the file. "You might know him from a couple of romps down Colombia way. Miguel Villanueva."

Bolan knew him. If there was a man outside the Stony Man project who had worked with the Executioner, no matter how peripherally, it was Villanueva. Mostly it was a ghost relationship, the Colombian cop keeping a line of cold drops open to feed the Executioner data about the situation in his country. Since Villanueva had operated in the two deadliest cities in cartel history, Medellín and Cali, the info that he gave to Bolan had proved vital.

Villanueva was a back-channel source that had been worth his weight in gold. Without that man, Bolan wouldn't have had a tenth of the success he'd gained against the Colombian cocaine cartels, or their allies farther up in Mexico and Central America.

"How is he?" Bolan asked.

"He caught a mild concussion, but by the time you get down there, he'll be on his feet," Brognola returned.

Bolan nodded. "You want me to head to Colombia first."

"The crime scene is fresher, and it's closer to home," Brognola explained.

"What about the other agent?" Bolan inquired.

"Zachary Winslow. Former marine. Current Secret Service," Brognola rattled off. "Good man, despite a stumble here or there."

Bolan shook his head. "I'm not worried about a misstep. In this case, it saved his life. The real equation is how many times he's fallen, and how many times he's picked himself up."

"Knocked down six times," Brognola said. "Stood up seven times."

Bolan smiled, allowed himself a half of a nod. "I'll work with him, if he's up and ready to fight."

"Bruised ribs and a torn muscle. Again, he'll be fine by the time you get down there," Brognola stated.

Bolan opened his file packet. "Chinese yuan. Colombian pesos. U.S. hundred dollar bills."

Bolan then squinted at the monitor, the damaged embassy. "Sixty people dead, scores more injured. Real dollars aren't worth one human life, so there's no way counterfeit is a good excuse for this."

Brognola nodded. "That's why I'm sending you. If anyone can collect the Devil's dues, it's you."

Bolan gathered up the file material that Brognola had assembled for him. He'd familiarize himself with all of it, burn it into his memory before he got on the flight to Colombia.

The murderers who had been so brutally active over the past few days were going to pay, and the Executioner would take compensation in blood and bullets.

CHAPTER TWO

"That bastard has the Devil's luck," Diego Millagro grumbled as he finished watching the documentation that his hit men had taken. It was the eighth time he'd watched the assault on the CNP station, and despite the glorious carnage wrought by light machine guns and rocket launchers, he was frustrated. The assault had derailed the raid on their printing presses long enough to get the equipment out and moved to a new, safer location, and it had gutted the investigative group under Captain Miguel Villanueva. But once more, that damned cop had survived, avoiding permanent injury and death, despite the searing, searching trails of autofire from machine guns firing armor-piercing ammunition.

"Are you having a problem?" Alfa Molinov inquired.

Millagro grumbled. "What is it to you? The operation is still secure."

Molinov nodded. While Millagro was tall and thin, with long ropy limbs and corded muscle, Molinov, who was the exact same height, looked as if he were three times the mass of the Venezuelan. While his stomach and face showed fat, a sausage-pinched stomach flowing around his belt and a second chin, which would make a pelican jealous, Molinov's forearms were a hint of the raw muscle hidden behind that soft exterior. Bulging muscles and flowing veins betrayed the power to snap a man's neck like a twig.

Millagro knew better than to upset the Russian, just for that. He hadn't fought his way to the top of the Russian mafia by being a weak sister or some gourmand with no strength to back his appetites. Despite the way Molinov was squeezed into his clothes, Millagro needed to be sharp to catch sight of the big German .45 pistol the man wore on his waist beneath the linen, tropic weight jacket.

"The printing presses are fine. But Villanueva still lives," Millagro admitted. "And that bastard has more life in him than a cockroach."

Molinov nodded with understanding. "A troublesome policeman. And he's survived this long?"

"He lived through Medellín," Millagro answered. "Back when we killed judges and elected representatives with impunity. Hundreds of cops caught bullets, or were left with our special neckties...."

Molinov's brow wrinkled for a moment. "Oh, yes. The Colombian necktie. You slice the throat from the chin back, then pull down the victim's tongue through the opening."

Millagro nodded.

"And you didn't attempt to give him this gift?" Molinov asked.

"He's got the knife scar on the tip of his chin," Millagro answered. "But he fought his way out. Against three men, unarmed, he was able to fight his way to freedom."

"You should have shot him in the head," the Russian stated.

Millagro sighed. "We did. The bullet didn't penetrate, so it skittered along his skull under his scalp. We thought he was dead."

"Fascinating," Molinov noted. "And so, he survives yet again."

"I have a person at the hospital. He's due to be released, along with the sole American survivor, tonight," Millagro explained. "I would love another crack at killing him off. We take down Villanueva, chances are that it will demoralize the CNP enough for..."

Molinov shook his head. "You won't do it."

Millagro felt the hairs on the back of his neck bristle. "Why not?"

"I will have my people make a move," Molinov stated. "Chances are, the authorities will be expecting cartel members. This matter shall require more subtlety."

"Subtlety might just expose your people's involvement in this," Millagro countered.

Molinov nodded. "Already, they are aware that you've gone further than simple old Soviet castoff equipment ferried through Cuba back in the days of the glorious revolution. We're no longer operating with fifty-year-old rifles and rocket launchers, but the newest of guns and bombs."

"So you want the U.S. and Colombia to be on the lookout for the Russian mob in their backyard," Millagro said.

Molinov smirked. "I want them to be afraid. The American public became squeamish at the losses they incurred in the Middle East for a decade. Loss of lives, targeted attacks by skilled, brutal attackers, will do the same work for us."

Millagro's eyes narrowed. "Are you…"

"The lack of stomach possessed by the North Americans is legendary. Because of that, they failed in Vietnam, they ran with their tails between their legs from Beirut, they buckled in Somalia and in Bosnia, and they eventually crumbled in Iraq and Afghanistan. We strike now, decisively, show them what they are against, and show them the losses we are willing to inflict, and the cowards will recoil in terror," Molinov told him.

"And if not?" Millagro asked.

"Then it will cause tension between Colombia and the U.S.," Molinov said. "The American military will want to send in their mightiest weapons, but that will grate on Colombia's nerves. We end up splitting the union between the two governments."

Millagro frowned. "You've only got a few hours to assemble the components for an attack. You can do this, right?"

Molinov chuckled.

Millagro bristled at that dismissive noise. "It took us a week to draw this damned team to where we could hit them, putting the presses at risk in the process. Now, you've got three hours to arrange a hit on a hospital!"

Molinov reached out and laid a calming hand on the slender Venezuelan's shoulder. "Your Villanueva will be a corpse soon."

MIGUEL VILLANUEVA PASSED by Zachary Winslow's room. His bag was sitting on the mattress next to him, but he wasn't packing his things. Instead, he was hunched over, head bent out of sight from the doorway, shoulders bunched up to totally obscure him. He stepped through the doorway, but left the door open, taking up only a small space, so as not to let the younger man feel suddenly penned in. He spoke softly, gently. "Zack?"

"What?" Winslow returned, his voice low, sullen, the words crackling through a raspy throat.

Villanueva took a step closer to the hospital bed. "Is something wrong?"

Winslow lifted his head. His hair was a tousled mess, strands standing up and poking everywhere. There was a slight turn, and Villanueva caught a brief glimpse of a livid, battered redness on the side of his head, just above his right ear. It looked like a blossom of raw colored petals, the newly shaved hair revealing the pattern of fist-size fresh bruises that would darken soon. Winslow looked away, hiding it behind his right shoulder.

"Zack, what happened to your head?" Villanueva asked, walking around the bed.

For a moment, Winslow turned, trying to hide the side of his head, his beet-red ear, his bloodshot eyes and raw eyelids.

"Don't look at me," came Winslow's response, this time a growl.

"Punching yourself in the head is stupid. It's not going to bring your team back," Villanueva told him.

Red-rimmed eyes glared out of Winslow's face. "It's the only pain I can control. It's the only thing I still have any control over, because God help me, I sure can't control my nicotine urges, and I sure can't control the aim of the guys who couldn't shoot me!"

"Zack…" Villanueva said. "Zack, I know how you feel.…"

"Really?" Winslow asked, snapping to his feet. His

sudden rise made him wobble for an instant, his balance unsteady, but he stiffened, held straight and tall, looking at Villanueva. "You know what it's like to watch as, for the second time in your life, your friends are blown up and you're, at best, only a spectator?"

"I've had people try to kill me for the past twenty-something years because of my job," Villanueva answered. "I know what it's like to have something miss me, and then hit someone I care about. I've lost too many damned friends to count!"

Winslow brushed Villanueva aside and walked around him, heading toward the door, leaving his bag behind. Villanueva could tell that the younger man was fuming, torn from within, and getting into a pissing contest about friendship and loss, who had the bigger right to survivor's guilt, wasn't going to get him anywhere quickly. The Colombian cop jogged toward the door after Winslow, reaching out and touching his arm.

"Zack, wait. Hold on," Villanueva said softly, apology flavoring his words. "Zack, come on, sit down."

"It wasn't just losing someone. I was there fighting with some when they were shot, when they went down," Winslow answered. "I pushed to reach them, saved one or two, but lost others."

"It was how you just missed getting killed this time," Villanueva intuited.

Winslow nodded. "In Iraq, it was a quick piss break against a wall, just out of sight of my Humvee. I'm painting the wall yellow, and the next thing I hear, the bombs are exploding, and people are screaming. My squad isn't in that group, because they took an RPG right through the door they left open for me."

Winslow suddenly went green, and he pushed past Villanueva, slamming open the lavatory door and losing the contents of his stomach into the sink, unable to reach the bowl just a foot beyond. Tremors shook through Winslow's body, racking heaves releasing loud cackles as abdominal muscles contracted violently, pushing out only air and pain after the acidic splash of bile into the basin.

Once more, Winslow's legs looked as if they were going to turn to rubber, but Villanueva took hold of his belt, the best handle available to keep the younger man from toppling to the floor, causing even more damage to his head. Even as he thought about Winslow's physical being, the puffy scar stitched closed at the back of his head reminded him that there was worse hurt present on his own skull. The chunk of ceiling hadn't fractured bone, but the impact had torn Villanueva's scalp. It had taken the doctors an hour to rinse all of the dust and concrete splinters out of the wound before bringing out that ominous hooked needle, which had looked for all the world like it should be used to capture half-ton tuna rather than poke through someone's skin.

The pain washed up, but Villanueva ordered himself not to allow his own nausea to overtake him. His body trembled once, as if in chuckling response to Villanueva's hubris at being the master of unconscious responses, but his stomach held.

For now.

Winslow leaned on his elbows, his forehead balanced precariously atop the sink's faucet. One trembling hand reached up and turned the spigot, water pouring from the tap and cutting through the greasy concoction that had been emptied into the basin. It was swirling into the drain, and Winslow whimpered once, then gasped in a breath to replace the one which had come out in a near-sob.

"We'd better get to the emergency room," Villanueva said. "Maybe you gave yourself a concussion...."

"Maybe I don't care," Winslow croaked.

He reached back and pushed Villanueva's hand off his belt. He was slowly regaining his strength as he managed to stand once more. Winslow regarded himself in the mirror, as bleary eyed as a jilted bride, his cheeks sagging and mouth slack and dumb.

"Good Christ," Winslow grunted as he took inventory of his half-wrecked body. His fingers ran over his clean-shaved head, the short hairs that had been there that morning scoured away by a cheap disposable razor and a handful of shaving gel.

Villanueva picked up the mess of hairs and shaving foam in the tub.

"Zack?" Villanueva spoke, trying to distract Winslow from his own visage.

"I don't remember taking off my hair," he muttered.

"Damn it, look at me!" Villanueva shouted.

Winslow turned, slowly, like a zombie hearing something that almost sounded like food. That half-awake quality was cast into Winslow's features, and Villanueva wondered if the man were dying inside, or simply wishing he were dead.

"This time, it was just sucking on a coffin nail. And then when the shooting started? Instead of running out with my dick in my hand, like when my Humvee was hit, I curled up on the goddamn floor. I hid instead of rushing out," Winslow said. "You know what I'm saying?"

"I was hugging that same floor," Villanueva said.

It wasn't registering with Winslow. He was caught in an unreeling loop, pouring out his words. Winslow saw himself as nothing better than a traitor, as guilty of killing his friends as if he'd been the one manning the trigger of the light machine gun, or firing the rockets that split the transport trucks asunder.

As such, he was on a total disconnect right now. He couldn't think rationally. Accusations flew, and he absorbed every one of them. No wonder he'd punched himself in the head; he was right. The absolute only thing that he could control was the pain he inflicted upon himself, and focus on that throbbing headache was his sole means of distracting himself from the silence that dominated his thoughts.

Orderlies were at the door, drawn by the shouting. Villanueva pulled his badge, snapping for the men to stay back. He hated pulling rank of that sort, but the last thing that Winslow needed was to be crowded, even by well-wishing friends or nursing staff. Villanueva did his best to direct traffic, pushing people out of the room, leaving Winslow to stand in the washroom, fighting off the urge to cry.

Villanueva knew that, despite his years, despite how inured to the pain he thought he was, he was teetering on the same edge of breaking down and crying over his own lost friends. Guilt was a vicious, hungry beast that never let go after it first smelled the blood in the water. He leaned against the wall in the hallway, taking deep breaths, his eyes closed. Even with them shut, he could feel the sting of tears starting to form, the faces and names of his fallen comrades coming unbidden.

He sent up a silent prayer to the Universe to send something to pull him out of his own inward spiral to depression when his cell phone buzzed in his pocket. Rather than get in trouble for using a cell phone in a public space in a hospital, he turned and walked into Winslow's room. He moved to the window, cupping his phone to his ear.

"Hola, Villanueva," he said softly into the microphone.

The voice was deep, strong and familiar. Villanueva had spoken to the man over the years, referring to him by different nicknames, as "La Mancha," as "Striker," as "Stone," as "Cooper" or as "McCormack." The Colombian cop had his suspicions as to who this man without a name truly was, but he kept it under his black fedora, another secret in a career already topped with them. Whatever his true name, lost to the annals of history may it be, there was one universal truth involved with this "stranger."

When Villanueva talked with the man, bad things happened to even worse people.

"Special Agent Matt McCormack, Justice Department," the man said, establishing the identity he was using for this mission. "I assume you remember me."

"Absolutamente," Villanueva replied. "I hate to seem rude, but..."

"You've had an extremely bad morning," Bolan stated. "And I've had a very long flight, Miguel. I just landed and I'm on my way to the hospital where you are."

Villanueva blinked. "You know?"

"I was alerted to your current situation only this morning," Bolan told him. "I figured after all the years you've been on my contact list, now was the time to meet."

Villanueva looked toward the washroom. "Things are very complicated at this moment."

"I know," Bolan said. "The problem is, they're so complicated that I needed to come down here. You had a near miss this morning, and judging by the way these things unravel, I'm concerned for your safety and that of Agent Winslow."

Villanueva felt an eerie déjà vu at the American's statement. "You *are* up on current events."

"I wish I'd been even more so. Maybe a lot of good people wouldn't have died this morning."

Villanueva took a breath, and in a moment of absentmindedness, gave away the farm. "I already have Winslow beating himself up, both figuratively and physically."

There was a grunt on the other end, and Villanueva wondered if this mistake hadn't been one that could leave his young American counterpart in even worse condition.

"The best thing we can do to alleviate all of this survivor's guilt is to occupy ourselves with something productive," Bolan told him. "That's why I'm coming to pick you two up at the hospital. Some other mutual friends have set us up with a safehouse so that you can advance your recovery, and I can be briefed further on the investigation that blew up in the first place."

A wave of relief cut through Villanueva when Mc-

Cormack said that. Action was usually the best therapy. That was one truth that Villanueva was keen on. "All right, then. How soon can I see you?"

There was a moment of silence on the other end.

"According to GPS, I'll be there in about forty-five minutes," Bolan returned.

"I'll be expecting you, then," Villanueva answered.

Winslow stepped out of the washroom. "Who was that?"

Villanueva regarded the young man. He'd let out a ton of self-poison in his system, vomiting, crying, venting his rage on the only target he was certain that he wouldn't hurt.

As such, Winslow was a little more sure of foot, standing tall and balanced. His face was still a wreck, but he'd washed the crud and tears off, and his cheeks were a little rosier for having been scrubbed. His breathing was even. Orderly. He'd be good.

"We're getting a visit from a friend of mine," Villanueva said. "And after that, you, me and he will go to work finding the bastards who attacked us."

Winslow wiped his mouth. "After all the shit I pulled here?"

Villanueva cut him off with a wave of a hand. "You need something to rage against. Let's put that energy to good use on the truly guilty parties."

MACK BOLAN HAD lied about being forty-five minutes away from the hospital. Sure, he was in his car, but the Executioner's instincts were jangling like a station house during a five-alarm fire. Villanueva was in danger, and from the vicious focus and the building-punching weaponry used in the attack on the police station, the goal of the ambushers was not just to cripple the combined CNP-Secret Service task force, but to utterly destroy it. It was a message the cartels of old would have fully approved. This was as much a demonstration of power and ruthlessness as had been the brutal attack on the U.S. embassy in Malaysia. No one was to be safe where this counterfeiting operation was concerned.

As such, Bolan, tired from his six-hour flight, had grabbed a satchel with an Israeli-made Desert Eagle in .44 Magnum, a 9 mm Beretta pistol and holsters and spare magazines secreted within. The soldier had come in on a chartered flight, and as such was able to go directly to customs officials. His badge and credentials, supplied by Hal Brognola, had been enough for the officials to think nothing of a foreign lawman bringing a couple of big, powerful handguns into their country.

As he waited in the parking lot, Bolan finished threading the hip holster for the Desert Eagle through his belt, then closed the belt. It felt good to have the weight of the .44 Magnum pistol on his right hip once more, balanced out by the Beretta tucked away under his hip-length, summer-weight dark blue linen jacket. A light white shirt beneath kept him in the fashion made popular by the neighboring president of Venezuela, an open collar with no tie and a stylish blazer.

While Bolan was well armed enough for a night on the town in Chicago, the violence of recent days, if not recent years in Colombia, might prove to be more than even the mighty, near rifle-range Desert Eagle and the high-capacity, sleek and quick Beretta could handle.

Even so, the reason the soldier carried such a pair of weapons was because, between them, they provided both the stopping power and the volume of fire necessary to handle most urban threats. He'd pitted these guns against opponents with AKs and other deadly enemy firepower in the past, and he didn't intend to fall today, so he'd go toe to toe with such foes again.

In the end, it was Bolan's reflexes and marksmanship that would either carry the day or end it with him lying in a puddle of gore.

There was one more factor, Bolan reminded himself. His wits. The ability to observe the landscape, to pick up details, to scan for threats and paths of action. His intelligence, battle savvy and force of will had carried him to victory on more than one occasion.

The soldier had pushed his schedule as hard as possible, within reasonable traffic laws, to observe the hospital, scan for threats. He wanted to arrive in time to intercept the two surviving lawmen as they departed the facility.

A half-dozen lawmen were waiting outside the building, but their alertness was waning as the clock ticked down to the release of their comrades. Earlier, in the excitement and confusion of the arrival of wounded, the guards posted were on edge, wide eyed and ready to repel any assault on the building.

Now, Bolan picked up on yawns from the men. The long day had been trying for them, and because it was nearing the time of Villanueva and Winslow's release, their commanders had opted against assigning fresh officers on duty. Bolan could sympathize with how tired these men felt, but he made use of self-discipline and the skills of years in the battle zone to relax his muscles.

No, he wasn't as refreshed as he would have been after eight hours of sleep, but he was limber now, and alert. Ready.

He spotted the delivery truck's arrival.

Its chassis was low to the ground, meaning that the vehicle was heavy. The driver had avoided parking, or even passing too close to the boredom-numbed guards on station. There were two men, one driving, one riding shotgun and, through a pocket telescope, Bolan could see the silhouette of a gun barrel, complete with the familiar front sight of a Kalashnikov-style rifle, rise above the window, but for only a moment.

The side door opened, and despite being a soft-drink delivery vehicle, there were only more men in the back, no stacked boxes of cans, no palettes of six-packs or plastic bottles. He saw one of the men in the back tuck the unmistakable boxy silhouette of a submachine gun magazine back under the folds of his long jacket, black metal showing up underneath the white fabric.

Bolan checked his watch.

Five minutes remained until Villanueva and Winslow would walk outside the hospital's door.

The timing was no mistake.

The doomsday numbers were tumbling, and there was only going to be one way to prevent a massacre in the hospital parking lot.

The Executioner fired up the engine and peeled out of his parking space, wheels screeching a banshee wail.

CHAPTER THREE

Villanueva was no fool. He had pushed Winslow as hard as he could to be up and ready to leave. The schedule said that they were due to be gone in about fifteen minutes, but the Colombian cop pushed it. If the man he knew as "Striker" were in the vicinity, then there was a damn good chance that something bad was about to happen.

The criminal conspiracy that had caused him to meet with Zachary Winslow in the first case had already displayed such contempt for the law that they had no qualms about firing heavy weapons at a police station. A dozen good men were dead, two more still dying in ICU on the floor above. Only luck and happenstance had kept Villanueva and Winslow from standing directly in the path of concentrated murder.

He knew that McCormack, as he was calling himself now, was on his way, and most likely already on the property, but Villanueva was hardly someone to let another person fight his battles for him. The Colombian cop had been disarmed of his SIG-Sauer P226 service pistol when the ambulance crew dropped him off in the emergency room. Unarmed, Villanueva had lain uncomfortably in his bed until one of his fellow CNP officers, a plainclothes man who had been assigned to watch his door, had poked his head in for a moment.

After some begging and cajoling, Villanueva had borrowed his friend's "throw down," a Taurus Millennium Pro in 9 mm Parabellum. The pistol was scarcely larger than a pocket .38, but it could hold a full twelve rounds in the magazine. It sagged a little in the pocket of Villanueva's trousers, but fashion wasn't foremost on his mind. He was otherwise unarmed, naked to any who would come to murder him.

At least now, he could fire a few shots in self-defense.

Winslow walked steadily beside him, over his emotional turmoil, having expelled it with the contents of his stomach in the washroom. Where before, his eyes had a glassy, unfocused quality, now they returned to life, flicking from subject to subject, scanning left and right. When something that was just entering the younger man's peripheral vision drew his attention, he imperceptibly moved his head to at least follow it from the corner of his eye.

Winslow was back. It might have had something to do with the promise of going after those responsible for the ambush on the police station, a chance for redemption at McCormack's side. It wasn't a strange concept; a purpose in life was what gave most people a reason to get out of bed in the morning, even in the worst of times.

Villanueva looked at the exit.

He saw the delivery truck that had pulled up. Something was eating at his instincts, but he didn't know what.

That's when he heard the squeal of tires and the roar of an engine.

All hell was breaking loose.

BOLAN RELEASED THE brake on the rental car and the screeching wheels grabbed on to the asphalt. The vehicle picked up speed instantly, taking flight as it hit a bump in the road on the path to the delivery truck. He'd hoped that this maneuver would at least catch the enemy off guard, and while it did so, one of the more alert members of the ambush team reacted by pulling out his submachine gun, a personal defense weapon—PDW—of some sort that fired powerful enough bullets to perforate the windshield.

Bolan didn't mind being the target. Every bullet directed at him and the bulk of the car was one that was not fired at innocent bystanders. Even though the PDW rounds went through the glass, the very effort of penetration caused them to veer off course, so the Executioner had a brief instant of protection just before the front fender of the vehicle impacted with the side of the delivery truck. Rubber shrieked as a 3000-pound missile hit the frame of the larger vehicle. Velocity plus mass, however, overwhelmed the inertia of the truck and shoved it sideways, causing tires to shred before the two vehicles impacted with the wall of the hospital, stopping them both.

Bolan pressed the release on his seat belt, a precaution he'd taken before throttling into the ambush vehicle. He'd been in enough collisions, accidental and intentional, to realize the importance of such protective measures. He'd also been prepared, braced for the sudden expansion of the air bags deployed from within the steering column. He'd kept his neck loose, and tried to keep his weight backward. As such, he didn't smack the suddenly inflating bag with his face. Too often, he'd seen allies with broken noses or eyes bruised and swollen shut from such an interaction with a safety bag.

The seat-belt release didn't want to respond, so rather than fight with the mechanism, he drew his Spyderco pocketknife. It was a tool that the Executioner rarely left home without. Not only was it a substantial blade, able to sever jugulars or puncture skulls with its well-honed steel, but it swiftly opened with its large thumb-holed hump. He could snap the blade from its folded position with a simple flick of his thumb. The first thing he did was to use its sharp, beaklike point to puncture and deflate the bag to give him a better view out the windshield, then he brought the blade down. The serrated portion of the knife edge attacked the nylon of the belt strap, shredding it easily. It took him only two seconds to deflate the air bag and sever the seat belt, his eyes up and searching for the enemy.

The gunman who had been alert enough to pour lead through his windshield was still down, shocked and stunned by the powerful collision. Bolan's sedan carried more energy along with it than all but artillery cannon. Had he hit a man with the same energy with which he'd struck the delivery truck, he'd have burst him like a balloon filled with tomato soup.

Bolan pushed open the door, which was already ajar. His left hand tugged the Beretta 93R from its spot in his shoulder holster. Even as he adjusted his grip on it, his index finger stabbed the fire-selector switch to 3-round-burst mode. Then his forefinger went to the frame as he aligned the sights of the sleek little machine pistol.

There was movement inside the back of the delivery truck, but it was halting. From what he could see, four men were back there, but they had been thrown into such a tangle that they were having a hard time getting moving. Even so, they had been lucky that the frame of the truck absorbed much of the impact, preventing limbs from being crushed, despite how they had been tossed about. Unfortunately for Bolan, the men in the cab seemed to be crawling out the doors with much more agility than the tossed mess in the back, and the rear doors of the truck flapped open, two gunmen having leaped clear even as the gunfire began.

Bolan swung to the rear of the car, getting the trunk and the wheel axle in front of his stomach and legs. He'd have preferred to have the engine block between him and the enemy, as their rifles could easily punch through sheet metal, while the heavy mass of the engine would provide more cover. Even as he positioned himself, though, he brought the front sight to bear on the face of one of the two gunmen who was drawing his AK-style rifle to his hip. One stroke of the trigger, and the Beretta spit its lethal payload out of its six-inch barrel. Bolan's hand loads meant that they left the muzzle at over 1350 feet per second, and the trio of 124-grain hollowpoint rounds impacted with the equivalent force of three-quarters of a ton of kinetic force.

The rifleman's head snapped back, a geyser of blood erupting from the tennis-ball-size cavity where his nose and eyes used to be. Struck in the fatal triangle, the gunman's brain was vaporized. He died, his body paralyzed and collapsing into a loose mass of folding and crumpling limbs. The second gunner had his rifle at his hip, as well, and he pulled the trigger.

The nonsighted fire was low, bullets tumbling into

the car and way off target from Bolan, but the shooter was turning, walking rounds toward the emplaced Executioner. The big American shifted his aim, took another step to the right and fired, pulling the trigger twice. Six bullets smashed into the hip-firing gunner, one 3-round burst catching him in the chest, zipping a line of destruction along his breastbone from sternum to throat, the second triburst touched off as Bolan tracked the tumbling gunman, spearing through his stomach and up into his heart.

Torn apart from two directions, the second rifleman was reduced to a cooling corpse on the asphalt. The Executioner took three steps, swinging around to use the other side of the car as cover, even as a heavy handgun bullet smashed into a side window and fractured the rear windshield from the inside.

Bolan straight-armed the Beretta, aiming right at the passenger. His long arm had been lost, but the guy was packing a .44 Magnum pistol, or something equally as large. Its fearsome slug had destroyed two windows, and was embedded in the windshield of a parked car. The soldier didn't want another round to be fired, if anything, the next time, he wouldn't be so lucky that the bullet would avoid civilians who were still in a scramble for their lives. The shooter, however, realized he was outgunned and ducked back into the cab of the delivery truck.

Bolan held his fire. The Beretta's hollowpoint rounds might stop in the truck's windshield, but he didn't want to risk lives any further. Instead, he lowered the machine pistol and pulled the Desert Eagle with his right hand. The mighty .44 Magnum autoloader could penetrate the steel shell of the delivery truck with killing force. The Executioner aimed the hand cannon at a spot just to the right of the door. He could still see the shotgun rider's feet kicking, and he tried to get back into the vehicle to slither out on the other side. Bolan lowered his aim and fired once, twice.

The two slugs, boat-tail hollowpoints loaded hot, struck the metal shell of the delivery truck at an angle, punching through the passenger seat. Bolan fired down, hoping to intersect the fleeing hit man's legs. The sudden wail accompanying shattered leg bones informed the Executioner that his aim was true. If there was one thing that he needed, it was the identity of the attackers, what cartel they were with.

Even so, the oddity of the man shouting in an Eastern European Slavic tongue, not Russian, gave the soldier more information than he'd expected so soon after landing in Colombia. Bolan stepped back around his accordioned sedan, moving toward the cab, Desert Eagle leading the way. Hushed curses in that same Slavic language were thrown at the broken-legged ambusher.

As the Executioner popped into view, he saw the driver duck out of sight, but a flurry of gunfire suddenly rattled. Sheet metal perforated under the onslaught of a machine pistol, the driver trying to discourage pursuit.

More gunfire rattled, and the soldier realized that the tired, end-of-shift policemen had suddenly entered the fray. Colombian National Police-issued Galil ACE rifles chattered, spitting their response to the armed killers on hand. A quick glance out of the corner of his eye showed two men among the police at the hospital entrance, both armed with tiny handguns, and he recognized Villanueva's black fedora. The Colombian cop was directing traffic, which was probably the only reason that he hadn't been blindsided by a storm of automatic gunfire from the national policemen.

"McCormack! Stand down!" Villanueva shouted. Bolan thumbed his Beretta 93R and the Desert Eagle onto Safe, returning them to their respective holsters. He raised his hands and stepped away from the delivery truck.

"Any survivors?" Bolan asked as the CNP men swarmed the truck.

Villanueva shrugged. "I thought you weren't going to be here for about an hour."

Bolan checked his watch. "You were early."

Villanueva grinned, but the sweat on his brow betrayed that he wasn't so nearly as glib as he was pretending to be.

"No survivors," one of Villanueva's protectors said. He wiped the back of his hand across his forehead. The CNP lived a life of danger, no one could ever deny that, but getting into a blazing gun battle was something that hit everyone's autonomic system as hard as a freight train. Pulse racing, nerve axons firing more quickly, fine motor controls thrown out the window, even the Executioner, despite his countless battles against hordes of enemies, still got the sweats and shakes from time to time. No matter how courageous, how used to it you were, the human body had its responses to stress and attack.

Bolan frowned. "They were speaking some Eastern European language, as far as I could tell."

"Eastern?" a man spoke up in English. Bolan recognized him from Brognola's files. This was Zachary Winslow, the lone survivor of the Secret Service team.

Bolan extended a hand. "Special Agent Matt McCormack, Justice Department."

Winslow took the offered shake, and Bolan noticed that he had a sidearm in his left hand. It was small and flat, but the slide was tall, indicating that it wasn't a blowback pistol. He finally recognized it as a Walther PPS, which was a full-powered 9 mm or .40-caliber Smith & Wesson handgun, one of the truly slim and compact pistols with a comfortable grip that filled the average-size man's hand.

"You must be Agent Winslow," Bolan said. "Nice to meet you."

Winslow nodded, and answered in a low monotone, "Under the circumstances. Thanks for taking out the ambush."

"I spotted their guns, and didn't think that Medellín SWAT had a soft-drink-delivery unit," Bolan returned. He called upon some of the off-the-cuff humor he'd been exposed to by countless allies. Maybe a little bit of amusement would draw the sullen, numbed Secret Service agent out of his funk.

Winslow smirked. "I don't think so, either."

The other lawmen on the scene checked Bolan over, examining his guns and checking his documentation. They regarded the telescoped front end of the rental car, clucking their tongues, exchanging a few words and laughter that was as tainted with nervous titters as genuine humor. Bolan wasn't concentrating on translating what they were saying, and they spoke quickly, hushed, just out of earshot. Bolan's Spanish was conversational, and he knew enough specific terms to be of use in military and police situations, but unlike Italian, the romance language he *was* fluent in, half-heard whispers only translated to gibberish.

"I've had other people try to kill me before, Mc-Cormack. What brings you here at this specific time?" Villanueva asked.

Bolan nodded to Winslow. "American Secret Service men are dead. Funny money is popping up in the U.S. and here in Colombia...and across the Pacific. Made this visit a little heavier than just a personal appearance for a friend."

Villanueva nodded. "All right, then."

"You two *have* met before, right?" Winslow asked.

Both men shook their heads. "We keep in contact via back channels," Villanueva went on to explain. "I'm his resource for Colombian cartel-related intelligence."

Winslow nodded. "But you recognized him immediately."

"No one makes an entrance like he does," Villanueva added.

Bolan sighed. "I only crashed my car into theirs because that was the quickest way to incapacitate the whole group. And even so, I had the beginnings of a raging gunfight."

He looked around, triple checking. Sure, they were in a hospital parking lot, and the emergency room would be able to treat wounded bystanders, but the whole purpose of Bolan's ramming speed ploy was to completely curtail such violence. So far, there was no indication of anyone other than the Slavic assassins having been injured. He still felt tense, because there could have been someone out in the lot, even across the street, who might have been hit.

"Other CNP units are on the way. They'll radiate out from the lot and look for anyone injured," Villanueva said. "I think you landed on things hard enough and fast enough to prevent any bystander casualties."

Bolan nodded. "All right. I would offer the two of you a ride to our safehouse..."

Winslow looked at the accordioned sedan and frowned. "That should buff out."

Bolan smiled. The Secret Service agent had recovered his sense of humor. "It's a rental...."

"Ah," Winslow answered. He shrugged. "Say it was like that when you rented it."

Bolan shook his head.

Villanueva wandered to one of the officers. *This* conversation wouldn't be so much of a mystery to Bolan. Villanueva was going to borrow a car, at least until the soldier could arrange another ride. Bolan also was glad that he hadn't actually deprived a rental agency of a vehicle that gained revenue. This was from another member of the Medellín police department, a drug seizure that the Executioner could abuse and destroy as necessary.

The policeman that Villanueva was speaking with leaned out and nodded. Bolan repressed a smile; it was the same officer who had been responsible for the "rental."

The cop nodded and handed over the keys to a car, no questions asked. He then gave Bolan a small salute. The soldier returned the gesture. Villanueva came back.

"That was Rudy Rojo," Villanueva told him. "He's kind of our 'used-car salesman.'"

"Yeah. Seizures from criminals, right?" Bolan asked.

Villanueva grinned. "Oh, that's who rented you the car."

"You know I'm not going to take food out of an honest person's mouth," Bolan told him.

"I'm glad he was here to get us a replacement so quickly," Villanueva noted. "But he said I had to drive the car. Something about not being made of cars or some such."

Bolan nodded. "That's understandable."

"Let's get to that safehouse," Villanueva said.

Winslow shook his head. "Justice Department guy comes in and only picks up two partners. Never had anything to do with this investigation until today. You bring a machine pistol to a hospital gunfight…and we're just going to continue working? No paperwork for a shooting or ten?"

Bolan frowned. "Where you are now, paperwork is going to be the least of your problems."

Winslow tilted his head. "We're going off the reservation."

"We're going on the warpath," Bolan cut him off. "This already is becoming something far bigger than I expected. I knew that there might be some Malaysian, maybe some Chinese involvement, but the addition of Eastern Bloc nations makes this something much worse than just a counterfeiting ring. This is big, and it's bad, and it has to be put down in the most agile means possible. It goes without saying that we've already got too many dead lawmen on the case…."

"We're living on borrowed time," Villanueva agreed.

Winslow remained tight-lipped.

"If you don't want to get bloody, I can appreciate that," Bolan told him.

Winslow shook his head. "I'm just trying to get my head wrapped all around this. You're Justice Department, and this changed from a counterfeiting investigation to a vigilante strike."

Bolan didn't say a word, only nodding in assent to Winslow's assessment. "I call it justice."

Winslow folded his arms. The Executioner knew that most lawmen took a chance to step outside the boundaries of normal operations, though the subject of many fantasies, as a serious step over a moral line. Bolan had never been a lawman before his career as a lone warrior against the hordes of Animal Man, he had been a soldier, and he had been assigned to search-and-destroy missions, as well as sniping behind enemy lines. To him, he came and brought the concepts and tactics of war to the criminals who had worked hard to place themselves outside and above the law. Arrest was never an option, though Bolan allowed men to escape, to turn themselves in, rather than face his grim wrath.

Winslow seemed to be conflicted. He'd seemed haunted when he'd come outside, and had retreated back into himself, evaluating the opportunity that the soldier presented to him.

"We're going to war," Winslow said softly.

"Unrestricted," Bolan added. "No…not totally unrestricted."

"No civilians, no cops just doing their jobs," Winslow stated.

Bolan nodded. "We're going to war, not engaging in mass murder. Folks have tried to equate the tactics I'm suggesting to a wild, crazed killer, but the truth is…"

"The truth is, you can't bear to even shoot a guilty cop," Winslow said.

Bolan didn't have to answer. The young American seemed to be adding it all up and drawing a conclusion.

"We're going to need guns that we know," Winslow offered. He looked down to the Walther that he'd tucked into his pocket. "Full-size service pistols, maybe some submachine guns, assault rifles…"

"I've got the tools to go to war. All you have to do is bring your own will to wage it," Bolan explained.

"You're good with this, Miguel?"

Villanueva nodded. "I've heard what he has done in the past, based on my offered intelligence. Now, I'm sure I want to have a go at the men who murdered my friends, and do it his way."

Winslow extended his hand, no longer cutting himself off from Bolan behind folded arms. "All right."

Bolan took his hand. They shook.

One man became three, though Bolan knew that he would do as much as he could to protect them. The Executioner was a hands-on leader, and wouldn't allow them to take any risks he couldn't assume himself. Still, three against a conspiracy was better odds than one.

CHAPTER FOUR

Alfa Molinov braced himself for what shit he knew that Diego Millagro was going to throw his way when the news returned that their hit squad had not only failed to eliminate Miguel Villanueva and the lone American Secret Service agent survivor, but had been completely wiped out. Once more, he was going to have to listen to a bout of backseat driving and planning that was spouted by a less-experienced man. He didn't mind listening to such vapid oral sputum, but he also didn't want to cause any rifts between the South American side of things and the rest of the organization. As such, he knew he'd have to bite his tongue.

Millagro entered the Russian's office, but his face was calm. Maybe he hadn't heard about the atrocious failure.

"You've received word that all of your men are dead?" Millagro asked.

The Russian swallowed. He didn't like it when people took such news with quiet, understated calm. "Yes."

Millagro nodded. Molinov scanned him. The Venezuelan didn't appear to be concealing any firearms, but guns could be made so small that they fit into a pocket. While useless for defense at range, Molinov had used a mere 6 mm bullet at muzzle contact range to eliminate several men.

Even so, Millagro was not attempting to close the distance, moving into a position where a single tiny slug could scramble his brains through an eye socket or a nostril. The Venezuelan nodded once more. "Do not worry, my friend. I'm not going to kill you."

"That's a relief," Molinov noted. "What now?"

"Now, we continue doing what we must. Protecting our assets," Millagro stated. "I'm having our presses left where they are, and doubling the guard. If we go probing and hunting for Villanueva and his allies, that will only give them angles with which to approach us."

Molinov frowned. "All right. Why are you suddenly so collected?"

Millagro's eyes flared for a second, the first real emotion that the Venezuelan had shown since he'd walked into the office. His lips were drawn tight.

"Because I have seen this happen before," Millagro answered. "One of the cartels gets a little too bold, a little too aggressive, and then they drop a five-ton hammer on American cops. Before the bodies are even buried, someone comes down here."

This was experience talking. Real nerves. Real fear. But Millagro was doing his best to keep it under control.

"Things go differently. Sometimes it's one man. Or three men. Or five. The worst was when there was an army, about ten of them. They hit a Colombian estate with assault helicopters and all kinds of deadly stuff. The place was razed, and that was when they were still utilizing some high-tech unmanned combat drones," Millagro said. "This time, it looks like we're only getting one of them, but it's that loner who is the worst. The most relentless."

Molinov's hairs stood up on the back of his neck. "I've heard similar stories. So?"

"They're not just stories," Millagro said. "But for the record, every time we've drawn this level of heat, then actively tried to stomp it out, we've ended up screwed seven ways to Sunday. This time, I want to try a different tactic. I want to button down, go on the defensive and not give those bastards an inch if we can help it."

"That might be good for you...."

"We call him *El Soldado*," Millagro said. "In the Middle East, he's Al Askari."

"A loner. A single man like that does not exist. It was the work of someone else...whole groups of people, but all carefully crafted. This way, we're looking in one direction for a lone, mad dog vigilante, and we crumble."

Millagro sighed. "You don't buy that any more than I do."

"So what are you saying?" Molinov asked.

"Whoever the Soldier is...he's bad news," Millagro said. "I hope that your men were smart enough not to have much identification with them."

"They were," Molinov replied. "They are...were, professionals. They knew about operational security."

"I hope so. Because right now, we are in a state of war," Millagro stated. "And once they come gunning for us, we have to hunker down and bear all that they can throw. There's going to be no turning this to our advantage, no matter what we pull in."

"But we can get outside help," Molinov replied.

"You're going to draw more attention?" Millagro asked. He was growing irritated now. Molinov eased off, just in case the Venezuelan had decided to bring in a .22 to put a bullet in his brain.

"No. We are going to call in some hitters who have no attachment to the current organizations on the ground," Molinov said. "A freelance squad."

"Who?" Millagro asked. "Who could keep this Soldier from recognizing that it's Venezuelans messing with Colombian money?"

Molinov shook his head. "We let the Colombians go after them. I drop a dime that an old enemy is in town, they sure as hell will set up a hunting party for him."

"The Colombians," Millagro grunted. "You mean, the cartels?"

Molinov nodded. "This way, you score either way. The enemy is already under the assumption that this has something to do with cartel cocaine operations, perhaps a branching out. A Colombian manhunt comes down on them, we could easily muddy the waters so that no one comes sniffing by our back door."

"That's a good theory. Can you make it work?" Millagro asked.

"There's only one way to find out," Molinov stated.

"This better work," Millagro growled.

Molinov didn't answer. He punched a number into his phone. This call had to go through channels to keep it clean and sanitized. If the man they presumed was after them was as good as the stories said he was, then there was a terrible possibility that even this measure wouldn't be sufficient.

Molinov knew that if this were the case, the next time that Millagro came around, he would not be so terribly patient.

BOLAN CLEARED the safehouse before allowing Villanueva and Winslow to enter. He didn't want them taking any unnecessary risks, but as his friends in Able Team and Phoenix Force often told him, he would play mother hen to a SWAT team even if they were armed to the teeth. Given his lifetime of experience, Bolan didn't feel as if he could be blamed for being concerned with the ability of others.

Sometimes friends with decades of conflict under their belts were taken down by the oddest of coincidences or accidents, while newcomers with no prior encounters rose to the occasion with natural ferocity and courage. Either way, Bolan was fully aware that Villanueva had been struck in the head, even though the X-rays showed little indication of traumatic brain injury. Winslow was an emotional wreck, as well as having to walk off near rib-shattering blows that had been stopped only by two brick walls and his bulletproof vest. Neither was going to be operating at peak capacity, despite how readily they brandished firearms and joined the CNP protection team in responding to the attacks.

Still, both men took to checking all the rooms, making a layout of the place, not quite trusting Bolan enough to validate that the safehouse was completely clear until they saw with their own eyes. That was a level of preparedness and professionalism that had been indicated in their files, and with interviews with their friends, all present in the data package that Brognola had assembled. They'd taken their knocks, but they still had a keen presence of mind, and a sureness of purpose.

Finally, after the safehouse was declared clear, and Bolan did a taste test on a pot of strong, locally grown coffee, the three of them rested at the kitchen table. The homegrown brew was not just strong, it was a diesel train engine, dragging blood through a tired man's veins with machinelike speed and efficiency.

"I knew there was a reason I liked being here," Winslow mentioned as he took a second sip, but only after adding half a glass of milk to dilute the power. "Coffee just doesn't get stronger unless you expose it to a gamma-ray bomb."

"And even then, you might like it if you're angry," Villanueva added.

Bolan once again settled into a state of relief that they were able to shake the stresses of the day.

The past eighteen hours had been terrible for the two men, having been attacked and having lost their friends in a brutal and vulgar display of power by the counterfeiters early in the morning, and then ending up as the targets of another assassination attempt only two hours prior. Bolan had grown accustomed to days when he'd been forced into battle more than once in an afternoon. "All right, McCormack. Do you have a plan for what we're going to do?" Villanueva asked.

"I would have asked you to get some sleep in the meantime while I shook out some leads, but this coffee…" Bolan began.

Winslow's jaw stretched open, and he let out a long, baleful yawn. "I'm a mutant, Agent McCormack. Caffeine makes me sleepier."

He took another sip. "I'll be dozing in ten minutes if the conversation doesn't improve."

"I'll try to be as boring as possible," Bolan returned with a grin. "What about you, Miguel?"

"I want to make a few calls around," Villanueva replied. "I know all the notes I have are trying to point this at being a Colombian connection, but it doesn't feel right. First off, the money being made is too perfect. It reminds me of the kind of thing that was being put out from the Bekaa Valley in Beirut back in the early nineties, I believe."

"The super notes," Bolan returned.

"On the one hand, the money was good for supplying the insurgent groups keeping the nation unstable, and supported operations into Israeli territory," Villanueva noted. "But the real threat was that the notes were so good, they posed a major threat to the United States currency it was copying."

Winslow perked up. "That's why we have holograms, watermarks, proprietary ink, even intelligent fibers woven into the fabric of the paper now. The bad guys are trying to keep up technology-wise, but even so, it's easier for them to make older money from older dollars."

"Go back to being sleepy," Bolan said.

Winslow shook him off. "That's what brought me and my team down here. I wasn't the lead on this operation."

Bolan could see a crack in Winslow's resolve. He watched the agent take a sip of coffee to wash those thoughts away. "I wasn't the lead, but I still was impressed with the reality of the notes being produced. They have the EURion constellation with the right ink, and showing up precisely where necessary. That takes some snazzy ink work and printing capability. And... here's the clincher. We've had the design in the wings since 2009, and there has still been trouble getting it off the ground."

Bolan frowned. "They're using a noncirculated bill as their basis?"

Winslow nodded. "That means they got deep, deep, deep into our holy of holies. This is like Dracula walking into a Catholic hospital blood bank in the Vatican on Easter Sunday at high noon. Shit ain't supposed to happen!"

"That should be stopped and blown up any dozen of ways before it got that far," Bolan returned.

Winslow sat back. "Sick skills, whoever thought that shit up. They release that money, you might as well kiss the American monetary system goodbye."

Bolan frowned.

"The Colombian *pesos* being fabricated are of equal skill," Villanueva said. "So, I know that the cartels prefer operating in U.S. currency, so why are they making billions, trillions of counterfeit bills that would wreck both Colombian and American monetary values?"

"Because it wouldn't be the cartels. They want to make a profit, and really, as long as there is a jungle, as long as people are hungry enough to give over their land for growing or processing cocaine, they're raking in all of the cash that they'd ever want," Bolan answered.

Villanueva nodded.

"So, who would like to see Colombia and America tank economically?" Winslow asked. "I'll give you a hint…"

"Venezuela," Bolan interjected.

Winslow raised an eyebrow. "That obvious?"

Bolan nodded.

"You're no fun to play with," Winslow grumbled.

"No fun to play against," Bolan corrected. "When you're on my side, things could go your way pretty well."

Winslow looked down at the cup of coffee, trying to stifle a yawn, but it stretched and slithered in through his nostrils, popped his ears and rustled heavily out his nose. The whole process made him blink heavily. "Well, you do get great coffee for your safehouse."

Bolan gave him a salute. "Just rest up. You've had a hell of a time."

"What about you?" Villanueva asked.

"I'm not half as bad off as you two," Bolan replied. "I've only been in one fight today. Not two."

Winslow nodded, his eyelids drooping. "Don't let me sleep too long."

He got up from the table, taking his coffee with him.

"Sleepy from coffee." Villanueva sighed. "I wish I were wired like that."

Bolan shrugged. "Who are you going to call?"

"I have my sources," Villanueva stated. "What about you?"

"I generally hang myself out to dry, but I think that I came down too hard and too quick on the attack against you," Bolan stated. "They might not want to draw attention by focusing more resources against me."

"So you're going to try and figure out the Eastern European angle on this," Villanueva responded.

Bolan nodded. "I'll rattle a cage here and there and get some answers."

"Things are going to get even more messy tonight," Villanueva mused.

Bolan tilted his head questioningly. "You worried about them?"

"Nope," Villanueva answered. "If they know who was behind the murder of my fellow officers, they deserve all the heat they catch for remaining quiet. Get them to sing, *amigo*."

"You're preaching to the choir," Bolan returned.

With that, Bolan went to a closet, retrieved a war bag and went to a spare car in the garage.

Medellín had plenty of rocks to kick over, but the thing about kicking over stones in Colombia was that there were all manner of poisonous spiders, snakes and scorpions that could come out and bite you to death.

IF THERE WAS one thing that Bolan counted among his many assets, it had to be the wealth of connections he had available to him. Through those people, he had the names and locations of various people of interest around the world. He had files on major international cities that, if they fell into the hands of the FBI, would clear the decks of all manner of global small-fry across the planet. Unfortunately, Bolan knew that the vast majority of these were middlemen, people who kept their ears to the ground, and when threatened with some rough treatment, would be quick to cough up names and addresses of even more important folks.

In a city such as Medellín, things would have been easier for a white man like Bolan. Seventy percent of the city was made of ethnic whites, in contrast to the more common *mestizos,* those who were the product of couplings between Spanish colonists, European refugees and the indigenous tribes of the nation. The thing was, as long as people kept their mouths shut, it would be relatively easy for Eastern Europeans to blend into such a populace.

As opposed to North American cities, where the downtown urban sprawl was usually where crime was the densest, in a metropolis like Medellín, the center of town was the richest, the most prosperous and the best protected. In South America, rather than being a "pioneer nation" like the U.S., where expansion moved outward, seeking more room, prosperity tended to "castle up" and the poorer, more lawless clove to the walls like barnacles. Despite still having one of the highest murder rates in the continent, if not the world, there were districts of the city that hadn't seen a homicide in over a decade.

Bolan didn't have exact statistics on Medellín itself, but violence had peaked in 2009 with close to three thousand violent deaths. In some outskirts of the city, gunfights out in the open and armed, paramilitary gangs were the norm. One thing that Bolan detested in this town was the presence of the worst kind of vigilante movement—*las Aguilas Negras*—who had no qualms about murdering prostitutes, drug addicts and alcoholics with the same ferocity as actual violent offenders. They were no better than the Brazilian thugs who used law and order as an excuse to murder the homeless in order to cleanse the streets of Rio.

Bolan knew that there had been some Russian mafia involvement in Colombia, but mostly it was importing arms to leftist insurrectionists such as the FARC, a gigantic paramilitary guerrilla organization looking to overthrow the elected government of Colombia. The

FARC had been responsible for decades of violence, working as muscle for the cartels while publicly despising the very capitalism that funded their war on democracy. The mafia didn't care to whom they were selling AK-74s, they just liked the money.

Even so, former Eastern Bloc countries did have a few ties to the country, but the most recent blatant example of that had been back in 2000. Russia's mob, however, wasn't the only one with the ambition to stretch out across the world. There was the Janev clan, Serbia's answer to the mafia, as well as the Bulgarian mafia, the Chechens, the Estonians…

That was why Bolan needed to get some answers from people on the ground in Colombia. Villanueva was going to call in his contacts, so the soldier was turning his sights toward the shadows he knew that only he could reach.

He stepped into a club, dressed for the role of walking angel of death. The black fingertip leather duster was smooth, shiny, soft, an affectation that Bolan wouldn't have normally worked with, and he had on a pair of polarized sunglasses. The lenses were designed to make things like the blazing flashes of a full-on rave or the laser sights and tactical lamps of many assault weapons dim while allowing him to see easily in darkened rooms. The technology was akin to the polarization used on state-of-the-art NASA helmets, and cutting edge. All in all, Bolan dripped the image of wealth and power, all the while being a big black pillar of imposing humanity.

The coat did little to hide the butt of Bolan's Beretta with its extended magazine, nor the flash of the Desert

Eagle in its hip holster, but concealment wasn't an issue here. He came as death on two legs.

A bouncer saw him coming and was like a deer in the headlights. The man had been hired because he was a bodybuilder, tall, with bulbous chest muscles that made the rest of his body seem tiny, including his head. His neck rose from a plateau of deltoids, sheets of tissue ending just behind his jaws. His bald head shone, almost comically as his eyes went wide.

Bolan walked up to him, put a hand against his chest and gently brushed the man aside. The soldier would have had more resistance from a cranky two-year-old, which informed him that the image he was projecting worked like a charm.

Now, all he had to do was find the owner of the club.

Bolan paused, scanning the crowded club. Men and women were pressed together in a living sea of amorous, drunk and drugged flesh. The salty tang of sex hung in the air, sweaty bodies wrapped in little or no clothing grinding against each other to the hypnotic, droning electronic music that provided a breathless atmosphere to the place. Bolan was glad he'd chosen to slip a few cooling chem packs into the pockets of his athletic shirt, otherwise he was certain that his core temperature would be soaring in such a humid environment. Those chem packs kept his forehead dry and his glasses cleared as he scanned through the crowd.

That was when he noticed the pair of men angling through the mass of hedonists. These were smaller, leaner than the bouncer, but their faces were ugly from scars, meaning that they had actually been in fights. The muscle was a steroid-packed totem, nothing more than a horseshoe hung for luck at the door. These two were the real deal.

Bolan could see the flicker of steel in one hand.

Violence was cutting its way through the crowd toward the Executioner.

He obliged it by meeting it halfway.

CHAPTER FIVE

Bolan sized up the pair. Both were just under six feet, which meant that they had a proportionately shorter reach than he did. That was one thing that could work in his favor, though they had knives and he was unarmed. Both sides of this conflict knew that their enemy was experienced, and capable. The knife men also knew that they had to move in quickly before the soldier could reach for his guns.

That wasn't going to happen. Certainly, logic would dictate that a big badass in black would pull his iron and begin blasting away at knife-armed killers, but the reality of the situation was that Bolan knew that his aim wasn't infallible, and in the deadly close quarters of the club, every bullet he loosed would invariably end up in a human body. Even if he used the Desert Eagle, one shot would punch through any target that he did strike decisively, and then roll on, burrowing into the crowd and wounding or killing more behind him. Overpenetration was a true and dangerous concern for Bolan. His very name, the Executioner, meant precision, that the right target was always killed. He wasn't the Mass Murderer, the Reckless Killer, he was a focused instrument of justice, not wanton murder. Certainly, this club would hardly be filled with saints, but until the soldier knew who surrounded him, there was only one course of action.

His hands versus the knives of the two bodyguards.

The first man darted in, breaking from the throng. There had been enough of an air of menace around Bolan that space had cleared out, and the soldier was glad for the long tails of his calf-length leather duster. Grabbing one lapel low, he brought up the fabric in a rustling flap, the flourish of supple cowhide rising and snapping to intercept the lunging point of the blade-man's thrust.

The knife artist paused in midstride, realizing that his initial attack had been blunted, deflected as if by a toreador in the ring. That brief instant of shock and surprise gave the soldier the opportunity he needed to bring down the flared wing of leather and piston out his right hand, middle knuckle extended to apply the most force to the smallest area. Going for the face in this brief moment would have been a foolish endeavor, because he would strike only bone, in which case, he'd get a fracture in his hand that would limit his gun handling later. Instead, he speared his punch into the notch below the man's rib cage. The force of the impact translated into an explosion of air, spittle and bile from the Colombian's lips.

The first club goon staggered backward, his face purpling as he couldn't gather a fresh lungful of air. The sudden and swift dispatch of the man made the crowd push back farther, and gave his backup another moment of pause. Bolan took advantage of the next instant and pressed his attack. The club guard saw Bolan's lunge and brought up his knife, whipping it in an

X pattern through the air. The sleek blade flickered in the intense club lighting, but Bolan halted his lunge just outside the reach of the knife tip. Rather than go in for another punch, the soldier snapped a kick into his foe's flexed knee.

The Colombian was good, as he hadn't gone stiff, allowing the limb to bend under the impact. Even so, he was knocked off balance, causing both of his arms to windmill to recover. Bolan sidestepped away from the knife-hand side and snatched hold of the guy's wrist. The soldier locked his fingers into a steel grasp, squeezing with all of his strength. The knife man tried to use that point of contact as leverage, but Bolan stepped back, drawing the off hand farther out, extending the man off balance to the point where the big American could knee him in the ribs with little concern of that weapon getting at him.

Folded over and lifted bodily, the guard grunted and was hurled to the floor, his trapped wrist finally released. Facedown on the floor, the second man was slow to move, and the first was still gasping like a grounded fish.

Bolan allowed his duster to settle down around him, standing straight. Even as he did so, the crowd parted like the Red Sea before Moses, only this time it wasn't a forty-year journey through the desert that awaited the Executioner on the other side. There was a table, gunmen bracketing it, women tucked in around the edges and a greasy, slightly chubby, fully balding man chewing on a cigar.

That was the man Bolan had come to see. He advanced, stepping confidently. The clubbers were drawn back in fear. Perhaps they'd seen violence in the club, had seen those two men end a scuffle with swift and brutal steel, and yet Bolan had been untouched. Tall, clad in black, the soldier was a cliché from an action movie, a tower of irresistible human force that stalked with impunity.

There was movement behind him, and the soldier cursed under his breath, stopping in his tracks. Already he was calculating the approach of the floored man, realizing that a knee to the ribs hadn't been enough. He took a handful of his coat and whipped around, fanning out the tail of his duster with the flourish of a master bullfighter. The rustling leather snapped and crackled through the air, slapping the second guard's knife and knocking it out of his grasp.

Even disarmed, the guy didn't want to give up, so Bolan brought up his elbow, swinging it like a club into the side of the Colombian's head. An ugly crunch sounded as the soldier's forearm bludgeoned the guard to the floor. Bolan took a step back, grabbed the bouncer's knife wrist and pulled up hard. The man squealed as his shoulder was pulled to its limits. All it would take would be a few more pounds of pressure, and the joint would crack open like an overcooked chicken wing. Bolan decided to be a little more merciful, giving a light kick to the shoulder and releasing the injured limb.

The jolt would be painful, but it wouldn't cause lasting damage. He'd be able to use his right arm again, if he gave it enough rest and physical therapy for a few months. What mattered was that he was left in no condition to continue the fight.

Finished with that little "distraction," Bolan advanced toward the table.

The bodyguards with their guns still holstered threw their boss a nervous glance. Half-naked women who had allowed the wealthy master of the table to paw them were now tangled in a mass of glistening smooth limbs, having fallen over each other in the attempt to crawl out of this back table. Frightened eyes locked on all of them.

The only one not scared was the man who chewed on his cigar.

"Sir?" one of his guards urged, his hand not quite reaching for the machine pistol hanging under his loose blazer.

"If you want to commit suicide, sure, go for your damned gun. Otherwise, let's just assume he's a faster draw than you, and get the hell out of the way," the boss growled.

Bolan folded his arms, frowning, remaining silent.

"I'm sure you have no intention of leaving without some form of information, right?" the boss asked.

Bolan nodded.

"Don't talk much?" the boss asked. "No smoke? No drink? No woman?"

Bolan shook his head.

"Hard-ass. A regular goddamn iron man," the boss muttered, tapping the ashes off the end of his stogie. "All right. Who are you looking for?"

"Eastern Europeans," Bolan answered.

"Oh. Not Russians?" the boss asked.

Bolan didn't react. He wasn't surprised that there might be Russian involvement in this. From what he'd noted from the Malaysian bombing, yuan from the People's Republic of China were being counterfeited along with the U.S. dollars. If someone was playing economic roulette with false cash, the lack of rubles in Europe was both telling, and concerning. Already, so far, the former Soviet Bloc involvement in this operation was starting to add up. The FARC, long a staple of conflict within Colombia, had received enormous support from the Soviet Union before its collapse. The Venezuelan government, who also appeared to be a major factor in this conspiracy, also had Communist leanings involving the nationalization of large amounts of resources, and the tried-and-true standard of "leftist despots" of killing everyone who didn't agree with them. It was amusing how "leftist despots" were really no different from extremists on the right, men like Allende who sent thousands to executions in Chile.

The real goals of these animals was all the same. Power. Either power through money, power through convincing the religiously uneducated to follow insane preachings, or anything that could give them support. Such discussions of fascists and socialists in American politics brought the taste of acid to Bolan's mouth, as over the years, he had been to countries where real communism and real Fascism had taken hold. Political pundits could spew whatever garbage they wanted to, but the truth was, there was no real fear in America that the government would grab them in the night and take them to be murdered callously.

"You know what I want," Bolan growled. "Keep delaying, and I'll grow impatient."

The boss looked to the left, and then to the right. He

was alone now in the booth. The women had scrambled their way to freedom. The allure of his money didn't outweigh the reality of the threat standing before the table. The bald man shrugged. If they didn't come back tonight, there would be more tomorrow. Women like the ones who had been curled against him were a dime a dozen, and he could score far more with just the drop of a few tablets on the table. "My apologies. I was simply trying to be nice."

"If I wanted nice, I'd have called to make an appointment," Bolan returned.

The boss nodded. "Thing is, if you wanted me dead, you wouldn't even have wasted the energy you did on my two knife men."

Bolan remained silent. Even if he weren't wearing his sunglasses, his features would have been grim and inscrutable. The boss was talking for the benefit of his remaining bodyguards, and the clubbers who were backing up as far as they could, trying to blend into the crowd around them. This was a business transaction, a product provided for a payment. The payment here was a relative act of peace. No blood had yet been shed in the dance club, and none would.

The boss would have no flies on him should this information be tracked back, and even if the Slovaks had known that they had been given up, the Colombian club owner knew the giant before him. He didn't know a name, but he displayed a facility with violence that was deadly and professional. The thugs who brought Bolan to his doorstep were the kind of scum who he'd give up willingly. It had been their actions that had awakened the soldier's wrath, let it land fully on their doorstep.

Once he was done, the boss wouldn't have much to worry about. Either the foreign gangsters would be dead, or they'd have suffered more than enough losses to cut and run all the way back to Europe where their stinking hides would no longer be in competition with him.

The boss wrote a name and an address on a cocktail napkin. He snapped his fingers and one of the bodyguards picked it up. It was carried to Bolan who barely moved, catching the napkin between two fingertips. The gunman stepped back, not wanting any physical contact, just in case the bastard in black were radioactive, or breathed anthrax out with each exhalation. The sooner the stranger was gone, the sooner the gunmen would feel safe again.

Bolan nodded. The boss returned the gesture.

With that, Bolan turned, enjoying a little showmanship as his duster flourished behind him. Though he was a man of business, there were times when theatrics were warranted. In front of a nightclub full of drugged and drunken revelers, the events that had transpired would mutate and change. Over time, they would tell tales of the day a seven-foot-tall vampire tore through the front of the boss's club, shredding minions as if they were made of wet newspaper.

The boss would receive a better reputation for having brokered a deal with a walking death machine, while the Executioner would foster more tales through the underground of a boogie man who was so terrible, none could stand before him. The capelike flow of his long duster would only add to the legend.

The world had forgotten the Executioner and Mack

Bolan, but they knew someone was out there, going bump in the night, hitting back for those who were helpless. With that story spreading, maybe some hard guys would think twice about stepping up to the plate to try some big scheme. If so, then the whole showboat was worth it to prevent a single life from being lost.

And if not, they had a date with some cleansing flame.

MATTY SORRENO, THE cigar-chomping boss of the club, watched as eventually the crowd, significantly thinned but still profitable for a night, returned to carousing and debauchery. In the booth next to his, the rhythmic thump of the padded bench told him that sexual desires had trumped fear of madmen. A smile spread across his face.

Things were returning to normal when he received a phone call. It was the Russian, and that was all Sorreno knew the man as.

"I'm calling to let you know that trouble was in town," the Russian said.

"Six foot plus, all in black?" Sorreno asked. He splashed some expensive tequila into a tumbler for himself. He slammed it back, straight. The burn felt good.

"You've seen him?" the Russian asked.

"I gave him the address of the Slovaks you sent after the Colombian cops," Sorreno answered. "But only after he asserted that he was the alpha male."

On the other end, Molinov sighed, a raspy sound of worry that stretched across the airwaves. Sorreno didn't need impressive cell reception to realize that his decision had inconvenienced the Russian.

"Did you say anything about…"

"He asked about the Eastern Europeans," Sorreno said. "I asked if he meant Russians. He asked me what did I think?"

"You gave him a sacrificial lamb," Molinov assumed.

"I'm looking out for my ass. Screwing my clients doesn't fall into that," Sorreno responded.

"Then you're going to want to do me one more favor," Molinov replied. "Get your craziest cartel friends, and send them to the Slovaks."

"To help?" Sorreno asked.

"No. Scorched earth," Molinov answered. "That's why I want your craziest. Tell them that… Well, you know who you spoke to."

"El Soldado," Sorreno stated.

"You actually want him banging around Medellín?" Molinov pressed.

Sorreno grimaced. "I made a deal with him because he came showing me respect. If I tell my friends to hunt him down…"

"You'll be bitten if he survives. If he survives hitting the Slovak mobsters in their stronghold, and a small army of cocaine cowboys," Molinov added.

Sorreno cleared his throat. This time he didn't pour the liquor into the glass. He tipped the neck of the tequila bottle to his lips and took a long pull, two full gulps.

"Who do I have to call to get this done?" Molinov asked.

Sorreno looked around the club. Betray the man who just left? Molinov had to be crazy. The thing was, Molinov was casting about, and Sorreno would be the one who the trench-coated war machine would look at, anyway. Sorreno could deny his involvement, but as an information broker, a deal builder and kingmaker, he would still be at the center of any web of intrigue in Medellín.

The big mystery man would come back for him, and ask questions. Harsh questions.

And when he returned, it would be when the club was empty, closed down, the vampiric nightlife crawling back to their homes to avoid the harsh reality of daylight. *El Soldado* wouldn't be limited. History and rumor both agreed, innocent bystanders, even drug-addicted rabble like the ones Sorreno catered to, made him take a lighter hand. Without noncombatants present, he was more willing to cause damage.

"Call them. Or I warn the Slovaks that he's coming. You won't like that," Molinov returned.

Sorreno sighed. "All right."

Sorreno just wondered if the Russian would betray him. If that were the case...

The Russian hung up. Sorreno rubbed his bald pate, took a third gulp from the bottle, then began punching in a number.

BOLAN HAD PEELED out of the long duster, folded it then threw it in the backseat of his car, a Porsche Panamera Turbo. He hadn't had the opportunity to drive one of these before, but it held a lot of similarity to the classic Porsche 911. It wasn't as fast as the legendary sports car, but for a sedan, able to top out at over 190 miles per hour in seventh gear, Bolan could live with second-rate speed and handling when the exemplar was the Porsche

997 iteration of the 911. Throaty power and quick response were everything that the soldier could hope for in a set of wheels, and for a visiting badass, Bolan could pass himself off as a hit man, a Russian mafia boss or whatever he wished.

No second-class ride would be the chosen wheels of a professional, accomplished criminal.

There was the danger that he would draw undue attention, but he didn't intend to stay still for long enough.

He navigated through the town, heading toward the address that Sorreno had given him, parking the Panamera out of sight. It took him a few minutes to find a good, darkened alley to secrete the car, but once he did, he moved around to the back of the sedan and opened the trunk. The cargo area back there, and the spacious door, allowed the soldier to store his war bag within and not be too concerned about having to collapse stocks or break down longer items. He'd contemplated setting up the rifle he brought, a Heckler & Koch 416, into its M27 Infantry Automatic Rifle configuration for a few moments, but knew that if he was going in for answers, he was going to have to make the compact rifle as short and deadly as necessary. He left the sixteen-inch upper in the trunk, but took the full complement of AR magazines for the weapon.

The 416 that Bolan chose to roll with was a special United Kingdom version. Where M-16 based carbines were often limited to how short their shoulder stocks could go by means of the buffer tube jutting behind the pistol grip, the HK416C had that item abbreviated greatly. Replacing the standard stock was now a clone of the original HK MP-5 or G3 stock, which when fully closed, added little more than the width of a human fist to the length of the rifle. The 416 also had a nine-inch barrel, which for close quarters was not only extremely quick handling, but required a muzzle-mounted suppressor, lest the sound of expanding gunpowder combustion shatter eardrums.

Bolan drew out the buttstock, pressed it to his shoulder and did a quick check of the iron sights. The weapon moved and pointed naturally, so he threaded a can onto the nose of the stubby subcarbine. While no attachment could make such a powerful caliber truly silent, the stubby contraption would reduce the massive overpressure of the muzzle-blast to tolerable levels, dampen the heat and light given off by the escaping gasses and keep Bolan from giving himself a concussion by firing it within the confines of an office.

He secured his spare ammunition, then brought up a night-vision monocle to sweep the terrain that the Slovak mobsters had chosen to inhabit. Here, skirting the edges of the city limits, he was looking at a failed urban renewal project, a century-old asylum that had fallen into disrepair. Most of it had been cleaned up, but incumbent corruption and political posturing had put the rebuilding of the campus on delay. This had been the ending place of too many life journeys, Bolan could sense. The place had such a stink of death that few wanted to stay close. Despite usable land inside a flimsy-looking fence, no shanties had been constructed within.

The locals knew better than to cross into the home of the dead. Bolan didn't believe in ghosts, not in any sense other than haunting memories that clung to him, recollections of family and friends who died because of his actions or inactions. However, he didn't discount tales of the supernatural, either, preferring to keep an open mind, and he could also recognize that there were "feels" to places, emanations that gnawed at the peripheral senses, like the ultrasonic whine of a security system in a store, or the buzz within the wires of a faulty electrical system.

Death and suffering could bring those kinds of feelings to the forefront. It was a possibility, and while Bolan couldn't confirm nor deny the presence of such things, one thing he did pay attention to was that even those desperate for a hovel to live in hadn't scaled or crawled beneath a fence to make use of empty offices and cells.

On the other hand, the foreign gangsters that Sorreno had put him onto would enjoy such privacy, and more than a few of them could fight off the feelings of superstitious fear with a strong pull of liquor, or just a grim chuckle and the weight of a loaded firearm.

So far, Bolan could see that there were four shifting shapes patrolling the grounds, distant shadows made indistinct by night and intervening overgrowth. He caught movement in four more different locations, peering at windows. Those flickered into being, then disappeared quickly, seeming ghostlike in their movements.

The trouble was, a sentry trying not to draw attention to himself *would* pop in and out, carrying the same appearance as an apparition. Bolan also could not recall the last time a spirit carried binoculars and a walkie-talkie.

Given that they were looking out of the buildings on

campus in the middle of the night, those binoculars were night-vision capable, as was the soldier's own scope.

The Slovak gangsters were on edge, and it wasn't because of Casper nor the gentleman spirit of Canterville.

No, the only ghost they were looking for was Bolan himself.

It wouldn't have been the club boss who let his arrival slip.

Something else was in the air.

The desperation of a man trying to burn down all leads pointing back at himself.

The Executioner began slathering on grease paint, blacking himself out.

It was time to go bump in the night.

CHAPTER SIX

Marlo Gruvicz listened to the rasp of a distant radio transmit a quick message to central. The different patrols were on separate frequencies, currently stuck in paranoia mode. Only one radio could read everyone's signal, and that was the one that coordinated the team. Eight men were on patrol, while the other two dozen were split into three areas of the old abandoned facility.

Gruvicz wasn't happy about this situation, alone in the halls, despite the contact to home base.

Molinov had given them a call. Sorreno had given them up, and now, a rival was coming here, loaded for bear, and not looking for something so neat and gentle as arrests. No, this was someone from outside, who had it in for the Families. The details were iffy, but he did say that the Russians had similar problems with this man. He was a vigilante, waging a one-man psychotic war on the various crime Mobs.

The whole thing sounded familiar, the kind of plot belonging in old American movies. The thing was, Gruvicz didn't mind. He and his Mob had dealt with guys who thought that they were one-man armies before. Sure, things were tense, but there were more than twenty hard men on this old asylum campus, packing the latest variants of the fabled AK-47 family, except these were chambering newer cartridges than the old rifle. Faster, lighter and easier to carry, the new AEKs also put out rounds at higher rates.

Gruvicz had hit a Polish GROM cop in full armor with an AK-101 on full-auto. Nine-hundred rounds per minute tore through Kevlar and trauma plates like a chain saw through butter, splitting the flesh and bone beneath in a bloody swathe of destruction. That was the last time he feared any living man.

The unliving, though, they troubled Gruvicz. He'd heard things in these hallways, caught glimpses of movement out of the corner of his eye. Sure, they were explainable things, the "matrixing" of sounds and images to something more familiar, so that the dripping of water or the whistle of wind became an unearthly human whisper or footsteps in the shadows. It wasn't helping that some of his friends were pulling up internet videos of ghost investigations in similar darkened buildings, coming up with rasps of noise that could be turned into actual words, especially once someone put subtitles running beneath the video footage.

Gruvicz grimaced. Here he was, holding an AK-101, one of the premiere combat rifles of the late twentieth century, and he was starting at superstitions thousands of years old. Old wives' tales of spirits and phantoms belonged in storybooks to read to uneducated children, not grown combat-trained and heavily armed men.

"You're an idiot, Marlo," he whispered to himself.

"Yes, you are," came a low, hushed whisper in response.

Terror poured between Gruvicz's shoulder blades like spilled ice water. He didn't even think of putting his finger on the trigger as he whipped around in the darkened hallway. There was a movement of shadow farther down the corridor, but instead of opening up on full-auto, he fought for discipline and clicked on his LED flashlight.

An old rag dangled on a doorknob, whipped up by the wind. Heart still in his throat, Gruvicz killed the torch and leaned against the wall.

"There's no such thing as ghosts," Gruvicz told himself.

"No," Mack Bolan said, stepping out of a doorway right next to where the Slovak gangster had braced himself.

Off balance and surprised, there was little that Gruvicz could do as the Executioner snapped forward with a powerful elbow to his jaw. The lower mandible violently twisted on impact, lights exploding behind Gruvicz's eyes as nerves misfired into his brain.

The elbow strike to the jaw wasn't intended to be lethal, but it would stay with the man, leaving him in pain and barely able to move, even an hour after he awakened from the violent launch into unconsciousness. The soldier needed prisoners this time, and he rolled the man so that when he awakened, his bile wouldn't back into his airway and choke him to death. The Slovak wouldn't be able to speak, but Bolan made certain he'd stay put through the judicious use of nylon cable ties.

He checked out the rifle. The familiar Kalashnikov controls, but the chambering in 5.56 mm NATO informed the soldier of the model number, and the fact that this was right off the line, but designed for export, neither the current Russian army issue, 1991 issue AK-74M nor the soon to be fielded AK-12. Bolan had encountered the more modern rifles spread throughout the globe, the end result not of the mass exportation of rifles to insurgents by the KGB, which would foster a revolution, but sold by the various Russian mafias.

Bolan gave the Slovak a pat on the back of his close-shaved head, then took the AK-101 with him.

He was glad for the ghostly feeling of this old place of madness and incarceration. Such general emanations had given him the edge he'd required. Guards, feeling themselves among phantoms, would be less on edge to the sound of feet whispering softly on a floor, especially through the kind of coated boot soles the Executioner had used to muffle his steps.

The ghost whisper he made had been a piece of misdirection that allowed Bolan to slip through one room to the other. He found himself within a short lunge, able to bring down the gangster in near silence. What racket that had been made had been without the telltale sound of gunfire, which would have brought the whole place down around Bolan's ears.

As he moved off a distance from where he'd left the unconscious man, he cradled the rifle. Bolan had taken an hour skirting the patrols of the outside guards, then moving in closer. He was running quiet, exploring the campus quietly in order to take the home-field advantage away from the Slovaks. It had been while Bolan was undercover that he'd been able to get a semblance of understanding of what frightened the men as they dealt with the "haunted" asylum.

With that, Bolan knew that nerves were on edge. All he needed to draw someone out of the shadows was a simple mistake. He had the unconscious sentry's rifle and the radio. He'd listened to the man speak in hushed whispers. All he needed to do was fake a few grunts. He checked the safety, then fired a single shot into the floor. In the close quarters of the corridor, if he hadn't equalized the pressure in his eardrums, the muzzle-blast would have deafened and concussed him. The gunshot would be heard for hundreds of feet, echoes bouncing.

The radio crackled. "Marlo? Marlo?"

Bolan grunted dazedly into the microphone.

There was a stream of curses in Slovak, some words that had crossed into Russian street parlance, so Bolan was certain that the man on the other end of the signal was questioning whether Marlo's parents weren't related by birth. Bolan grunted again. More words came streaming through the speaker. Bolan placed the radio on the floor, then stripped the magazine and bolt from the AK. He faded into the shadows, slipping the suppressed Beretta from its holster.

Footsteps came rushing as the radio continued to spew out insults, curses and the unconscious Slovak's first name. Flashlights speared through the darkness, scything through the blackness as they searched for the fallen guard. Hushed whispers and wary grumbles issued under breath. Bolan smirked as their lights fell upon the radio and the dismantled AK on the floor.

He heard the name of Jesus muttered by one of the men, and the man who said it began to back away from the mess on the floor. Another shouted for Marlo Gruvicz.

Silenced Beretta in one hand, a hooked Emerson Combat Karambit knife in the other, Bolan sidestepped through the shadows, slipping into the common bathroom between two of the hospital rooms. Bright LED lenses flared, blazing through the night, sweeping the hospital rooms. Bolan remained stone-still, his breath slowed to a halt, remaining silent, despite the rise in his pulse rate. His body was preparing, revving up for combat. Things were going to explode in a few moments, but the Executioner had to do this right. One wrong move, and he could find himself riddled with bullets, or being stormed by all of the European mobsters at once.

Bolan eased out behind the searching group. Their attention was focused ahead of them. He peered into the hall, and, looking out the window, he could see another group of gunmen advancing along a perpendicular hall. They walked swiftly, but they weren't running. They didn't want to be out of position if they should stumble across an enemy in the dark. Their flashlights were off. No one wanted to blind their allies, or give away their position with those glaring beams.

This was Bolan's cue to slip into the hall. He advanced on the last man of the group, the hooked talon of the combat knife rising. This was going to be a swift, brutal bit of butcher's work, but the Executioner was going to use fear as much as firepower to bring down the gangsters. He tucked the Beretta away as he drew within striking distance, freeing his left hand.

In a flash, that hand was clamped over a mobster's mouth, thumb mashing the nostrils shut against his index finger's knuckle. Bolan scythed down with the knife, the needle-sharp point sinking into deltoid muscle, the inner curve of the blade providing the leverage to turn its razor's edge into a bloody gutting tool. Skin, clothing and flesh parted under a design that had first shown its brutal effectiveness in the age of the dinosaurs. Bolan pulled the knife free, then brought it up to the dying man's throat, slicing deep to the neck bones.

The two cuts took only a few moments, and Bolan's twist of the dead man's head spun the corpse so that he landed with a grunt, his neck yawned wide-open, his body slashed deeply. Bolan ducked into a hospital room, but before he was through the doorway, he let out a high-pitched shriek, echoing the death cry that the Executioner had muffled when he took out the sentry.

Stampeding feet thundered to a halt. Flashlights sprayed their blaze down the hall, coming to rest on the gutted, nearly decapitated corpse of the man who had been only a few steps behind the men scanning it. There was a cry of horror as the lamps illuminated the gory mess, more muttered prayers, pleas to saints and savior at the sudden death just at their heels.

"In the rooms!" Bolan understood as he reached a windowsill inside the hospital room. The glass had long ago been broken by idly thrown rocks, so it was clear sailing through the opening, his coated boot soles silent as he climbed onto the ledge only moments before LED beams speared out the window he'd vacated.

The chatter of an assault rifle split the silence, firing through a room two windows over. The gangsters were firing at shadows, and in the backwash of the rifle-mounted light, Bolan could see the fluttering of a threadbare, neglect-rotted curtain out of a hospital window.

The chatter of frightened, bewildered men was insistent in the hallway. Flashlights were shut off in answer to hissed commands, the pop of radio static burping from hand radios as men called in to central command. Bolan ducked and lowered himself back through the window he'd rapidly exited. The group in the hallway was being accompanied by the men who had been rushing up to meet the first search party.

The splash of boots in a growing blood puddle prompted more light, more cursing, more prayers.

"Turn off the lights!" another man snapped.

Bolan picked out the term "playing with us," from one of the gunmen.

Another mentioned a ghost.

Bolan entered the hall quietly, then watched as the group of guards muddled about, grumbling among themselves. The soldier made certain he was far enough away from the enemy, then wound what seemed to be a pillowcase around the suppressed Beretta. It wouldn't be as efficient as a true slide lock installed on a purpose-built "hush puppy" pistol, but Bolan had put in a slightly underpowered round right under the hammer of the sleek pistol. The lower gas volume produced by the reduced charge was a mere pop, ejected casing landing in the loosened folds of the pillowcase.

Downrange, Bolan's target jerked violently forward, the back of his head cratered by the subsonic round. At 180 grains, but only thumping along at a mere 800 feet per second, the ballistics weren't anything earth-shaking, but the results were still dramatic. The solid, flat-nosed slug met skull and punched clean through, tumbling into brain matter. The precision of the shot, as well as the sheer mass of the quiet 9 mm round had combined for a quick silent death.

The drop of their comrade, poleaxed by the hushed bullet, created a flurry of activity.

Lights flashed on, this time LED lenses blaring straight into the eyes of fellow gangsters, inducing blindness. Bolan tucked himself into the shadows of another doorway as a scuffle broke out. Curses sounded, there was even the sound of a fist striking a jaw. Voices tried to bellow over the cacophony of panic in order to bring the sudden melee under control, but Bolan's planted seeds of paranoia were growing wild, untamed.

One rifleman spit out something angrily, then pulled his weapon to his hip and cut loose, ripping a long burst along the hospital wall. The aluminum doorjamb near Bolan's head popped, bursting into oxidized splinters of neglected rust, spraying him. Dust burned in one of Bolan's eyes, but he gritted his teeth to bear it. He simply backed farther into the hospital room as the blaze of the autorifle died out, its magazine spent in blind rage.

Bolan knew what he had to do to fix the irritation in his eye, and he pulled the tube from his back-mounted water container. He gave the bulb a squeeze and blasted himself in the eye, rinsing the caught dust away. Bolan blinked and no longer had to worry about irritation. The last thing he needed was to be half blind in the midst of a firefight.

Vision restored, the Executioner was able to see enough so that he wasn't being rushed. It'd been only a few moments since the salvo of AK fire raked across the doorway. The enemy gunmen were backing away from where their friends had died. They wanted distance between themselves and whatever was in the shadows, stalking and killing them.

That was smart of them, but at this point, caution seemed to be a controversial last resort as the gangsters shouted and bellowed at one another. Bolan knew that there was going to be division among his foes, which was why he decided to attack by the means that would inspire the most dread. That fear finally led to another gunshot, a booming shotgun blast. Bolan peered around the doorway with a small pocket mirror. There was enough light for him to see that no one down the hall had been shot, but he could also see the crater in the ceiling.

The man with the shotgun was a brawny, grim-faced man with a nose like a hatchet and his head blanketed by a uniform depth of scruff from balding pate to scraggly chin. He stood his ground, speaking softly, quietly, just out of sight. Bolan knew that he was going to be the man to take down to knock the legs out from beneath the unity of this group.

It was time to mix it up, anyway. The gangsters were clotted in the corridor, bunched up and making for easy targets. There were probably other groups around the abandoned campus, but a blow here, now, would either draw the entire force running, or give the others a good excuse to stage a hasty retreat.

Bolan took out his Desert Eagle and stood, all the while keeping the leader of the gangsters in sight with the pocket mirror. He calculated trajectories, panicked response and who would fight back. Bolan would have liked more answers, so his first shot was going to be with the most accurate weapon he had with him.

The Executioner stepped into the open, visual focus transitioning from pocket mirror to the night sights installed on the big .44 Magnum auto loader. He brought the glowing green front fiber optic down to the center of the leader's thigh and triggered the pistol. With a thunderous boom, the head gangster's leg was whipped from beneath him. Two hundred and forty grains of flat-point lead struck the gangster's femur after punching through clothing and muscle. The bone, the heaviest and strongest of the human body, snapped in two, and that sapped the will to fight straight out of the man. And if the leg hadn't done the work, then getting slammed nose-first into the floor helped some more.

The powerful boom of the Magnum, and a second of their leaders falling from an unseen gunner, started another scramble. An assault rifle chattered in the distance, but the bullets had to go through the rifleman's own comrades to get to the Executioner who swiftly transitioned from Desert Eagle to the HK 416. Even as the muzzle of the carbine ran parallel to Bolan's gaze, the warrior tripped the trigger and threaded the needle between jerking, dying gangsters to blow off the face of the panicked shooter behind them.

Bodies toppled to join their leader, except this time, they fell with far more holes and much less life and blood. Where there had been one injured thug on the floor, there were now five bodies.

Punches were flying among the men as survivors tried to scramble out of the path of the madness that had erupted within the group. Two men smashed through the remnants of windows and leaped out of the building. One more stood his ground, focusing his fire on where the muzzle-flash of the Desert Eagle had exploded in the shadows. The criminal hadn't counted on Bolan moving laterally, sidestepping away from where he'd fired his initial salvo, nor that the 416 in the soldier's hands had a suppressor that damped any flare produced by a burst of 5.56 mm rounds from a bright white fireball to a dull red pencil.

The Executioner decapitated the second gunman with a burst that struck him first in the throat, then split his lower mandible wide-open, both sides of the jaw flapping open like flower petals of rancid meat. On the other side of the abandoned asylum's courtyard, the windows suddenly blazed with weapon-mounted lights, LED lenses putting off intense beams of light that cut through the corridor in front of Bolan. The Executioner, however, had been aware of his surroundings, and moved himself to a section of wall between the banks of decrepit, glassless windows, and thus, he was now in the shadows between the portable spotlights.

He could hear the screams of injured men, perhaps a couple who had only been nicked by the crazed response of Bolan's first 416 takedown, maybe someone who had broken a leg leaping from a window. Either way, the men across the courtyard opened fire from their positions, bullets punching through empty windows and raising clouds of dust and broken plaster as they struck home. Bolan shouldered the HK carbine, stepping to the right, farther down the corridor, and out of the line of fire.

The Executioner tapped off short bursts, two- and three-shot growls of bullets, toward the flashlights and muzzle-flashes from the enemies across the way. They had given themselves away, pouring out all manner of illumination and noise, making themselves easy targets for the warrior. He'd taken down four of the riflemen before they realized that they were under attack and dived for cover. Even as they did so, they still hadn't turned off their LEDs.

Bolan wasn't going to run a clinic on how not to be a target in a firefight. If the enemy survived this, it would be because they ran like hell. He let the HK drop on its sling, drawing the Desert Eagle once more. Bolan took aim at spots below windowsills and cut loose, punching single rounds into walls where gunmen had hidden. The 5.56 mm rifle round of the 416 might have had a chance against old brick and mortar with a longer barrel at a shorter range, but the Executioner needed penetration, so that meant nothing less than a .44 Magnum round.

Brick dust clouds vomited up from where the Eagle's eggs landed, and screams issued as men died or received ugly wounds. One rifleman had been out of the line of fire, and he whipped his weapon around, aiming at the muzzle-blast of Bolan's hand cannon, but the Executioner was already moving, working closer to the enemy rifleman. On the way, he ripped the partially spent magazine from his pistol, turning a spare stick into the mag well. There was a round up the spout, so he could have fired while on the move.

The gunman's light not only made a huge glowing sign of where he was, but it was also betraying where the shooter was focusing on. Bolan was yards distant from where the LED spot glowed, but he wasn't going to let the fool know where he was, not until the last moment. He came to a halt, brought up the Desert Eagle in the two-handed Weaver grip then fired twice. The massive slide rocked back on its rails twice, each time ejecting an empty .44 Magnum casing, but Bolan's grasp on the weapon kept the muzzle on target for both quick shots. Twenty yards away, the rifleman received both high-powered slugs in the upper chest. His shirt, pale in color, was now splashed with dark gore. The light-equipped enemy rifle tumbled from nerveless fingers, toppling out the window and crashing to the ground below.

Wide bloodshot eyes locked on his executioner, glazing over after a few moments. Finally his boneless corpse slithered over the windowsill and continued on in pursuit of his lost weapon.

The Slovak gangsters had been routed, and Bolan turned toward the boss of the group. The man's face was drenched with sweat, his skin pale beneath the dark bristles. He was going into shock, his stare glassy as he looked up at Bolan's arrival.

"Sit," Bolan told him. "Stay."

It was a moment of levity amid a thrash of gunfire and death, something that Bolan rarely engaged in, but the gang boss seemed like a good audience for such a quip.

Bolan knelt by the man's side, drawing a set of cable ties from his web belt. A couple of them were going to splint the broken thigh. The man was bleeding, but it wasn't high pressure, or particularly bright blood. With a kick, he snapped off the stock of a fallen AK and bound it along the shattered limb with the ties. He used a third to keep direct pressure on the bloody bullet hole. It wasn't a comfortable bit of first aid, and the gangster passed out from pain because of all of the manhandling.

That was good for Bolan. The less this guy struggled, the less likely the soldier was to cause him further harm.

Automatic weapons erupted to life outside the asylum, jerking the big American from his bout of mercy.

Bolan's fight with the Slovak gangsters hadn't gone on long enough for the police to have been called, and even so, there would be the flash of mars lights, or the distant sound of sirens. The gunfire sounded one-sided, as well.

The Executioner brought up his night-vision monoscope and swept the perimeter of the campus.

The fleeing gangsters were nothing more than piles of lifeless trash. A twisting Slovak was approached by a figure in the shadows and shot through the head by a suppressed submachine gun.

Though the soldier couldn't make out faces in the dark, he knew where these men had come from, and who they likely were.

The Russian that Sorreno had omitted to mention as being on the scene in Medellín had sent them. He was playing scorched earth, killing all ties. And to make sure that Bolan would hit a speed bump on the road to taking the fight to the real mastermind behind the counterfeiters and their death squads, they had let the Medellín cartels know that an old enemy was in the neighborhood.

An army had assembled outside the asylum, and they were preparing for a deadly siege, armed to the teeth, and gunning for Bolan.

It was going to be murder getting out of this old haunted campus alive.

Bolan checked his gear and confirmed that he had

a good dozen magazines, which would be necessary to punch through the Colombians. Now it was just a matter of distribution.

He traded the night-vision scope for his 416, lining up the glowing tritium front sight of the compact 5.56 mm carbine on the shadow of the man who killed the wounded gangster.

CHAPTER SEVEN

Cruz Cordova gave the order for the fleeing Slovaks to be cut down. Matty Sorreno had told him that *no one* should leave the abandoned hospital alive, and that meant the foreign scum who had rented the place to conduct their business. The thugs were the kind of people that gave organized crime a bad name, Cordova thought, slovenly, looking as if they groomed themselves with rusted ax blades and smelled even worse. He was elated to have the opportunity to be the instrument of the Slovak mobsters' destruction, and even though he'd been able to cut down a few of them, the thugs had only been finished off.

Someone else had arrived early, had brought down a hammer of destruction upon this lot of killers and would-be international drug traffickers. They had come, with the grudging allowance of Cordova's cartel, to open a pipeline into Eastern Europe. They had sought to establish themselves, to be the power to rival the heroin traders who were growing fatter on Middle Eastern opium sales.

That dream, however, was dashed. Rather than having any coordination to bring in guns or other profitable trades for cocaine, their capabilities made them useless as business partners. The Vallejo cartel, Cordova's employer, wondered if it was worth the effort to evict these fools when Sorreno gave them the call.

The Slovaks were a liability, and they had drawn the attention of *El Soldado*.

Cordova had heard rumors about the man and his allies, and had been aware that he, or others claiming to be him, had been responsible for the deaths of friends and allies across Colombia, as well as bringing down rivals that allowed the Vallejo cartel to expand into the wreckage of their operations. *El Soldado* was a legend, and if half of what had been spoken was true, then Cordova was glad he was with some of the worst, most heavily armed soldiers in the cartel's barracks.

Cordova brought up a pair of night-vision binoculars to scan the darkness when the light amplification turned the dull red smear of a suppressed muzzle-flash into a bright gleam in his eyes. Instants later, the crackle of the weapon resounded, and men were scrambling for cover. Almost everyone who jerked at the racket was all right, except for Paz Bonilla. Bonilla had just put a bullet into one of the Slovaks when most of his face and a part of the side of his head disappeared in a burst of shattering bone and vaporized flesh and brain.

"He knows we're here!" Cordova hissed into his hands-free radio. "Lay down suppressive fire!"

On cue, Cordova's men opened fire, shooting in unison, even as he read off the coordinates of the brief muzzle-flash picked up by his goggles. Rifles chattered lines of fire punching into brick. The assault rifles were simply to keep the enemy busy. Other weapons were being set up to provide a knockout punch.

One simply did not go up against *El Soldado* with

conventional small arms. He scanned his line of men, nodding as he saw the familiar silhouettes of APILAS rocket launchers being shouldered and FN MAG light machine guns lowered onto their bipods belts were swiftly being locked into breeches.

Cordova didn't want to wait. "Hit him with the thunder."

Five men armed with the launchers, a French GIAT copy of the American Javelin anti-armor missile, cut loose. Five 112 mm warheads were launched, sizzling across the ground toward the abandoned asylum. The four-inch-diameter missiles struck hard, and almost in unison, their payloads detonated with earthshaking force. These missiles were meant to take on modern tanks and bunkers, punching through two meters of concrete with a solid hit.

The wing of the decrepit hospital shuddered violently, huge clouds of debris billowing on impact. Walls collapsed, and the roof tumbled down, blowing out even more smoke.

This was a storm of destruction. No one could have survived that, but Cordova wasn't going to take any chances. Maybe *El Soldado* was alone, or maybe he had a small mercenary force along, with only one man shooting to draw the attention of the Colombians so the others could flank and bring down the hammer.

"Keep your damn eyes open," Cordova hissed. "Anything moves, and it's not wearing one of our markers, you kill it, confirm the kill, then shoot the remains. Rocket team, reload!"

The cartel commandos followed orders.

In a few moments, when the smoke cleared, he was going to send in a recon team to check for bodies.

There would be no mistakes made. When it came to *El Soldado,* even overkill was not enough.

As SOON AS the Colombian gunmen opened up en masse, Bolan knew that he was going to be in deep danger. The group had the campus cordoned off, and they were applying suppressive fire, not looking for hits, but to keep the soldier from peeking over a sill and finding targets among them. Bolan gave a quick flash with his pocket mirror and was able to see cartel soldiers moving up with bigger, bulkier weapons than the assault rifles that were pouring so much lead into the building.

He wasn't so interested in the belt-fed machine guns, though those would be a concern. What anchored his thoughts were the fat tubes with bell-shaped muzzles. At this distance, in the dark, he couldn't make out the exact kind of weapon it was, but it was going to be a four- or five-inch anti-tank, anti-bunker missile, which could smash a hole in the side of this building big enough to drive a jeep through. There was more than one man with the heavy weapon.

Bolan, in a crab crawl, made for the room where he'd stashed Gruvicz, and picked the man up. The broken-legged gang boss was away from the wing where the enemy gunmen addressed their attention. Rifle rounds zipped through the open doorway of the hospital room, but the soldier had kept his prisoner well out of sight. He turned toward the room's window, which was facing away from the hail of lead pouring into the building. He heaved his prisoner through the window, hoping that he didn't inadvertently snap the man's neck with a rough landing.

Bolan grasped either side of the windowsill and hauled himself through, right after his prisoner. Even as he released the frame of the window, he heard the unmistakable loud grunts of shoulder-fired missiles being launched. With a kick, the Executioner was airborne, dropping through empty space even as the warheads struck the side of the building and detonated.

Shock waves ripped through the air, overpressure hammered Bolan's senses even through the bulk of the asylum wing. He struck the ground and felt his ankle bend sharply, but it snapped back straight as he toppled, partially blind and deaf, into the grass. There was no time to worry about himself if he could still feel his toes, so he cast about, hands finding the unconscious Gruvicz. A quick check of his pulse proved that the Slovak gangster was still alive.

The wing that they had just escaped from suffered a far worse fate. The wall that faced them groaned, dumping bricks, but the collapse of the building drew the crumbling face inward, not dumping death on their heads. Bolan hauled his prisoner up against a remaining ridge of brick. Long grass flowed around them, so the man would be out of sight and out of mind.

The Executioner's instincts were to break and retreat, but he had to learn what he could, not only from his Slovak prisoner, but also who had sent the Colombians. Bolan was analyzing the dozens of potential variables as to why they had come, even as he surveyed the landscape, looking for cover and fields of fire against the enemy. His mind was working on different levels at once, knowing that once he was finished battling the ambushers, he would have to deal with who had sent them. Still, those thoughts bubbled beneath his conscious assessment of the situation.

It was at that moment that he was able to determine the kind of weapon that the Colombians had used. As it was one man carrying each launcher, it couldn't be the Javelin, which was traditionally a two-man weapon. It had to be a French-build GIAT APILAS, which was in the Colombian military's inventory of anti-armor arms. The coordinated fire of five of those missiles had been enough to completely gut the hospital wing behind him.

Luckily, the explosions and collapse of the building had produced more than sufficient dust and smoke to provide the soldier with a shroud he could hide in. He worked his way through the rubble, crouched, HK 416 reloaded and at the ready. The cartel rocket men would be reloading the reusable launchers. The light machine guns would be ready to sweep the darkness, looking for targets.

But to save ammunition, some of the cartel cowboys would be moving around, flanking the collapsed building and looking for him as a target. They had been ruthless in eliminating the fleeing gangsters, and from the firepower they brought along, they were on the warpath. It had to happen sooner or later. The cartels didn't know who Bolan or his allies in Stony Man Farm's Sensitive Operations Group were by name, but there had been a reputation built up from the occasional survivor of Bolan blitzes or Phoenix Force and Able Team raids. Colombia had seen several visits by the Executioner over the years; it was how he'd gotten in contact with

Villanueva at first, and why he stayed in contact as a forward resource.

The cartels *knew* someone terrible was stalking them, someone who was tireless and utterly destructive. The cartel strike force sitting out on the perimeter of the campus was akin to the American mafia's response to Bolan's vendetta against them, and later in dealing with other ethnic criminal gangs moving in on their business.

But they were operating from rumors. Bolan would have to adapt and scale his response accordingly. He regretted not taking the time to affix an M320 grenade launcher to his rifle, but this was supposed to be a stealth mission, not an all-out war. However, the Executioner was nothing if not one of the best at reacting to sudden shifts in odds or situations.

The first thing, though, was that he had to take the most advantage he could of the debris cloud before it settled. He couldn't see the enemy approaching, but he could hear movement. Bolan kept low, and away from the broken ground. His ankle throbbed from where he'd landed on it, flipping his foot almost ninety degrees sideways. Fortunately, Bolan was strong and limber. His overstretched tendons were limber and spry, able to take this punishment and spring back. It was a common tenet of sports medicine that a body that was pushed to its limits could recover quickly.

Bolan knew he hadn't broken his ankle; it hurt, but he could easily put weight on it. Even so, its range of motion was going to stiffen, and using that foot too hard might result in another failure, a fold under pressure.

Quickly, he knelt and took a look at it. His combat

boot was ankle-length, but it was a more flexible kind. Bolan took the spent magazine from his Desert Eagle and bound it to the inside of his ankle, tucked into the cuff of the boot, securing the whole thing with more cable ties. It made him stiffer, less agile, but it gave him some support so that the shocked, untangled ligaments wouldn't come loose.

The fix ate up precious time, but it also kept the soldier low and out of sight as a squad of gunmen stalked around the rear of the building, into the lot where Bolan had leaped. He changed over to his silenced Beretta 93R machine pistol. If he could keep the enemy from knowing where he was, then he would have that much more of an advantage over them. He wasn't certain if they had forward-looking infrared to help them penetrate the smoke and dust, but even so, he waited until the group was at its closest before rising into a crouch, following the group.

These men were packing Heckler & Koch G-3s and modern Israeli Military Industries Galil assault rifles. It was a lot of firepower, and the men had scopes and lights on their weapons, but lacked the discipline to not splash beams around in order not to give away their presence and approach. Bolan kept close to the group, moving up on the last man in the squad. He swept the shadows behind him, and noted that there was another patrol, thirty yards trailing, just coming into view.

Perfect.

The Executioner moved forward, hooking one arm across the last rifleman's throat, then twisting him bodily. Bolan had about twenty-five pounds and surprise in his favor, so wrestling the gunner around to face the pursuing group was easy. Bolan's forearm crushed into the man's windpipe, reducing the noises he could produce to a low wheeze, then he grabbed the man's gun hand, forcing his grip on top of the Colombian's. Two fingers mashed down on the trigger of the Galil, which fired from the hip, a long raking burst that swept the group of Colombians coming around the side.

Once the burst was fired, the warrior released the choke hold on his opponent, jamming the butt of his Beretta into the gunman's kidney to insure paralysis and keep the sudden, violent break of one of their own confusing the Colombians.

Bolan instantly dropped to the ground next to the man, rifles snarling in the darkness and raking the first squad. The cartel soldiers were shooting at their own, and in an instant, the two groups opened fire with speed and discipline, separating and seeking cover. Even so, gunmen shouted and twisted as bullets slammed into them.

"Stop! Stop shooting!" Bolan said in Spanish.

The stunned rifleman next to the Executioner had his radio on, and he could hear a man in charge barking orders.

"Stand down! Stand down! Cease fire!"

A Colombian gunman poked his head out as the weapons fell silent. He was looking for the other group, wide-eyed and unsure of what was going on. Bolan leveled the Beretta and fired a silenced triburst into the man's face, obliterating his features and tossing him into the darkness.

Curses rose and the squad that the man had been part of unleashed a salvo of automatic fire in return for the assassination of their partner, but it was blind panic fire, as they hadn't seen Bolan's muzzleflash.

"No mas! No mas!" Bolan shoved the stunned man to his feet. The guy, half choked to death, still reeling from the agony of the punch to his kidney, stood drunkenly, hands fumbling as he tried to reload his Galil.

Even as the man did so, Bolan brought around the HK 416, and rising behind the staggered man, he used the gunner as obfuscation and a scapegoat. The 416 ripped loose at over 800 rounds per minute, chattering rifle fire swinging across the wrecked hospital wing and out toward the perimeter. Bolan could see the silhouette of an APILAS-armed rocketeer, and he drilled him with a tight quartet of 5.56 mm bullets.

The rocket man toppled backward, gurgling as his chest was perforated by high-velocity projectiles that whipped his lungs into a foam that ejected from his nose and lips. A light machine gun opened up, its heavy roar resounding as Bolan's patsy was stitched with a dozen slugs. A volley of 7.62 mm NATO rounds crushed bone to dust and turned flesh into stringy pulp, and hurled the lifeless Galil rifleman to the ground in a gory mess.

Bolan had shifted position, moving away from his lifeless victim, triggering a salvo of 5.56 mm rounds toward the muzzleflash of the MG. The suppressor at the end of the HK 416 made Bolan nearly impossible to see at this distance, but the precision bursts that took out two of the perimeter guards had pulled the plug on fire discipline.

Light machine guns opened up, rattling off long and ragged bursts that speared into the darkness, chewing through the remnants of brick walls, sweeping the wreckage of the collapsed building.

Colombian drug soldiers wailed and, while a few of them shouted into radios for restraint, others simply turned and cut loose with their own weapons.

Chaos exploded among the ranks of the separated cocaine cowboys, but there was a voice barking over the radios, demanding discipline and cease-fire. Even so, Bolan could tell that there were plenty of bodies littering the ground, nerves left raw and jangled by the sudden cross fire.

Sowing confusion had suddenly brought down at least eight of the opposition in the ensuing panic, two more taken down by Bolan himself. This was a good start, but the commander of the strike force seemed to be pulling things back under control. He was ordering the Colombians to get back out of the campus.

His plan was to lay waste to the compound from without. They would rain hell upon the abandoned hospital campus until they'd exhausted their ammunition.

Quickly, Bolan mingled with the Colombians as they broke from position and headed back to their perimeter. Moving among the herd, looking frightened and scanning back for an enemy who was not there provided him with more than sufficient cover. Unfortunately, Bolan had to ditch his HK 416, replacing it with a Galil, but that wasn't much of a problem. Both weapons were good, solid reliable models. Trading out magazines was easy, and he had plenty of 5.56 mm ammunition, which the Galil used.

A little smeared blood and dirt across his face obscured Bolan's features, helping him to look like someone who had just survived a terrible attack. It was a risky ruse, but right now, the cartel gunmen were more interested in consolidating their forces as night-vision-equipped riflemen swept the darkness, looking for the ambusher who'd started the melee among them. He recognized the leader of the group, a man who was on Colombian and American law enforcement's radar, as Cruz Cordova, the leader of the security forces belonging to the Vallejo cartel.

Bolan frowned. The Vallejo cartel hadn't been linked to the counterfeit money. In fact, the cash had been distributed by their competition, Rio Negro, at least within Colombia's borders. Rio Negro was a controversial group, its funding and history digging back deep into the days of the Communist FARC. In order to wreck capitalism, Rio Negro had been keen on all manner of piracy, counterfeiting and nontraditional cartel matters, in addition to running cocaine and heroin.

The presence of the Vallejo cartel's soldiers was a little confusing. Or at least, it would have been if Bolan hadn't just hammered Matty Sorreno hard enough to send a message—one which had spread much more swiftly than anticipated.

A Colombian came by with a box of hand grenades.

"Gracias," Bolan thanked him, taking four of them, hooking three on loops of his vest.

"We're going to blanket the remaining buildings with explosives. Just let fly at anything that isn't standing after the rockets go off," Cordova announced.

Bolan thumbed out the cotter pin on his grenade. Now, only the pressure of his grasp kept the safety lever attached to the side of the miniature bomb. He eased around the back of the group, getting closer to one of the SUVs that the Colombians had arrived in. The engine was idling, and the driver stood beside it, not behind the wheel where he belonged. The man had chosen the engine block and the hood of the truck as his protection when the gunfire had gone off before, and he still wanted a lot of metal between him and *El Soldado*'s return fire.

Bolan lobbed the hand grenade through the passenger window, walking behind the cover of a second SUV in the moments that the fuse took to tick down.

The driver's thoughts of protection disappeared as a wave of windshield glass burst from its frame and slashed across his face, carving it into a million strips. The explosion shook the ground, and the door of the truck had been blown off, turning into a cartwheeling guillotine that slashed through three men on its way toward the perimeter.

Fear took over, the Colombians scattering everywhere. Bolan used another of his issued grenades, rolling it between two of the cartel light machine guns before bringing up the Galil, barking orders in Spanish.

The rolling fragmentation grenade came to a stop between the six men who formed the two machine-gun teams, a gunner, a loader and a security/spotter. They had bunched up too close to each other, only five yards apart, which was well within the deadly radius of the fragger. The bomb detonated, and the standing spotters were ripped with segments of broken, notched wire that tore through skin and carved in bone like a million little knives. One of the loaders threw his arms out wide as his back was reduced to hamburger by the same wave of shrapnel and overpressure that flattened the others.

Cordova's head whipped around. In the space of four seconds, hand grenades had obliterated another eight of his team, hand grenades that he'd just ordered into the hands of his teams.

Bolan could see the sudden shock and realization on the cartel hit man's face. Damnation and devastation burned all around the two men as the Executioner emerged from the shadows, Galil locked to his shoulder.

From the stories told, Cordova recognized the unmistakable form of the deadly soldier who plagued the cartels, but before he could call out a warning, command others to gun this man down, Bolan punched a half-dozen 5.56 mm rounds into the cartel hit man's chest. Lungs and heart chopped into a slurry, all that issued from Cordova's lips was a fountain of blood and tissue. The other Colombians were opening fire, sweeping the darkness along the perimeter, thinking that Bolan was outside, not in among them.

The Galil snarled and kicked against the Executioner's shoulder and cheek weld. He popped off short bursts into confused and scattered gunmen, raking them with high-velocity projectiles. He paused only to rip another grenade from his harness and hurl it beneath yet another of the trucks that had brought in the troops to scorch the Earth in the wake of *El Soldado*'s arrival. The vehicle split in two, snapping apart as the grenade erupted, using the volatile contents of its diesel tank to provide extra oomph. Flame and metal flew from the lifted truck, the bulky frame forming a deflective surface that only increased the focus of shrapnel into a fan that raked the gunmen.

Bolan was glad that he'd taken cover behind yet another SUV, otherwise he would have been cut to ribbons.

Even as he took cover, the soldier scanned around. Those who weren't nursing shrapnel wounds or slumped as bloody heaps on the ground were running for the hills.

Bolan contemplated letting the gunmen flee unmolested, but then he remembered the slaughter that they had inflicted on the Slovaks. Sure, the Executioner had ended the existence of many of the gangsters, but he didn't shoot them in the back while they fled.

Bolan decided to deny the enemy resources, dumping his last grenade into the cab of another truck. The vehicle shattered, blown apart violently. Anyone who looked at Bolan caught a 5.56 mm bullet between the eyes.

Within a minute, it was all over. Engines had been smashed by rifle or .44 Magnum slugs when he'd run out of explosives to wreck the fleet of vehicles that had brought in the death squad. Bodies were strewed about, torn by bullets and shrapnel.

Some who were slowly expiring were in agony. The Executioner provided a mercy bullet for each of them.

The body count was huge, Bolan figured, which meant that the Vallejo cartel wouldn't be waging war anytime soon. Maybe that would have worked in the favor of the men running the counterfeiting conspiracy.

Bolan would have to ask Sorreno about that. But first, he had prisoners to recover.

CHAPTER EIGHT

It was nearing dawn and Sorreno drained the last of his bottle of beer. He let the empty roll off the table, landing on the floor. His booth was empty, scattered with "dead soldiers" and pill packets. After the call from the Russian, Sorreno decided that he didn't have much of a life left, so he'd live it to the hilt.

He'd heard the reports of what had happened at the abandoned asylum. The police were trying to pass it off as a territorial dispute between newcomer Slovak mobsters and Vallejo cartel locals, but that was only a fraction of the story.

Sure, Sorreno had sent them to throw the lethal knockout punch against the gangsters that the bastard had come for. But they had been set to rout by the lone gunman.

There had also been no way that the thugs from Europe could have stood enough of a chance against Cordova's small army to cause the casualties that had been reported.

No. *El Soldado* had added more notches to his belt, if that was what the American gunslinger did. He doubted that the scary bastard kept count, though. There were legends that he'd slaughtered thousands of enemies. What were a few back-alley gunmen—or backbiting snitches like Sorreno—to someone like that?

There was a knock at the door. Sorreno mopped his brow, then realized that he didn't need to look good for anyone anymore.

"Come on in!" the club boss shouted.

There he was. This time he wasn't all style and flash. The American was dirty, grimy, walking with a stiff ankle, but bristling with firepower. He looked like he'd just put boot to ass against dozens of men, which was exactly what Sorreno calculated from the reports of the war at the abandoned hospital.

"The Slovak gang knew I was on my way. And then, a bunch of cartel cowboys tried to round me up," Bolan told him. His hand rested on the receiver of a stubby, nasty-looking gun which was one hundred percent business, all black and jagged with rails and clipped-on magazines.

"The Colombians and the Slovaks were warned by me. But they had been bought and paid for by…"

"Do you know the Russian's name?" the Executioner cut him off. "Or is he keeping out of the spotlight, letting everyone else do his work for him?"

"I just know him as the Russian," Sorreno replied.

"That's a shame," Bolan mused.

Sorreno shrugged. "I had a good time."

"I doubt you could walk two steps, and that's even without the alcohol in your system," Bolan noted.

Sorreno grinned. "I banged a whole lot of box tonight. I don't think my balls have a drop left in them."

Bolan remained silent.

For some reason, Sorreno felt his cheeks redden in embarrassment. "Sorry, big man."

Bolan shrugged. "Why'd you send your bodyguards away?"

Sorreno smirked. "Because they don't deserve you."

"But you do," Bolan countered.

"I'm the one who put you in between the Slovaks and the Vallejos."

"You can recover some favor from me," Bolan said.

"Like what?" Sorreno asked. "I'm tapped out. The Russian probably already ditched the burner that he used to call me. He knew that I was going to take the heat for all of this."

Bolan nodded. "I could use whatever you have on the Russian. I'd also like to pick your brain on Rio Negro."

Sorreno frowned. "Those Commie assholes?"

"They have help from outside?" Bolan asked.

"I wouldn't say that they were getting help from a government, at least, nothing local."

Bolan walked to the booth and sat. He rested the rifle against the seat, but Sorreno knew that he had no hope of doing anything to harm the man. Sorreno was blitzed, humming along on Ecstasy, and physically spent from the best sexual workout he'd been through in a decade. Meanwhile, the American looked a little battered, but his arms were lean and powerful, knuckles and the edges of his hands callused. The American had killed men with his bare hands, so any funny business would end with Sorreno gagging as his windpipe collapsed.

"Local?"

"In decades past, they had the nodding approval of Cuba, but that's long since dried up with the end of the cold war," Sorreno stated.

Bolan nodded. "I see. But the infrastructure is still there, to get through to Cuba, perhaps beyond?"

Sorreno tapped his nose.

Bolan folded his arms in front of him. "That explains why there's funny money showing up in more than just South America."

Sorreno tilted his head. "Where else?"

"Malaysia," Bolan replied. There was no need to hide anything from him. The man was already on that cold, desolate plane where nothing mattered anymore, on the verge of rolling over and putting a gun into his own mouth.

Sorreno narrowed his eyes. "There was something going on. I was called to arrange a meeting so that someone could get some product from Santa Marta to Buenaventura or Tumaco."

Bolan nodded. "From the Atlantic Ocean to the Pacific."

"That is why Colombia has become such an international hub. We have coasts on both oceans. Drop stuff off from Europe, and with just a little overland transfer, you've got a way to send stuff to the Orient," Sorreno said. "I didn't know who wanted to make the deal, at least they didn't identify themselves...."

"But you found out, anyway. Who was it?" Bolan asked.

"The Slovaks made that request," Sorreno answered. "I can't figure out what the transport was. You'd think that sending contraband to Malaysia would be easier from somewhere like India or East Africa than across two oceans."

Bolan looked at the table. Even as he was thinking

about the implications of a world-circling, he heard the thumps of car doors closing. He looked toward the door he'd left open, his right hand falling to the fast-draw Desert Eagle rig on his hip.

"Better find something solid to hide behind, Sorreno," Bolan whispered.

Sorreno didn't look convinced that he had a life still worth living. "You'll need help."

"Not in your condition," Bolan said. "Besides, you gave me enough assistance already. Find cover."

Sorreno began to scoot out. Bolan slid from the other side of the booth, then hooked his hand under Sorreno's meaty arm, lifting him out with a little more alacrity.

"Why save me?"

"Because you hear things. I can use that," Bolan growled. "Scoot! Also, find the circuit box. Shut down all of the lights."

The chubby man's first couple of steps were uneasy, off balance, staggering. But after the fourth step, he was back on his game, ducking into a back room. Whether Sorreno would abandon him, follow his wishes or, worse, get involved in the gunfight, there was one less worry now on the soldier's mind. Anyone who came in was going to catch a lot of lead in the face.

He left the rifle in the open by the booth, skirting into the shadows. He'd plotted the layout of this place before, when he'd first arrived, only a few hours ago. The club was laid out so that it had only a few truly negotiable entrances, the main one being the front entrance through which the party goers could arrive. He'd also spotted two service entrances back by the kitchen, and another along the hallway down which Sorreno had disappeared. The Executioner was glad he restocked the partially spent magazines in the big pistol.

The HK 416 would have been preferable as a defense weapon, but Bolan opted against that, simply for the fact that its presence would give the men coming after him a pause.

Sure enough, figures darkened the doorstep, the first glow of dawn backlighting them as they sliced the pie around the sides of the doorjambs. Bolan calmly, carefully aimed the Desert Eagle at the gunman on the left, the one farthest from him, but also the one who would have a straight shot at Bolan in the shadows. The other would need to take two steps to get into firing position.

Only four pounds of force was needed to trip the mighty Magnum pistol's trigger, and the hammer fell. The primer, pierced, spit a jet of hot flame into the packed gunpowder in the cartridge. That gunpowder began turning into energy, burning, expanding, creating enough pressure to accelerate a 240-grain chunk of lead and copper to almost 1500 feet per second. The bullet was in the air for only a moment before it struck the left-hand gunman on the bridge of his nose. Slightly over a half ton of kinetic energy caused the cartilage and bone beneath the wide-mouthed hollowpoint round to collapse in on itself, pushed out of the way as if it were garbage being bulldozed into a landfill.

The pressure in the man's skull increased exponentially even before the round touched brain matter, its shock wave compressing the wrinkled cluster of neurons flatter than a pancake against the back of his head. The 240-grain slug struck the back of the skull, and the man's head popped like a balloon, vomiting gore in a thick syrupy spray.

All of that happened in less than half a second, but the surprise and terror elicited by the violent, bloody death would buy the Executioner a few more moments. He was out and moving, reaching another tier of tables for cover, adjusting his aim in anticipation of the rush of the second assassin. Bolan didn't have to wait long as the stunned gunman staggered into view, sweeping the area that he'd vacated only a heartbeat ago.

Again the Desert Eagle thundered, and Bolan punched another powerful .44 Magnum slug into a Colombian's body, the bigmouthed shovel of a bullet striking the man in the juncture of his neck and shoulder. Muscle and bone parted in the path of the heavy slug, spine severed by fragmented vertebrae.

With two gunners slumped to the floor in mangled heaps, the enemy strike force answered the Executioner's sudden violence with a storm of return fire that speared into the shadows of the club. Even as they shot, the lights died instantly. The whole club had gone from dimly lit to pitch-black, illuminated only by the muzzle-flashes of the intruders. Bolan kept on the move, skirting the wall, but closing the distance between himself and the enemy. One of the gunmen had betrayed his position with the flare of his rifle, the splash of light also spilling on a gunman next to him.

Bolan snapped the Desert Eagle to point of aim and fired twice, one bullet crashing into the side of the rifleman's head. His left cheek cratered inward, his face snapping around and away from the soldier's position. Bolan's second shot took the other assassin in the side of his chest, his ribs splintering, lung tissue rupturing under the hammer-blow impact. This man wouldn't be down instantly, not like the others who had suffered significant central-nervous-system trauma.

Even so, he could hear the retching of the gunner who suffered a sucking chest wound. Raspy, ragged breaths resounded in the darkness. Another of the death squad had the bright idea to turn on the LED riding parallel to his rifle's barrel. The high-intensity beam burned to blue-white life, casting its brilliance in a cone ahead of him. Bolan had been only a shadow, disappearing at the edge of the splay of illumination, but even as he stepped beyond into the darkness, he turned on his own light—the muzzle-flash of his Desert Eagle.

The rifleman caught two .44 Magnum rounds, both of them spearing into his chest. Bones turned to splinters under their impact, and the spotlight swerved, swinging downward as lifeless hands lost hold of the rifle's grip. Those two muzzle-blasts drew attention, though, but the Executioner was on the move, rifle reports crackling, the enemy muzzle-flashes looking nearly perfectly circular, meaning that they were on target for the Executioner. He thumbed the magazine catch, clearing the way for eight fresh rounds of 240-grain missiles, shouldering a table to turn it over.

The riflemen heard the sound of the tabletop striking the ground and opened fire on it, meaning that the Executioner's ruse worked. Few tabletops could deflect assault-rifle rounds in close quarters, but the common belief was that anyone who did flip furniture was looking to use it for cover. Bolan, however, was still on the rush, Colombian gunfire covering the sound of his boots on the floor.

With a pivot, Bolan brought up the Desert Eagle on another pair of the attackers as they were cutting loose. Their own muzzle-flashes were flickering bright enough to illuminate their faces. They were European in appearance, but considering that more than eighty percent of Colombians were ethnically European Spanish, light eyes and Caucasian profiles did little to identify them. He would puzzle out all of that later.

Bolan shot the closest gunman in the ear, the muzzle of his .44 Magnum pistol only a foot away. He threaded the needle through the man's skull, but the trajectory didn't put the bullet through both heads, although he scored a splatter of blood across the second man's features, the salty fluid stinging the gunner's eyes shut.

The Executioner lunged, shoving the skull-blasted first target into his blood-splashed partner, the two bodies colliding hard enough to throw them both to the floor. With a sidestep, Bolan fired into the gore-smeared face of the second shooter. This time, the blood on his features was his own, his brain and chips of skull sprayed out into a fan on the dance floor.

"Jesucristo!" one man shouted, his cry of terror accompanied by the sound of retreating footfalls, not return fire. The last of the assassins was on the run, fleeing from the slaughterhouse that the rave club had become. Bolan was tempted to grab a flashlight to follow the escaping killer, but there was no guarantee that there wasn't at least one other killer, biding his time in the darkness while their partners expended ammunition on phantoms and shadows.

The runner threw the door open, but he was met with the thundering crash of two shotgun barrels. The escape artist was folded over violently, chest and belly burst open by two charges of 12-gauge buckshot, one atop the other. That had to have been Sorreno's gun, an expensive duck hunter rather than a side-by-side. Even so, the end result was two fist-size craters in the torso of the running killer, the vertical muzzle-flash a key-shaped spear of light that tore into the assassin.

Sorreno stepped back, breaking open the action. Spring-loaded ejectors kicked out the empty shells, and with the sound of the spent ammunition striking the floor, an automatic weapon sprayed, tearing a scythe of light through the darkness. Sorreno had been the primary target, and he'd shown himself.

He simply hadn't shown himself enough. The balding, chubby man pressed against the wall, shielding his eyes with his forearm as the doorway he was in was flooded with high-velocity slugs.

Bolan whirled and ripped off two more .44 Magnum messengers, the twin bullets bringing a message of eternal darkness to the killer firing his rifle.

The shadows returned to an eerie, gun-smoke-scented silence. As the sun began to rise above the horizon, the Executioner could see the butcher's work in this battleground club. Nine corpses lay on the floor, the bloody messes evidence of the power of the Desert Eagle and an over-and-under double shotgun.

Bolan edged sideways, scanning the doorway. This was a large assault, a ruthless one at that. He wanted to figure out if it was the Colombians plugging a hole, especially the Vallejo cartel, or if this was the work of the Russians. Right now, however, he had to make certain that the club boss was all right.

"You still alive, Sorreno?" Bolan asked.

Sorreno grunted. "They tried to shoot me. They failed to hit anything important."

Bolan kept a watch on the front entrance, then the way to the kitchen, where two other service entrances had been. So far, there hadn't been any activity from that direction, but the Executioner hadn't survived this long without being aware of all possibilities. He reached the hallway to Sorreno's office, and saw that the man had a hole through his biceps, yet he still clutched the over-and-under shotgun tightly. He'd reloaded it, and there was a fire in his eyes that showed that he wasn't going to die.

Not after being a reprieve from execution by the big American.

"What about the back way?" Bolan asked, nodding behind Sorreno.

"I popped one who came through there. Missed with the top barrel, hit him in the neck with the second," Sorreno growled. "Guys did the stupidest thing in the world coming at me through my back doors."

Bolan pulled his pocket light and swept Sorreno for any other injuries. Just one bullet hole, and even that was a shallow through and through. Bolan tapped the back of Sorreno's hand, and the Colombian flexed his fingers. No bones had been broken, no nerves had been damaged. The soldier took a swatch of duct tape, pressed some sterile gauze in the center, and used the whole strip as a gigantic adhesive bandage. "That will take care of the bleeding."

Sorreno sneered. "Might not be enough. I took too much X. Losing blood, losing sweat…."

Bolan grimaced. "Sit down. I'll get you some water."

"There's real water in my office," Sorreno grunted.

Bolan hooked an arm under his, and he guided the man to his lair. Sorreno staggered over and plopped onto a comfortable-looking leather couch with overstuffed cushions. The soldier was able to see a minifridge behind the desk and opened it. He grabbed three bottles of water, one for himself, and two for the hungover, drugged out and wounded Sorreno.

He cracked the cap off Sorreno's first bottle, and the Colombian drained it so quickly, he had it down in one pull, and was gasping for breath at the end.

"Take it easy with the second," Bolan said.

Sorreno nodded.

Bolan opened his own bottle and rehydrated. Combat took a lot of fluids out of the system. He thumbed open one of his pouches and tossed down a couple of multivitamins in order to restore more than just the lost fluids.

He took a seat on a chair perpendicular to Sorreno's.

"You don't think they'll send any more?" Sorreno asked.

"They'd thrown an army at me at the asylum. The Russian, or the Colombians he suckered into working for him, must have thought that they would be enough. Otherwise, they would have nailed this place with grenades or firebombs," Bolan explained. "Instead, they just sent ten guys with assault rifles."

"And a machete," Sorreno added. "At least, on the one I cut down."

Bolan thought back. He'd noted a few long blades adorning the belts of other men in the attack group.

"They'd shoot me, probably in the gut or in the knees," Sorreno said, sipping slowly from his second bottle. "They would want me alive as they cut pieces off me one at a time."

"The Medellín way," Bolan agreed.

Sorreno lifted a bottle in a mock toast. "I knew the job was dangerous when I took it."

"You mentioned Tumaco before we were interrupted," Bolan stated.

Sorreno nodded. "That sounds familiar to you?"

"Yeah, 2011. The FARC, at least the Western Bloc, was violently active," Bolan noted.

Sorreno grinned. "You keep up on your Colombian violence."

Bolan returned the smile. "Knowing what to expect is what makes me so successful. Nine soldiers and seven civilians were murdered. And the FARC stormed a prison and 'liberated' fifteen of their own."

Sorreno grunted in assent. "Sometimes, the idiot FARC doesn't know when to lie down and die."

"Neither do you," Bolan replied. "But I'm grateful for that bit."

Sorreno's grin returned. "There isn't any solid confirmation that Caracas is giving money and support, but the Venezuelan president did call for Colombia to declare the *'Ejercito de Pueblo'* a legitimate military force, not terrorists."

"His explanation was that this would force the FARC to abide by the Geneva convention, which in turn would cut back on their kidnapping," Bolan said. "The man is not the sharpest tool in the shed, but I don't think, after such a proclamation, he'd put anything solid into supporting those people."

"No. But this wouldn't have to be official and from on high," Sorreno explained. "Especially with the influences from the Caribbean."

"Cuba," Bolan concluded. "So Caracas makes a request of Havana, and now we've got Cuban support for a military force. Even so, the FARC seems to be getting along well enough with drugs and kidnapping to fund their operations."

"You said the counterfeiting was showing up around the world. What better way to foster an economic collapse, the end of capitalism in Colombia, than by flooding the market with devaluing notes?" Sorreno asked.

Bolan nodded. He'd been adding this up all along. The counterfeit money wasn't a means of bolstering a revolution. It was the monetary version of a hydrogen bomb, making an underdog of an army into a powerhouse that could smash the legitimate Colombian government with a well-placed blow. "Do you think you can give me some information on Tumaco?"

"You're going there," Sorreno stated.

"Just to take a look, rattle a cage, see what floats when the sediment is stirred," Bolan returned.

Sorreno pursed his lips. "And then, you're going to look and see how far the road back to Venezuela goes."

Bolan nodded. "And then, I'm going to do my best to wreck any future traffic."

Sorreno lifted the water bottle once more, this time in a real toast. "God speed, *Soldado*. Kill the bastards."

With that, the club boss wrenched himself from the

sofa and headed toward his desk. He had notebooks full of information for the big American.

Knowledge was power. In Bolan's case, it was worth a hundred times its weight in firepower.

CHAPTER NINE

Zachary Winslow was waiting at the safehouse door, a 12-gauge shotgun tucked almost out of sight behind his leg, leaning in the doorjamb. Irritation was painted all over his face as Bolan pulled the car into the driveway.

"Help me with these guys," Bolan said, crawling out from behind the wheel. He decided to defuse the situation the easiest way he knew how. He limped, exaggerated enough to be obvious. He also counted on the dirt, the dust and the blood spatter to add to his shell-shocked appearance.

Winslow's irritation disappeared to first shock, then concern. He rushed over to the vehicle, opening the back door and seeing two men within. "You found the Slovaks?"

Bolan nodded. "This is all that's left."

"You killed the rest?" Winslow asked, hooking the arm of the gang leader over his shoulders and pulling him from the backseat of the sedan.

Bolan shook his head. "The Colombians cleared out most of them. These two, I caught as prisoners."

"Colombians," Winslow repeated. "Any idea who?"

"Cruz Cordova, of the Vallejo cartel," Bolan answered.

Winslow's eyes widened. "How did you get away?"

Bolan pulled out Gruvicz. The man had recovered

enough to be slapped awake. He jerked his thumb and ordered the dazed gangster out of the back of the car. The Slovakian did so, with some difficulty, though, as his wrists were bound behind his back by nylon cable ties. Bolan held the man's head down so the gangster didn't hit it on the door. The last thing they needed was to stitch the man's scalp closed, or deal with a concussion.

Villanueva was at the door to help Winslow with the gang lieutenant. It took only a matter of minutes to seat the prisoners, bind their ankles together and for the boss to be awakened with smelling salts. As Winslow watched the pair, both groggy and not in the mood to speak, Bolan caught them up on the events of the night.

"Looks like you attracted the attention of every scumbag in Medellín," Villanueva said. "Tumaco and Venezuela, eh?"

Bolan nodded. "It was what I was counting on."

"Sorreno's a good source of information, though, I've never tapped him," Villanueva admitted. "He's generally not into snitching for the law."

Bolan fixed him with a stare. "I'm not the law."

Villanueva took a deep breath, which transformed into an "oh" of understanding. "You just have a legit-looking badge."

Bolan patted his wallet. "It's real enough. I just don't care much for using the legal powers it provides. By the time someone crosses my desk, they've gone and passed out of the realm of being taken down by the law."

"But Sorreno…"

"Has been a useful asset. Plus, they came gunning

for him, not me," Bolan said. "I decided he paid enough for sending the Vallejos after me."

"Being scared to death?" Winslow asked.

"Being frightened is being three-quarters dead," Bolan said. "I gave him a twenty-five percent discount for last night."

Winslow smiled, but he looked dubious, not certain whether the man was joking or not.

"Where's our next port of call?" Villanueva asked.

Bolan rubbed his chin. "I'm tempted to go back toward Venezuela to look for the source of this, but Sorreno told me that there is a huge shipment heading out of Tumaco. I want to intercept it."

"I do have friends in town," Villanueva said.

"There's one thing keeping me from endorsing that tactic," Bolan said. "The counterfeiters showed no compunction about killing cops."

"I'm going to do this off the grid," Villanueva answered. "Surveillance only. Besides, according to Sorreno's notes, the pickup won't be coming for a week."

The corner of Bolan's mouth rose in a wry grin. Gears were turning in his mind.

"Are you going to tail the ship, or maybe hitch a ride on board?" Villanueva asked.

"I haven't taken a cruise in a while," Bolan mused.

Winslow nodded. "Of course, this might just be a slow boat to China."

Bolan shrugged. "All right. So we can wait a short time on the exportation. What about to the east?"

"I have the layout of the place we were supposed to hit when we were ambushed at the station," Winslow broken leg isn't going to affect your ability to think, or make phone calls."

Trenkov's jaw set. "And if not?"

"I call Sorreno and tell him to put out the word that one Slovakian escaped the massacre," Bolan said. "And that there's a lot of money on your head."

"Why not kill me yourself?" Trenkov asked.

Bolan shook his head. "You're unarmed and badly injured. I don't pull the trigger on the utterly helpless. However, I don't have a single damn concern about letting murderers kill other murderers. Then, there's the fact that we're in Colombia, and the cartel boys, they're crazy. They'll chainsaw your head off while you're still alive."

Trenkov turned ashen.

"Turning rat on someone who sold you up the river isn't so bad, is it?" Bolan asked.

"You have a clean burner?" Trenkov returned.

Bolan smiled.

MOLINOV GRUMBLED AT the phone calls coming in. Sorreno was still alive, and he wasn't happy one bit. He was spreading the word that any Russians in Medellín belonged in only one place—a meat locker, preferably with a hook through the neck.

Millagro poured himself another tumbler full of liquor, glaring across the desk at his partner. "So, we send out the Colombians to deal with our leaks and the Soldier, and what happens?"

"Shut up," Molinov snarled.

"Correct. We get shut down," Millagro returned. "Every bit of good credit you had with the Vallejos is gone, and the Vallejos are sending word to Rio Negro that you're so full of shit, your eyes are brown."

"I thought this plan was foolproof," Molinov replied. He tossed his cell phone onto the desk and stood up from his chair. He could feel the blood pressure roaring in his ears from pure rage. How many men had he thrown at the bastard in black?

The local authorities had claimed it had been a gang war between foreign mobsters and a local cartel. There were at least sixty corpses on the scene, with more presumed dead within the wreckage of the missile-smashed hospital. Molinov grimaced. That in itself hadn't been the worst of the news received.

No. It was the ten corpses that had been discovered, dumped in a sewer-runoff ditch, ten dead bodies that had last been seen on their way to take down Sorreno. There was no chance that it was a coincidence that those ten trained and hardened hit men, gunslingers of the highest order, were slaughtered to the last man the same night as another army had been destroyed.

What kind of magical powers did this Soldier have?

"No, it's not magic," Molinov growled out loud, finally.

Millagro raised an eyebrow. "Magic?"

"Being able to take on all of that. He's not magic, just very crafty. Sneaky," Molinov added. "He cheats at fighting."

"You're just learning this now?" Millagro asked.

Molinov glared at his local partner. "Oh, this was no secret to you?"

Millagro raised a hand. "Calm down."

The Russian grimaced. "You're the one making me feel like a fool for..."

"No. The Soldier is the one making you feel like a fool. This kind of frustration between partners, it's been used before. He turns us against each other, losing trust. Making moves behind each other's backs," Millagro explained.

"Psychological warfare."

"He must have tricked them into thinking he was one of their number, and then shot them in the back while they weren't looking," Millagro added. "You have grenades and bullets slamming out of nowhere, you're going to have the element of surprise and plenty of mayhem on your side."

"And the men sent to kill Sorreno?" Molinov asked.

Millagro ran his thumb over the bristles on his chin. "Again, the element of surprise. He could have had an excellent vantage point, or been working within the shadows."

Molinov nodded, regaining his confidence.

"He's been fighting this battle his way," Millagro followed up. "We have to have him come to us on our own terms."

"Us?" Molinov asked.

"Me," Millagro said with a scowl. "I'm going to mobilize my FARC allies, and together, we're going to consolidate forces and defenses. Can you work with my people on the other end?"

"What, in Tumaco?" Molinov asked.

"Yes," Millagro answered. "We need someone to meet the submarines and protect them. There's a good chance that the Soldier might be in position to interrupt them, but the best place for him to hit is actually at their base or at their destination. Trying to track one of our subs in the river is going to be too tough."

"But finding the origin base will be the tough part," Molinov mused.

"He would have to get all the way to Venezuela to find the source of the submarines," Millagro added. "But considering how well he did here in Medellín…"

"He'd make it all the way to the prime sub base," Molinov concluded.

"He will have to make it past the border, and once there, he'll be operating illegally in another country. The Americans will be accused of an act of war," Millagro said. His mood was improving as he thought about it. "This will be even better for our long-term goals, no?"

Molinov smirked. "If your people can handle this…"

"They will," Millagro said. "I have Western Bloc holding down Tumaco tight. And the Orinoco base has more than just FARC. We've got Ecuadorans, Bolivians, Argentinians and Brazilians on our side there, not to mention my people."

Molinov nodded. "All right. Just to be safe, I am going to make a few more calls."

"Let them know what's up back home?" Millagro asked.

Molinov grunted in assent. "And see if we can get some assistance in Tumaco."

"More assistance?" Millagro asked.

Molinov took a deep breath. "Not to insult the Western Bloc…or the army you've got at Orinoco…."

Millagro poured himself a cup of coffee, taking a dainty sip.

Molinov tilted his head, trying to gauge the Venezuelan's response to the offer.

"Send them. Better to have them and not need them," Millagro uttered, obviously tasting ashes in his mouth.

The Russian grinned.

Malaysia

NIK ONN PICKED UP the phone as he rested his other hand on the back of the young woman who had come to the big city for opportunities, only to end up with a face full of his dick. She'd wanted to be in the movies, part of the Malay soap-opera scene, but one taste of Onn's street product, and she was just another bitch on her hands and knees, trying to make him happy.

"I'm busy," Onn grunted.

"Too bad. Solyenko's not answering his phone," Molinov grunted.

Onn sat up, and the young woman between his thighs grabbed a breath. "Bitch, did I tell you to stop?"

"But…"

Onn swatted her on the back of the head, then leaned back.

"Working hard at the office?" Molinov asked.

"Fuck off, Alfa. I don't see you wrecking a goddamned embassy," Onn snarled, pressing the woman back to matters at hand.

"Oh, excuse me," Molinov replied.

Onn smirked, ignoring the sarcasm in the Russian's

voice. "Solyenko's talking with the Thais. It's a quiet, hush-hush meet. Any cell phones are frowned upon."

Molinov cursed in Russian.

"What's wrong?" Onn asked.

"We've got outside interference coming in. Tell Solyenko that we've gone Code Black."

"Code Black," Onn repeated.

"Don't screw it up," Molinov told him.

Onn clucked his tongue. "Code Black is simple, bitch. I can remember that."

"Even through a blow job?" Molinov asked.

Onn lapsed into Malaysian, cursing the idiot on the other end of the phone. He then took the phone in both hands, and texted both himself and Solyenko. "Texts sent, to remind me and to get through to Solyenko."

"Good," Molinov growled.

"What does Code Black mean?" Onn asked.

Molinov paused for a moment. "It means we've called down the thunder. Someone is after us, and he isn't bound by laws or treaties."

Onn pushed the would-be actress away from his crotch. "What did you say?"

"We have someone here in Colombia. He's already torn through dozens of men sent to kill him, and he's looking for the network," Molinov replied.

Onn felt cold sweat break out on his neck, trickling down his spine. "One man?"

Molinov repeated a curse word in Russian. "Did I stutter? English, knave! Dost thou speak it?"

"What do you think we're speaking here?" Onn asked. "You said it was one man!"

"Do we have to worry about the Thais?" Onn asked.

"No," Goomabang returned. "Now what's Solyenko all uptight about?"

"Interference in Colombia," Onn answered.

"Really? So why the pissy mood to me?" Goomabang asked.

Onn debated letting the man in on it. "Just get Solyenko to the arsenal. It's a *big* emergency in Colombia."

"That does not sound good," the bodyguard muttered.

"It isn't," Onn replied. "Just get him and his people the guns, and hope that they can take care of it."

"You mean, this interference is going to come here?" Goomabang asked.

Onn gritted his teeth. "It will get here if you don't do what I asked!"

"Fine," Goomabang snapped back.

Onn took the phone and hurled it at the plasma screen. A lightning crack appeared in the surface. The young woman screamed and ducked. He'd only just missed her head. Tears were flowing down her cheeks.

He spoke to her in Malay. "Hold on, baby. No need to be all upset."

She looked askance toward him.

"This wasn't your fault, honey," Onn told her.

"Soldiers?" she asked.

Of course. The stupid aboriginals had only a bare bit of understanding of true Malaysian. How this bitch hoped to become an actress with a vocabulary of...

Onn glared at her. He'd never said the term "soldier" in Malaysian. Only English or Arabic.

"Come here, honey," he muttered, this time in English.

"Uh?" she returned, feigning stupidity.

"Come over here," he growled at her.

She took a step forward.

"You speak English, too, eh?" Onn asked, pinching both of her cheeks with one hand. Her eyes widened.

"Some," she answered. "Just...some."

Onn pushed her back against the wall.

"Are you a cop?"

"No," she sputtered.

Onn slid his thumb under her chin, finding the stiff tube of her windpipe. She swallowed, the muscles trying to dislodge the pad of that finger, but he pushed a little harder.

"You're a cop, sent to spy on me," he grumbled.

She blinked.

"Fuck soldiers...yes," she returned. "Be good lay."

Onn glared into her eyes. She was terrified. Was it just paranoia ripping through his mind?

"Go to the table and do some lines, bitch," Onn snarled.

She gasped as he released his grasp on her throat. She staggered away from him, then looked at the table. Cocaine was piled in a heap. She was already a tremble.

"You heard me," Onn ordered, switching back to Malaysian. "Snort some coke!"

Erra Majid blinked twice, then walked toward the table.

She had to maintain her cover. She was already on thin ice, and the only way to do it was to get blitzed out of her mind. She hoped that it would be enough, other-

wise, they'd find pieces of her in garbage bins across Kuala Lumpur. And if she were really lucky, she'd be torn apart post-mortem.

CHAPTER TEN

Using official channels to find a pilot was going to be tantamount to suicide. Luckily, Villanueva had been around Colombian law enforcement long enough to gain access to some aviators who were off the grid. This also kept Bolan from having to summon Stony Man pilot Jack Grimaldi from back in Virginia. Villanueva put Bolan and Winslow in touch with Lupe Magdalena. She was a Caucasian, with some Irish or Scot in her history, as her smooth, pale skin was dotted with freckles. Her hair was black, cut in a boyish style, her blue eyes at once inviting and full of burning intelligence, promising a hefty challenge when it came to any debate.

She had a Cessna 150 on pontoons, which Bolan knew would be perfect for navigating the Orinoco River, one of the waterways that would allow the traversal of contraband from Venezuela through Colombia, all the way to the coast.

The other great riverine transit system was the branches of the Amazon, which extended into the country. While the Orinoco itself didn't reach Tumaco, it sprouted dozens of major tributaries that reached as far as Medellín. Colombia was riddled with river basins, having both the Orinoco and the Amazon flowing through the nation, water splaying out like the branches of lightning bolts. In Venezuela, the two massive deltas crossed in the Casiquiare River, which formed a natural canal between the two mighty causeways.

From the Orinoco to the Amazon, there was one river that made it nearly to the west coast of the nation, the Caqueta. Its tail end petered out miles to the east of Tumaco and Buenaventura, but the river met with numbers of roads that could easily bring waterborne freight to the two port cities. Right now, they were flying east from Medellín along the Rio Medellín, which would take them toward the Orinoco, and then would cross into Venezuela.

Bolan rode shotgun with the pilot while Winslow was in the back. Both men scanned the countryside beneath them. The jungles of the river basin were thick, but they could easily see settlements, towns and cities along the shores. In places, there was more than sufficient room to navigate an aircraft carrier, though at other times, it was more suited to something the size of a large fishing boat.

Bolan turned and looked to "Mags" as she requested to be called. She threw him a glance from the corner of her eye, her wide mouth turning up in a smile. She showed a little wear and tear from a pale person's life in the sun. She wasn't wrinkled, but there were the beginnings of crinkles that only accented the beauty of her smile. She was closing in on her late thirties, by Bolan's estimation. Her hands showed easily ten, twenty more years on them while she maintained a semblance of youthful freshness. He averaged the eyes and the hands together for his estimate.

"See something you like, Mr. McCormack?" Magdalena asked.

Bolan returned the smile. "Perhaps another time, Mags."

Her teeth were bright, and Bolan tore himself away.

He let out a long breath, then turned away from Magdalena to look at Winslow. "So, where along these rivers was that way station supposed to be?"

"On *my* river," Magdalena said. "Rio Magdalena."

Bolan turned back to her and rewarded that comment with a smile. "Ah."

"She's right. The Magdalena has a turnoff where it has a few tributaries that angle off toward the Orinoco 'family,'" Winslow stated.

"You knew about this?" Bolan asked Magdalena.

She nodded. "I was the one who Miguel tapped to scout ahead."

Bolan narrowed his eyes.

"If I was a double, Villanueva wouldn't trust me to take you where you have to go," Magdalena returned. "Miguel thinks that this was someone inside of his organization, part of why he's going to Buenaventura, then Tumaco to make certain."

"You didn't 'smell' like you gave us up," Bolan stated.

Magdalena smirked at him. "What do I smell like?"

Bolan narrowed his eyes, a smile creeping across his lips. "Not in front of the kid."

"Hey," Winslow said in jest.

"Sorry, Agent Winslow," Magdalena spoke up.

"This is still awfully far from Medellín," Bolan mused. "Though, we're approaching the turnoff."

"What would you like to do?" the pilot asked. "I could come and help...."

"No," Bolan replied. "Not that I don't doubt you can handle yourself."

Magdalena shifted to display an Argentine Sistema Colt, a big, burly .45. But still, for all the size and power of its bullets, the Sistema had a handle perfectly fitted for a woman to use. "You'd like me to keep the motor running, in case we have to, as that adorable robot used to say, 'cheese it.'"

Bolan nodded. Winslow was smirking. "What's amusing?"

Winslow's cheeks reddened. "She likes the same adult cartoon I do."

Magdalena peered over her shoulder. "Ah, comedy is universal."

She turned back to Bolan. "All right. I'll land us a ways distant. I have an inflatable raft, in jungle colors, that you two can use. What is your plan, then?"

"Look for clues, traces leading back," Bolan replied. "If there's anyone on the scene, we try to ask questions."

"I doubt that will work," Winslow mused.

"That's why we'll be bringing along some firepower," Bolan added.

"Good luck," Magdalena.

She brought in the pontoon plane for a water landing.

THE EXECUTIONER TOOK the lead as the two men worked their way along the riverbank. It had taken them half an hour to travel the four miles to the alleged way station that the counterfeit smugglers used. Even as they closed with the station, both Bolan and Winslow could smell the unmistakable reek of a cocaine lab processing the latest harvest.

The two men were on the ground, moving slowly, softly through the brush. They had both opted for jungle warfare kits for this infiltration. In the close, dense forest just off the rivers, neither man needed to engage opponents at more than two hundred meters. And as such, both were carrying M416 carbines, the Heckler & Koch upgrade of the classic Stoner AR-15, with which they were intimately acquainted. With only a nine-inch barrel, the rifles were quick and handy to maneuver, a vital necessity in these tight quarters. Stubby, blunt suppressors added only a few inches to the length of the weapons, but went a long way toward rendering the muzzle-flash and blasts much more endurable without eye and ear protection. Without such accoutrements, the fireball put off by a 5.56 mm NATO round out of the muzzle had been known to sear eyebrows off and leave a sunburn on an operator's face.

Bolan had his traditional sidearms, the mighty .44 Magnum Desert Eagle riding in a fast-draw rig on his hip, the sound-suppressed Beretta machine pistol under his left armpit.

Winslow had his SIG-Sauer P229, its .357 SIG barrel and ejector traded out for a 9 mm tube that Bolan had on hand. He also had spare updated magazines, flush fit ones that held 15-round, and 17-round rubber-capped extended sticks. The Walther PPS was also on hand as backup for the bigger SIG-Sauer.

The two men moved quietly, Bolan glad that Winslow's time in Colombia had given him some skill in navigating the dense forest floor. Even so, the sun lowering in the sky so that no rays of light touched down from the leafy canopy above, both were assailed by biting flies and mosquitoes. Fortunately, most of the critters were being kept at bay by duct-taped collars and sleeves and liberally applied grease paint. Even so, ninety-five percent of thousands still numbered in the hundreds, and both men were glad for their preparations against malaria and other fevers.

They stopped, kneeling about one hundred yards out from a small hut that was surrounded by several tents and tarps. By now, the only illumination was the dull reflection of the sun against the sky, its burning golden disk sunken behind the horizon.

Bolan eased closer to Winslow. "Stay here and provide over watch."

Winslow looked at him, and the soldier could sense the disagreement forming. Bolan cut him off with a raised finger. He handed the man a longer suppressor, this one meant for muffling the report beyond comfortable from a snub-nosed carbine to something truly stealthy.

"Switch out for that," Bolan told him. "Your night-vision optics should allow you to follow me. If someone comes close to me and I don't acknowledge them, you put one in their lethal triangle."

Winslow nodded. "Dead meat."

Bolan smiled. With that, he stalked toward the camp.

At least two people were moving about under one of the tarps. In the growing shadows, Bolan's eyes acclimated to the dimmer light and he was able to make out the rows of tables where coca leaves had been set out to dry. On the other side, vats sat idly. It was too early in the processing schedule for them to be fired up, especially as sundown made the firelight easier to spot. In daylight, the smoke might be a giveaway, but the tarp went far toward stifling that giveaway. The Colombian coke labs had learned that operating at night was harder to hide than in the day, simply by dint of the amount of heat given off exposing the operation to infrared cameras that could be fitted to drones and helicopters.

In the heat of the day, with the sun beating down on the top of the forest canopy, reflected heat energy went further toward camouflaging the tarps and the vats from aerial surveillance. Even so, the best way that the Colombian JUNGLAs and their American allies could discover these jungle processing plants was strictly by informants and diligent patrols. As such, enough cocaine was produced along the rivers and in the forests to supply the habits for a dozen countries.

Flashlights clicked on, and Bolan crouched low to the ground, fronds of a fern breaking up the pattern of his bulk with their swordlike leaves. In black, he was a phantom in the shadows just out of range of the torches, but neither man was scanning the forest. They were checking their inventory, making certain that none of it would be dislodged as it was pressed beneath canvas sheets in the night.

"Seguro?" one of them asked the other.

The partner nodded. *"Sí."*

The two clicked off their lights and moved back toward the shack. Beneath the chirp and buzz of the jungle's ambient noise, Bolan was now able to pick up the low rumble of a generator. He caught the brief glimpse of a light shining within the blacked-out shack before the two slipped inside and closed the door behind them.

Bolan kept on his toes, skirting the camp's perimeter, looking for trip wires or hidden traps as he circled around, hoping to locate the generator. He found nothing, once more the enemy seeming to prefer seclusion as their armor rather than booby traps.

He advanced closer to a second, smaller shack. While the other was thirty by thirty, this was long, about twenty feet by five feet. Cables came out through a wall, bundled together and secured by nylon ties before they disappeared under the muddy ground. Bolan was tempted to cut those cables, but that would be a little too obvious. These men had flashlights, which meant that they would see his sabotage. No, the best way to separate this crew was to simply turn off the generator inside the shack.

He touched the door and turned the handle. It moved easily. Too easily, his instincts screamed to him. Even as the door cracked, Bolan realized that something had to be in there, something dangerous. The slight movement of the door, the rush of air coming through the crack, caused something to stir within the hut.

That tiny bit of stimulus would not have alerted most men or even a dog.

However, 100 million years of evolution had made the crocodile, specifically the thirteen-foot American crocodile that had been laying quietly, in wait, yearning for the next meal.

Two weeks ago, a live chicken had been tossed through the door, an event that occurred every fortnight. Crocodiles possessed the largest brain-to-body ratio of any reptile, with a four-chambered heart and a cerebral cortex, all of which combined to make the ancient predator not only a skillful hunter, but a creature capable of learning from its environment. Even as it was intermittently fed, the beast that lay on the floor of the generator shack was tired of living within the confines of the hut.

It had been born free in the wild, and it longed to feel and hunt the waters of the Orinoco River. With a mind and instincts that were spawned from a bloodline reaching back to the age when dinosaurs roamed the earth, the crocodile had bided its time. Every two weeks, when it ate the chickens, it grew tired, logy, unable to move.

It realized that the presence of the chickens was closely associated with the smell of the two-legged mammals. Given the chance, the crocodile would fill its belly with a choice hunk of one of the mewling, greasy mammals who kept it imprisoned.

Unfortunately, the predator, gifted with 100 million years of hunting heritage in its genetic structure and a good twenty-five years of memory and experience in life had come across the one mammal who could ever hope to stand a chance against it.

The door creaked slightly open, and the crocodile threw itself forward, its strong legs digging into the ground to get more than sufficient traction to help it leap forward five feet. However, Mack Bolan, on the other side of the door, had already sensed that something was horribly awry and was pushing the door back closed.

Unfortunately, 850 pounds of reptilian magnificence was too much for even the strength of the Executioner's own 220-pound frame. The door split in two vertically as the powerful snout of the beast struck it dead center. The split was shallow, a mere crack, as the door was sturdier than the hinges that had held it in place. Those had snapped off the frame, screws pulling out curls of wood as man and beast toppled into the jungle trail.

Bolan pushed hard against the door, realizing that right now, it was the only thing between himself and the snapping jaws of one of Colombia's most powerful predators. Even though the wood provided a crude shield, there was no way he could handle the mass of even the forward half of the deadly apex predator. Gathering as much strength as he could, he planted both hands next to each other on one edge of the door and pushed. The door tilted across Bolan, the ground now holding up the other end as the thirteen-foot mass of muscle, armor and teeth scrabbled, claws trying to find purchase on the relatively smooth surface.

A grunt of rage exploded from the beast, the vocalization having all the sound and force of a .44 Magnum pistol going off indoors. Bolan winced at the bellow, even as he squirmed out from under the panel of wood and rolled to his hands and knees on the forest floor. He glanced sideways as the angry crocodile whipped its tail around, a slab of muscle capable of hurling its kind an entire body length out of deep water used as an offensive weapon.

The soldier saw the oncoming slash, the tail moving lightning fast, far quicker than he could hope to react. All he could do was allow himself to go limp. The flat limb slapped hard against Bolan's right leg, and if he'd stood his ground or had braced himself, the force of the impact would have dislocated his knee, tearing ligaments around the joint like strands of thread. Even so, Bolan was whipped to the ground like a rag doll, and he knew that he would be sporting a two-foot-long bruise from midthigh to midcalf if he happened to survive. Fortunately, his quick thinking and reflexes had allowed him to avoid muscle or skeletal damage.

Bolan pushed himself off the ground, groggy from how he was slammed around. He peered out of the corner of his eye and saw that the beast's eyes were bright yellow, the tiny mirrorlike structures absorbing light and turning those orbs into Hell's own spotlights. He sprang from the ground, throwing himself sideways as 850 pounds of jaws and scales rocketed toward him. Bolan was in midair when the cheese-grater back of the crocodile slammed against his shoulder. Bolan's blacksuit was snagged and torn, the skin beneath scoured until it was bloody in the monster's passage.

The soldier rolled, ignoring the pain of his body sandwiching his sore shoulder and leg against the ground. If he paused, he knew that the reptile would be on him in an instant.

Bolan rolled to one knee, his foot planted so that he could spring erect in a single movement when the other shack's door opened, light spilling out into the night-blackened forest. Colombians backlit by an ancient yellowed bulb suddenly saw the drama playing out in the jungle, a battle that had been told since the first primates came down from the trees and trampled the grass beneath their feet. Man and crocodile were facing off in a brutal conflict.

"Chingada!" one of the men shouted, clawing for a revolver in his belt.

Bolan grimaced and went for the Desert Eagle on his hip, the HK 416 carbine twisted around his back on its sling, tangled in its nylon strap too much to quickly draw. The .44 Magnum pistol sprang into its master's hand and the Executioner raised it, thumbed off the safety with a single smooth motion and pulled the trigger. Two hundred and forty grains of hollow-nosed, copper-jacketed lead screamed through the night and into the upper chest of the guy who tried to get the drop on Bolan.

Bone splintered in the path of the mighty slug, bronchial tissue rupturing from the hydrostatic force unleashed by the hollowpoint round opening in fluid mass. Blood vomited through the dying gunman's mouth as he toppled backward.

Now that the shooting had started, Bolan no longer felt the need to hold his fire in this conflict, but he was still loathe to shoot the reptile who was trying to kill him. It could have been an Orinoco crocodile, whose numbers in the wild had dribbled down to a dangerously close to extinction scale of a mere five hundred, while its near lookalike cousin, the American crocodile, was still vulnerable in the wild. He tossed a glance toward where the thirteen-foot predator had been moments ago. He saw only flattened vegetation, and the hairs on the back of his neck rose.

Now he was in the darkened jungle with only a handgun with armed cocaine thugs on one side and a prehistoric horror on the other. He grimaced at his luck, but just for a moment. He fired two more powerful rounds into the shack's doorway, but the enemy had scattered, fleeing from the horrible thunder and flash of the Executioner and his Desert Eagle.

One figure was racing away in the dark, his feet snapping fronds and stems, slapping and splashing mud as he fled. His flight was swift, and he was almost gone into the shadows, well out of the spray of light that hampered Bolan's night-vision

But where even the soldier's keen, night-fighting eyes had limitations, the crocodile had none. It caught the movement of the frightened mammal in the forest, and its nostrils picked up an all-too-familiar stench, the stink of sweat and grime that had marked the hairless ape that threw those chickens to it. The crocodile didn't care that the chickens had been thrown to it because the men needed to maintain the generator, having figured out a safe way to refuel their electricity producing motor from the outside to spare them the wrath of their "guard dog."

The crocodile cared only that this was its tormentor, and that the tormentor was made of protein under those false skins about its limbs and torso. The man was fleeing the gunfire, unaware that it had now entered the realm of a stealth hunter with millions of years of hunting instinct hardwired into it.

With hunger and savagery, the crocodile launched itself into the path of the fleeing man. Jaws stretched wide, then snapped shut on the lower leg of the Colombian, a ton of bite force applied through spikes designed to crush, not cut or pierce, clamping down. Shin bones snapped and cracked as the crocodile pushed with its legs and tail, spinning on the jungle floor.

The man released a horrific cry of agony, skin tearing, muscle separating, blood vessels bursting as those insanely powerful jaws worked like a pair of pliers, twisting about everything from the knee down like the stem of a fruit on a tree. Hot gore splashed across the crocodile's eyes, and the lower leg of the Colombian was no longer attached to him. With a surge, the beast threw its head up and allowed gravity to drop the mangled half limb down its throat.

A few more snaps, and the single sign that the crocodile had eaten was hidden by the shadows, blood smears only giving off a coppery stink in the pitch-black forest. The Colombian, however, didn't see anything, didn't hear anything. He was gibbering, his mind snapped by the agony and shock of having his leg amputated by a living thresher. Fingers clawed in the foliage-littered jungle floor, lips bubbling with bloody spittle as the man had bitten his tongue, as well.

The crocodile had food sliding down its gullet, but hunger was now the least of its concerns. It eyed the trembling, whimpering heap of mammal flesh before it, the former jailer now at the mercy of the beast.

The Colombian blinked, looking at the monster it had once used as a tool, had kept as a prisoner.

He had been monster to it; it was only natural that the crocodile sought revenge.

With another lunge, the jaws snapped down, snatching the Colombian's head and shoulder between them.

Bolan took cover behind a tree trunk even as he heard the brutal slaughter in the jungle. The shrieks of terror and agony, the roars of the beast washed through the trees like a sudden flood, one that was poisoned with terror that froze two of the gunmen in their tracks as it splashed over them.

Considering that the pair was packing AKs, however, Bolan decided to give each a pill to calm their nerves. The .44 Magnum doses of oblivion struck both men as they were shocked still. Both were bowled over, one man cored through the center of his face, brains spewing volcanically out of the back of his skull, the other whirled with a heavy impact to the shoulder.

Bolan was set to send another round chasing after the fallen man, to end his pain and suffering when the crocodile surged past the big American, sprinting on the jungle floor, its deceptively short legs allowing it to run at ten miles an hour, nothing much compared to a world-class, record-breaking athlete, but against a fallen Colombian, it was the blitzing freight train of death that leaped on him, jaws crushing the thug's remaining good arm before incredibly strong neck muscles whipped him around.

Bolan held his fire, fascinated by the carnage, realizing that this angered monster was no threat to him.

The only other threat was betrayed by the subsonic "thump" of Winslow's rifle firing in the darkness. The last of the cocaine processors had been trying to flank the soldier in the darkness, but Winslow's night-vision scope had found the gunman and put an end to him.

The crocodile thrashed until the torso separated from the arm in its mouth. The mighty thrashing and the brutal wrenching of the limb, severing arteries, left only a battered corpse behind. Out of convenience, more than hunger, the predator swallowed the Colombian's arm, then turned back toward the Executioner.

Bolan quickly reloaded the Desert Eagle, but refrained from opening fire. Those gleaming eyes, reflecting the tiniest amounts of light like beacons to an inferno, glittered momentarily.

The crocodile had reacted to Bolan, thinking it was

initially a tormentor, but the mammal had only sought to protect itself. Indeed, the mammal had to defend itself from the same two-legs that had imprisoned it. Now, the Executioner made no hostile moves toward the great reptile.

Vengeance sated, the beast whipped around and bolted off into the forest, disappearing behind a curtain of shadows, trees and ground clutter.

"What was that?" Winslow asked over the radio.

"That," Bolan said, taking a deep breath, recovering his composure, "was a display of rule number one about abusing your guard dogs. It's something that will bite you in the ass. Fatally."

Winslow let out a low whistle. "Amen."

CHAPTER ELEVEN

There was nothing left to interrogate once Bolan, Winslow and the crocodile had finished their rampage through the little processing lab. Fortunately, there was communications on site, as well as cell phones and a laptop, complete with a satellite dish modem to allow contact with "home base."

Bolan had his cracker thumb drive ready. The little portable flash device was so tiny, he could have carried dozens of them without putting on a pound of gear, but this drive was equipped with powerful algorithms capable of breaking open and scanning any email or other form of communications. It would strip these messages off the hard drive or from the browser's "cookies" and transform them into a viable, easy-to-read electronic word-processing file for the soldier's perusal, as well as allowing the transmission of this information inside the laptop back to Stony Man Farm, the home base of the world's most covert action teams, located in Virginia.

The thumb drive did its work, and now the screen filled with the document, giving a rundown on all of the activities that the laptop had been used for. The cocaine processors had been using map programs to scan through the surrounding jungle, plotting paths along the rivers until they could reach someplace farther upstream.

They'd also been connecting with a bulletin board server, the address of which had been made into a clickable link in the document. Bolan tapped the touch pad, and the board popped to life, opening in the browser. It was the central clearing house for the cocaine distributors. It came as no surprise that the men stationed here were members of the FARC's Western Bloc, according to their profiles and passwords.

Bolan spent two hours reading everything that the thumb drive had stripped, Winslow pacing back and forth behind him, occasionally glancing out into the forest.

"The crocodile isn't going to return. It's free, it's fed and it has killed the humans who had kept it confined," Bolan said, noticing the activity out of the corner of his eye.

"Well, while you're playing Bruce Wayne in front of the Bat computer, we're burning night time. There's no telling when…"

"A relief team will be arriving tomorrow morning. They messaged that 9:00 a.m. was their ETA," Bolan responded.

"So you're not reading online Harry Potter slash fiction," Winslow mused.

Bolan smirked at the sarcasm. "Occasionally I do a little more than just put a Magnum slug into a head. If I didn't…"

"You'd be dead meat," Winslow returned. "I wasn't wrong about the whole Bat computer thing. You're pretty obsessive about knowing your enemy."

Bolan nodded, going back and scanning more information. This wasn't a glamorous part of the job, but every bit of information, every byte of data, was one more thing he could use to his advantage. He'd already located several waypoints, which extended farther up the river, all the way to the Meta and then the Orinoco. They, like this, had multiple purposes. Along the river shore, there was a mooring and resupply post for one of several submarines that the Western Bloc was utilizing in their efforts to fund revolution and violence.

According to the bulletin board, there were five vessels in the fleet, and they weren't true submarines. When they traveled along the river, there was a small canopy, much like the cockpit of a World War II P-51 Mustang, sticking above the surface while the main part of the craft was submerged. They were one- or two-man jobs that were able to move along stealthily, even amid riverine traffic. Each could carry up to a half ton of product, meaning that each trip provided $16 million in profits, more than making up for the cost of these craft's use in Colombia and Venezuela, let alone the initial purchase price.

There was also news about other subs, real ones this time, capable of full submersion and were truly seaworthy, able to make long-distance runs from South American coasts to the United States and back. These could carry five tons of cocaine, allowing the Western Bloc to profit in the range of $150 million or more. The return trip also would be beneficial, according to the BBS. The next coastal journey—straight into Tumaco—would be hauling in high explosives and ammunition that Western Bloc needed to continue its reign of terror.

Once ashore, the sub was going to be turned around, loaded and fully fueled, and destined for the South Pacific, a weeklong journey to deliver freshly minted counterfeit notes.

The BBS had given up secrets, but not to the identity of the Russians. This was all in-house notification to the local submarine tenders. Details such as who, and what exactly was going on was going to have to wait until Bolan caught up with the masters of this lot.

The Western Bloc sub would not arrive for another six days, which meant that scuttling this expedition was not an option. Bolan could continue his border crossing into Venezuela if necessary, bringing down the hammer on the FARC commanders working in concert with the foreigners. Bolan translated all of this information to Winslow, then pressed in an eight-gigabyte condensed flash memory card to save those files. The device could be plugged into Bolan's personnel computer or into any printer to disgorge the information within at a later time.

Further study of what was happening in the FARC's ranks was going to pay in dividends that would hamper their cocaine trade.

Winslow listened to what was going on and sighed. "We've still got a long way to go."

Bolan nodded. "I'm not sure if I warned you how..."

"Can it. I got a taste of this fight earlier," Winslow replied.

"Did it make you feel better?" Bolan asked.

Winslow shook his head. "It didn't make me happy, but it helped me not feel like a useless hunk of meat."

Bolan nodded.

"You know what taking that first step toward vengeance feels like," Winslow stated.

"I want you measured. Keep that fire in your belly,

be ready to fight, but you can't let that anger get you stupid."

"How many times did you learn that lesson?" Winslow asked.

Bolan thought about it for a moment. "Enough times not to go off half-cocked all of the time, but not enough to keep me from overreaching at times."

"Thank you," Winslow said.

"Not necessary. I need you sharp, otherwise my ass gets shot off," Bolan countered.

"We'd better call Magdalena," Winslow said. "She might be worried about where we went to."

"I gave her a ring on the radio an hour back when you were looking for crocodiles," Bolan answered him.

"Do you usually have this damnable prescience, or are you just an out-of-control psychic?" Winslow asked.

Bolan shrugged. "Maybe it's paranormal, maybe it's just awareness. Of course, I also could just be polite to the kind lady who dropped us off."

Winslow smiled. "So when do we start our hike back?"

"She's drifting the plane up to us in the river," Bolan said.

"And the crocodile?" Winslow asked. "Or his friends on the river?"

Bolan frowned. "Let's hustle and make certain things are safe for her."

The two men took off into the forest, back toward their raft.

LUPE MAGDALENA WAS waiting at the Cessna pontoon boat. If she'd suffered any difficulty with crocodiles, piranhas or any other creature larger than a mosquito, it hadn't shown. She had a smile for Bolan and Winslow as they approached, paddling their raft out to the middle of the river. It didn't take long to return their gear and the inflatable craft to storage.

"How did your expedition go?" Magdalena asked.

Winslow went wide eyed. "We rowed up the river, then walked in the jungle and then there was this big crocogator eating gun thugs! It was so exciting!"

Bolan grinned. "He's a little overstimulated. When he's like this, I give him a beer and put him to sleep."

"Woohoo! Beer and sleep!" Winslow said.

Magdalena chuckled at the banter. "So things went well? A crocogator?"

"It was hard to tell in the dark, but it was some species of crocodile," Bolan said.

"They'd been keeping it as a guard dog for their generator shack," Winslow added. "McCormack opened the door and the next thing we know, it's 'two-fisted tales of jungle action' out there."

"Oh, my," Magdalena returned. "Neither of you look injured."

Bolan shrugged. "Just some bruises and scrapes."

"I took care of them, but he could always use a little more nursing," Winslow commented, crawling into the back of the Cessna.

Magdalena smiled at the implication. "It'll be hard to do that while I'm flying us to the next port of call."

Bolan nodded. "It also makes things a lot less complicated."

Magdalena sighed. "All right, everyone buckled in?"

"Off we go," Winslow muttered. He laid his head

back, and within moments, he was breathing deeply, with the occasional snort of a snore, fast asleep.

Magdalena peered over her shoulder and smiled. "Aw. He didn't even need the beer."

"Thank heaven for small favors," Bolan replied. "You good for this?"

"I caught a cat nap while you two were exerting yourselves out in the forest," Magdalena responded. "I'm well rested, and have flown this river plenty of times at night."

"Fair enough," Bolan said.

"Sleep well," Magdalena told him.

Bolan was asleep as soon as the pontoons left the water.

DAWN CAME AND the Cessna had set down for refueling. Bolan and Winslow had both gotten an hour's sleep in the air, and were awake for the landing and resupply.

They were on the Orinoco River now, docked in Puerto Carreno, one of the towns farthest to the east in Colombia, a literal border town, with that limit being defined by the wide and powerful Orinoco. Across the water was the neighboring town of Puerto Paez, Venezuela, which despite the coolness between Bogotá and Caracas over the sanctuary provided to the FARC, were still on good terms of trade. Bolan stretched his legs and looked around. So far, there didn't seem to be much attention paid to them, but they had been noticed coming in.

The soldier wandered along the docks, speaking to locals in English and broken Spanish, if only to better identify himself as an outsider. He could have gotten along conversationally with any native Spanish speaker if he'd wanted, thanks not only to immersion training in the language, but also the assistance of one of his best friends, Rosario Blancanales, something of a linguist with various dialects of Spanish, and with Rafael Encizo, one of the oldest veterans on Phoenix Force and a native born Cuban.

Even so, this municipality's total population was a shade over 10,000. Except for importing and exporting crops and local fishing, the only other major economic feature of the town was mining. Gold and silver mines were in the area, but modern methods had not yet been introduced to this *departmento,* as the Colombian states were named.

Bolan had left most of his firepower back on the plane, but he kept a standard Beretta 93R holstered under an untucked safari shirt. Concealed carry wasn't the man's priority, as he stretched and bent to betray the presence of the firearm. He hoped that the news of an American, an *armed* American, would spread quickly.

He wanted to make certain that he was on the right track, and if any place had FARC and drug thug activity present, it would be the shores on the border-defining river.

Bolan thought about the position here and the things that were afoot. Venezuela had a lot to gain from an economic collapse of Colombia. There were rich mineral and fossil-fuel deposits that would go far toward increasing Caracas's stature on the world stage. Gold, silver and oil were major bargaining chips, which would increase the nation's political power. It was no wonder that Blocs of the FARC organization were given safe haven and political support from Caracas.

Once again, Bolan recognized how politics was so much empty bullshit, especially those governments that espoused "socialism" while engaging in wanton violence and bullying to achieve their ends. Venezuela claimed to be Communist, but in the end, it was money and power that made the world go around, even among the Marxist revolutionaries. There was profit, even in the most political of movements. That was where the violent and the greedy flocked. Any "purity" in these movements was quickly superceded by thugs who saw a venue to flex their muscles and engage in warfare on the helpless.

Even when Bolan was fighting the last of the "old guard" of the KGB, he could see that those men, those hollow, greedy men, were only looking to maintain their position in life in a case of "cold war profiteering."

There was only one "true belief" among those the Executioner warred against.

What I want is mine, and those in my path will die if they resist.

True, sometimes the ultimate goal was political power or just the enactment of old vendettas, wounds that should have healed over, forgiven by time and tribulation or allowed to fade into the dark channels of history, best forgotten. Those men were often the worst.

Bolan was doing the mental mathematics. So far, he had American-economy-destroying amounts of bills having been rumored at—those notes having been traced all the way down to Colombia, which itself was in its own feud with Venezuela, with oil fields and gold mines at stake. On the other side of the Pacific, the Chinese were also on the lookout for yuan notes of equally damaging capability. It was an attack that could devalue the People's Republic of China, which itself was fully embracing capitalism, becoming an economic powerhouse so great that the United States borrowed money from them. An attack on the economy of one would be a global disaster. The crippling of both superpowers, however, would be a financial apocalypse.

It would be the monetary equivalent of an all-out nuclear assault.

And throughout this ran the thread of the involvement of a Russian criminal. Or was he a criminal? What if he was someone who was still so old guard that he was around for the one maneuver that the USSR had attempted, and miserably failed at.

The KGB had orchestrated a devaluation of the U.S. dollar. It was a bold move that could have crushed the United States, especially after the gas crisis of the seventies. Instead, that ploy imploded, a SNAFU that made the already cash-strapped Soviet Union stumble even further. The counterstrike had been in effort to curtail American defense spending, which was bankrupting the Russian military's attempts to keep up.

Colombia was merely a detail, a side trip in the course of this mission. Venezuela was offered a chance at its own economic resurgence, and a chance to bury a hatchet, right into Bogotá's wallet. Naturally, in an assault on Colombia's capitalist economy, the pro-Communist FARC would be champing at the bit, making it easier for a socialist system to be installed. At least, that was what the leaders would shovel to the true believers. If the FARC had been truly Communist, they wouldn't have been so keen on aligning themselves and pulling in enormous profits from being enforcers and transporters of the cartels' cocaine billions.

Here, Bolan knew that there would be at least a few members of the Eastern Bloc of the FARC on patrol, looking for troublemakers, outsiders like the big American, or at least how he bumblingly presented himself. He didn't know how much longer he could fake being an inept field operative, not because of the effort, but because of the small sting of pride and common sense that told him to not be so blatant.

"You getting any interest yet? It's painful watching you fumble around," Winslow said over Bolan's earpiece communicator.

"I've got nothing," Bolan mentioned. Though he appeared to be oblivious to his surroundings, as well as to his own appearance, the soldier's senses and instincts were alert. Ears were keen for the sound of anything preceding oncoming violence. Eyes were flitting about, scanning for people who might have been trying to conceal their armed status, or avoiding Bolan's own line of sight. Even his nose was sharp for someone who stood out scent-wise, either smelling like imported muscle with colognes, or smelling of firearms lubrication or explosives.

The soldier's senses had been the fine line between life and death on far more occasions than he cared to count. It was that attention to detail that made it seem as if he had a sixth sense, a canny sensitivity to danger and imminent disaster.

"Maybe it's time to pack it all in, if that's the case," Winslow stated.

Bolan folded his arms, leaning against a post. He gave no indication that he was speaking to anyone, thanks to the sensitivity of the throat mike accompanying his earpiece. "There's something around. It's only logical."

"So maybe they're playing it smart and avoiding you," Winslow suggested.

"Definitely," Bolan agreed. "The 'boss' knew enough to keep an arm's-length distance between anything I've stumbled across and their main operation."

"More than an arm's length," Winslow said. "This place is dead."

Bolan looked at the river. "I don't think we'd get anything more on the Venezuela side of the river, either."

"What makes you say that?" Winslow asked.

"The water's too busy here. If you're moving the normal riverine submarines, then those subs are only barely submerged. It'd be too easy for them to be struck by fishing boats along the dock fronts," Bolan mused. "Sure the subs would pass through, but they'd be avoiding the boat traffic pulling up to the piers."

"We're looking for something that is more isolated, and directly purposed," Winslow concluded.

"That's my feeling. Submarine bases aren't too secretive and worthwhile, but I couldn't have known that without being here," Bolan said. He pulled out his Combat CDA, looking over the map. "This place was marked as a place for the submariners to stop off, someplace to get out, stretch their legs and resupply."

"Maybe get their dicks wet," Winslow added.

Bolan looked up and saw a couple of members of the world's oldest profession, two young women. At least, they looked young from the neck down, but prostitution was something that wore on a person, burning them out quickly. Sleeplessness, hunger and illness had left their faces lined, and one of them sported a broken nose.

"Thanks for the heads up."

"If you're interested in that, McCormack, Magdalena is definitely…"

"Quiet, Zack," Bolan cut him off.

"Con permiso, por favor," Bolan spoke to one of the pair. He fumbled in his pocket.

"We're off duty," the woman replied in passable, if thickly accented, English.

Bolan shook his head. "I don't want that."

The two women paused, looking him over. "You're a cop."

"American Secret Service?" one asked. "Eighty bucks, U.S."

She was smiling, but Bolan could feel Winslow fuming on the other end.

"Nope," Bolan countered. "Just wondering if you, or anyone you know, has had contact with some submarine sailors of late."

"We're on a river, man," one of the women told him, but her demeanor had changed drastically. "Not the ocean."

The other grew deathly silent.

Bolan nodded. "So, you're not working with the Eastern Bloc of the FARC, not servicing them here nor in Puerto Paez?"

The silent woman couldn't help but look back over

her shoulder. There was nothing directly across the joined forks of the intersection of Meta and Orinoco Rivers, at least nothing that looked like an actual river town. The first turned to her partner and gave her a hard shove.

"You don't have someone pick you up on one of the runabouts and take you to the other shore," Bolan said.

The talkative woman narrowed her eyes. "You have all the answers. Why are you asking us questions? Trying to get us killed?"

"Who's going to tell them that you didn't tell me where they were?" Bolan said. Her sudden rush to answer showed that Bolan had been off on where they went, but the talk of the runabout motorboat had hit close enough.

The quiet woman spoke up, cutting loose with a spiel in Spanish. "Listen, I don't want any trouble, and I don't particularly give a shit about them. I've got makeup covering bruises, and this crease in my nose is new."

"Emelda…"

Bolan rested a hand on her shoulder, then gave them a response in Spanish. "Your best chance is letting me know exactly where they are. Otherwise, my friends and I won't have the best chance of nailing the sub base."

Emelda nodded. "That's why I'm talking to you."

"Emmy…" the other said.

"You like having a knife pressed to your throat?" Emelda asked.

"No," she answered.

"Let me know how you get there," Bolan said. "I'll fake things, and storm off. Make it look like you stiffed me."

Emelda looked around. "Even better, I'll go get my brother. He has a boat…and no love for those Communists."

"Emmy…" the other woman said.

Emelda lifted her hand. "I will break your face."

"I'm not going to tell them anything," she answered.

Bolan cupped the other woman's chin, glaring into her eyes. "If things go wrong, I will be back."

That elicited pure terror in the other woman. She was paralyzed by his stare.

"Tonight, this spot an hour after sundown," Emelda said.

Bolan nodded. *"Putas chingados! Ellas vale pa pueras vargas!"*

He drew his hand back, but Emelda grabbed her friend and both of them recoiled from him.

The sudden flash of rage drew dozens of eyes to Bolan, and he glanced around. The role camouflage expert suddenly switched to shame and embarrassment, backing away from the pair. He jogged off, avoiding having to strike either of the working women.

Bolan hoped that bit of obfuscation would give the girls a reprieve from reprisals in the coming days.

CHAPTER TWELVE

Emelda was there at the promised time. Bolan and Winslow had been there since before sunset, paddling their raft from the pontoon plane's mooring to the lonely stretch of pier where the soldier had met her. The boat that they had was a wood-bottomed scull with oar moorings and a small outboard motor.

A slender young man was sitting beside her in the craft, a nine-foot-long affair that had seen better days. The inside was bare of finish and scuffed up with all manner of equipment, and the outside had been painted and lacquered over dozens of times to keep the hull watertight. The young man was named Emmanuel.

One thing that set Puerto Carreno apart from Medellín was that this part of the country was still the frontier, where the native peoples thrived. Both Emelda and Emmanuel were *mestizos*—a mixture of native blood and European genes, and they more closely resembled the dark, compact Mexicans who often crossed the border. Medellín was simply a microcosm of Colombia. The heart of the country was predominately white, while the "suburbs"—those parts deeper in the jungle and closer to the frontier between Colombia and Venezuela—were darker. Less European. To some, less pure.

Emmanuel assisted with moving gear into the nine-foot boat.

"We're going to motor away from the docks," Emmanuel told the Americans. "But once we get on the tributary where the Commies have their submarine dock, we're going to have to paddle."

Bolan looked to Winslow. The Secret Service agent flexed and stretched his shoulders. "Why not? It's the best exercise I've gotten in months."

"We're good," Bolan said.

He turned to Emelda. "You should go back."

The woman shook her head. "I'm going to make sure things are safe. That means I'm staying on hand."

"You could catch a bullet," Winslow noted.

"Better than having those bastards come to pick me up, than beating me to death, or raping me," Emelda said.

Bolan nodded. "If she's on the scene, then things will go quickly for her."

"You're letting her go into harm's way?" Winslow asked.

Bolan shook his head. "They'll stay with the boat. And you'll be between the base and them, working as sniper over watch."

"Leaving you alone in the middle of them. Last time that happened, you got slammed around," Winslow noted.

"Yeah, but I doubt that this time they'll have crocodiles pulling guard duty," Bolan replied. "This isn't anything new for me."

"You've raided a submarine base before?" Winslow asked.

The soldier thought back to his kayaking in Norway and his unintended discovery of a cold war–era submarine base built into the underside of a glacier. He also thought of an operation in North Korea, where a renegade cadre had installed its own sub base, this one designed to transport a deadly prion, a brain-eating protein.

The first had been collapsed with effort. The second had been obliterated with a near-nuclear-powered detonation of fuel-air-explosives, Bolan barely escaping the firestorm on the back of a motorcycle hurtling to the surface at top speed.

And there'd been others....

"I'll improvise something," Bolan told him.

Winslow swallowed. "You've had a ride on this merry-go-round before."

"If I told you..." Bolan began. He left him hanging, but the implication was clear.

Winslow concluded the phrase in his mind. *I'd have to kill you.*

MACK BOLAN STALKED through the jungle once more, silent and alone. This time, his assault rifle was ready for full-on conflict. The 416 had been converted from its compact PDW to its full length M27 IAR heavy barrel, and beneath the forearm furniture, an HK M320 grenade launcher. He had a bandoleer of 40 mm shells for the stubby little under-barrel cannon, as well as extended magazines for the HK. The IAR was short for Infantry Automatic Rifle, and as such, the design was made for sustained fire, churning out its brutal message of 5.56 mm destruction at 640 rounds per minute. The barrel was capable of quick change, but Bolan didn't anticipate leaning on the trigger and going all out like someone out of a third-rate action movie. The heavy barrel would take the sedate rate of fire easily, absorbing the abuse in a close-quarters melee. He'd change, *after* the battle, despite the speed and efficiency with which the barrel could be swapped in prolonged conflict.

With high explosives and a full-auto, full-length barrel combined, the soldier didn't need the suppressor on the end of the weapon. This was going to be a loud, brutal strike. Already, he'd placed a charge into the breech off the M320 grenade launcher, a thermobaric XM1060, which would spread a brutal concussive blast over a small area. The soldier was coming on full force, and he wanted the FARC submarine team to think that they were under attack with artillery. The next rounds were also anti-personnel in nature—both 24-pellet loaded "shotgun shells" and air burst M397A1s. He wasn't of the delusion that even a "homemade" submarine was going to suffer significant damage from a grenade launcher. Winslow, hanging back, also sat on a cache of moldable plastic explosives for the purpose of crippling the fleet.

The forest site ahead of him had lights on, but they had been diminished by the camouflage netting stretched between trees. No one would be able to see them from the air, simply by dint of that netting. Bolan scanned the area of shoreline, and things looked no more active than a small outskirt of a town, at least on infrared. The netting, however, was not as useful at close range. Just peering through the mesh he was able to see a full-blown camp. The lighting was low to the ground, as far from the camouflage as possible to avoid transference of heat, thus lowering the signature of the camp if it were caught in an infrared camera.

This place was much busier, and once more, Bolan referred to his mental map, the one he'd assembled after poring over the documents captured at the jungle coke lab. There were easily forty people present, many of them armed, and trucks idled to one side of the netting canopy. They were loaded with pallets, and workers were busy pulling rolling platforms up to them to transfer the cargo to the waiting submarines.

A quick scan with a pocket telescope informed Bolan that this wasn't the phony money, but simply cakes of coca and heroin that had been grown elsewhere and trucked this far, at least so far as the first packets unloaded indicated. He decided to hang back for a few moments, observing the off-loading.

The men worked in shifts, workers taking a break and trading their heavy-duty gloves for assault rifles. Everyone here was a soldier, even the women. There were radio communications and nervousness. He could hear chatter among the group. The drug workers were nervous because one of the way stations on the Meta river hadn't reported in since late the previous night. Eyes were wary, looking around, but Bolan currently was moving with all the urgency of a three-toed sloth on the other side of the camouflage netting. Quick, jerky movements would be what betrayed his presence, this close to the camp's perimeter.

A man wandered along the netting, his rifle slung over one shoulder, his hands cupped in an effort to start up a match to light his cigarette. Bolan lay low, remained slow and deliberate, drawing little attention to himself. It would have been tempting to take out this perimeter guard with a quick slash of a knife, but that would be wholly opposite of what he wanted now.

He continued to scan and watch the camp, allowing patience to settle in, to give him enough information of the layout, the numbers of people and their armament, to grant him the vital advantage he needed. The camp population was five men for every one woman, and the females on the premises were hardscrabble, either hefty women with wide hips and commensurate strength, or scrawny with arms lined with bulging veins from hard exercise. All of them looked strong, and mannish, sweat and grime having stained their faces and clothes.

It was little wonder that they sent out for sexual partners. Even if the women here enjoyed the attention of other men, there simply weren't enough of them to go around. One cuddly, yet burly armed woman sidled up to a similarly compact and stout man, whispering into his ear. The man grinned at what seemed to be the promise of some post-labor recreation.

Others were thrown into their work, drenched with sweat despite the cooling breezes coming off the river, though those were interrupted by the camou webbing draped over the facility.

The FARC rebels were peons, but they were armed and determined. They showed a powerful work ethic, doing their job with little complaint and plenty of focus. It was easy to see them as true believers in the cause, and for that, they all looked ready for the kill, each having at least one revolver strapped into a makeshift holster, and the majority sitting near or having slung a folding-stocked rifle over their shoulder.

Despite the admirable qualities among this group, he remembered Emelda's face, the punishment she'd endured over the time this camp had been here, the fear the other prostitute had shown when Bolan voiced his intent of raiding the sub base. These rebels were brutal, cruel.

If they chose to turn tail and run, fleeing the destruction Bolan intended to unleash within a few moments, then he'd allow them to escape with their lives. He'd made that clear to Winslow. Anyone who threw down their arms, or were just simply running as fast as possible into the jungle, would be allowed a chance at continued survival. However, anyone moving with the intent to flank the soldier was fair game for the Secret Service rifleman.

Winslow was working with his own 416, and though this one had been given the IAR heavy barrel, a suppressor was affixed to the muzzle, and a precision low-light optic had been put in place. The M27, by dint of its closed-bolt operation, could be used as a designated sharpshooter's weapon when coupled with the proper optic. Earlier in the afternoon, they had run some rounds through the weapon to make sure that the automatic rifle would shoot to point of aim, especially with the can in place.

Winslow had been able to squeeze a minute of accuracy out of a firearm that was intended for supplying a high volume of suppressive, automatic fire. That was one thing that Bolan liked about the HK designs—they were able to do anything asked of them, and more. Bolan crept closer to observe the submarines. There were four emplaced. On the dock that they surrounded, crates of arms had been unloaded. He could read the old Cyrillic script, Russian black-market firepower, probably having made it through countless hands before ending up on these shores. It didn't escape Bolan's attention that the rifles that these FARC guards were carrying were new, with black polymer furniture as opposed to surplus arms with wooden stocks and hand guards.

There was that Russian angle. Venezuela, however, was awash in Russian firearms, having imported a hundred thousand AK-103s from the former Soviet Union. If this wasn't a sign that the FARC had the specific backing of Venezuela, then there was little more that could be evidence to the most jaded of observers. This was likely under-the-table weaponry, all things considered. Caracas could hardly afford to have Colombian terrorists captured with equipment that could be traced back to their arsenal. Even so, ammunition, magazines and spare parts were going to be plentiful on the Orinoco River for the soldiers of revolution in Colombia.

Bolan moved back to where he could observe the trucks. They were nearly empty, but now he saw huge stacks of paper accompanying the pallets of drugs. He used his pocket scope to get a closer look, and sure enough, they bore the color scheme of Colombian peso notes and U.S. hundred-dollar bills.

He keyed his throat mike.

"Business is about to pick up. Choose your targets, and on my mark, open fire," Bolan whispered.

"Got it," Winslow replied.

The soldier leveled the M320's sights onto one of the idling trucks. He could have gone for the stacks of illicit product, but Bolan knew that an explosion in the open, atop a pile, would do very little, while a detonation of his thermobaric grenade in the back of the panel van would produce a jet of superheated air and shorn metal much more conducive to mayhem.

He squeezed the trigger, and the launcher chugged off its load, the grenade spiraling into the back of the panel truck.

An instant later, hell broke loose in a sheet of flame and fragmented metal.

McCORMACK'S MARK WAS unmistakable—the rear of a panel van rupturing as a thermobaric explosion created a turbo-jet of overpressure that crumbled the vehicle like a beer can. The vortex of flames spiraling out the back of the vehicle swirled around a spike of forward force that bowled over four men and a woman standing in the open.

Winslow swept the five of them, looking for signs of hostility, but they were down, unmoving, skin mangled and darkened under the incredible heat given off by the grenade. The rest of the camp was suddenly up in arms, scrambling crazily around the area. Some of them rushed to the scene of the explosion, worried looks on their faces. Winslow couldn't bring himself to pull the trigger on a group that was made up of rescuers, trying to save their friends, but he didn't hold his fire. He fired a long burst across their bow, and the men were held up in fright.

One of them looked toward the source of gunfire, while the others scrambled for cover. Winslow saw the man go for his gun, and the rifleman galvanized, switching to semiauto and firing two shots, center of mass. Heart blown out, the gunman flopped lifelessly backward.

Winslow kept an eye on his falling target long enough to make sure he wasn't getting up. Through the optic, the spray of blood and the ugly mangling had been blatantly obvious. His other eye, however, was open, peripheral vision picking up movement as he tracked for another target.

Below, at the edge of the camouflage netting, another of the HKs opened up only instants before the unmistakable chatter of a couple of Kalashnikov rifles thundered from inside. McCormack had attracted some attention, but Winslow didn't dare slow down and keep an eye on the mysterious super-Fed sent by Washington. Instead, he saw that a quartet of gunmen was moving into position to get to the remaining delivery trucks. All were armed with rifles, and they'd extended the stocks on the folding assault weapons. Murder, not salvage, was in their demeanor.

Winslow shifted the IAR's aim, centering the cross hairs on the leader of the pack. He pulled the trigger once, and a 5.56 mm round hit the FARC combatant at the joint where his neck met his shoulder. The projectile punched in, and thanks to the quirks of the high-velocity slug, as soon as it hit fluid mass, it turned from pointy object to tumbling mass of bent and flattened copper and lead. The 5.56 mm round cartwheeled until it struck the clavicle, then broke in two, forming two smaller, yet equally violent buzz saws tearing through flesh and sinew.

Blood exploded from the lead gunman's lips as he stumbled, legs tangling with each other and suddenly stealing his forward momentum. The man immediately behind him tripped over the collapsing corpse, but the other two skidded to a halt, splitting their paths and turning toward Winslow's side of the camp.

The Secret Service agent brought his rifle around and fired again. He pulled the trigger twice, this time using a pair of 5.56 mm tumblers to make sure he'd stop. The first round smashed into the join where the gunner's collarbone met in the center of his throat. Bone and muscle exploded on impact. The second bullet arrived only a moment later, striking the Colombian in the center of his face. What were once human features imploded into a crater of gore and mangled tissues.

Two down from this group, but the third man triggered his rifle. The suppressor did a lot to take the muzzle-flash away from the M27, but Winslow knew that he was a sitting duck as he rested in the crook of a tree's bifurcated trunk. A volley of 7.62 mm ComBloc rounds snapped through the darkness, some of them striking one of Winslow's support trunks. The young American swung his M27 on target and fired as quickly as he could work the trigger. Bullets slammed into the gunner's stomach, folding him over, sending the AK-103's payload into the dirt at his feet. Even so, the gunman didn't topple over.

Winslow fired more. Three, four, five rapid shots. The 5.56 mm rounds had done more than enough to kill the Colombian rebel, smashing through vital organs, severing major arteries, but that wasn't enough to completely unplug the body, not like the heart or central-nervous-system hits he'd scored before. The

FARC guard was a stumbling corpse, and Winslow punched a sixth round into the toppling form.

"McCormack!" Winslow rasped.

"Keep your shirt on," Bolan replied from the other end. Winslow flinched as a bellow resounded down below, a 40 mm grenade spewing its deadly payload of shrapnel and concussive force.

Men and women screamed, firearms crackled and chaos ruled in the FARC camp. Winslow could follow the trail of the Justice Department's agent, as much as by the way people had been set to flight, as well as by the unmistakable rattle of his IAR, chewing through magazines at 650 rounds per minute.

"Zack! Subs!" Bolan barked.

Instantly, Winslow turned his attention to the dock. There were men scrambling along the platform, and he flicked the fire-selector switch to full-auto once more, sweeping a 10-round burst along the pier. One of the escapees tripped, diving off the walkway, making a loud, hollow metal sound as he crashed face-first into the hull of the docked submarine. If Winslow's rounds hadn't killed him, the sound of that impact made it certain that either his neck broke or he was drowning from being knocked unconscious.

Two more men turned and opened fire on the forest, their weapons slashing through the branches of nearby trees. Winslow ducked as a 7.62 mm slug smacked into the bark too close for comfort. He leaned out behind cover, but he already saw the unmistakable, grim black form of the Executioner come out from behind a building. The thunder of the grenade launcher beneath the barrel of Bolan's IAR was loud and sharp. Almost instantly, the men who had scrambled onto the pier were swept away by an unseen wind.

That invisible force was a buckshot round loaded into the breech of the M320, twenty-four steel bearings striking flesh, having spread out three feet by the time they'd reached the Colombian gunmen on the dock. Bodies splashed and crashed into the water.

Bolan paused, breaking the breech and letting gravity drag the empty case from the grenade to the ground. He pushed another fat, thick shell into the weapon and closed its action. He dumped his partially spent magazine and looked around as he fed the hungry rifle once more.

"It looks clear…" Winslow mused.

The Secret Service agent's attention was drawn by a sudden movement. He turned and opened fire on a shape sliding through the river's surface. Bullets struck the surface and clanged off the canopy of the mostly submerged craft. Motors were pushing the vessel out, but its glass was substantial, too much for even the IAR to penetrate at range.

"Armored glass," Bolan's voice hissed over the radio. He let the M27 hang on its sling, pulling out his Desert Eagle. The .44 Magnum pistol bellowed, producing massive streaks of light and thunder in the darkness, slicing through the shadows. The FARC semi-sub was picking up speed, though, engines muffled by the water's surface.

Bolan triggered the M320 under his weapon's barrel, sending up a large plume of foam. He'd just missed the cockpit of the low-slung craft on the surface of the water.

"They didn't load anything on board!" Winslow called.

Bolan wasn't listening. He had run up to the end of the dock, pushing another shell into place. The thermobaric and air-burst rounds were hell against normal infantry, but the enemy submersible was moving away, too swift, too protected by the shadowy darkness of the waters.

He fired again. The water roared, spitting up more foam as the grenade went off. The FARC sub was getting away.

The Executioner looked back, then jogged toward another of the subs. "Don't move into the camp. I haven't made certain the area is sterile."

"But…"

"Stand your ground and keep over watch," Bolan growled, crawling into the canopy of an unattended submarine. "Nobody comes back for the rifles left on the dock. If they do, kill them. If they're back to give first aid, then let them be."

Winslow grunted in assent. "All right."

With that, Bolan's sub slid away from the pier, his combat knife having made short work of the mooring lines.

CHAPTER THIRTEEN

The controls of the smuggling sub were simple enough. It steered like a car, and had a throttle like many standard motorboats, something he'd familiarized himself with, thanks to the assistance of Phoenix Force amphibious warriors Calvin James and Rafael Encizo. While there was no way that Mack Bolan could consider himself a professional speedboat racer, he could pilot them if necessary.

The throttle was pushed to its limits, but even so, the smuggler subs were capable of a good ten knots, something that surpassed even World War II military submarines, but the difference here was that these craft were smaller, and were not fighting against the depth pressure that those diesel giants could.

Inside the canopy, Bolan could hear the ugly grunting and snarl of the motors that worked the Colombian craft's propeller screws. The watercraft stunk of diesel, and he could see two vent pipes behind him, poking up like periscopes. They belched out their exhaust, bubbling along the surface and dissipating in the misty fog that clung to the river's surface at night. Waves splashed against the windscreen, even as Bolan pushed his ship in pursuit of the other craft.

"Mags, one of the subs got away. Can you get eyes on the river?" Bolan asked.

One of the things that the soldier had been prescient enough to anticipate was the need for aerial surveillance. In the air a few thousand feet, Lupe Magdalena was invisible and inaudible in her Cessna pontoon plane.

"I'm trying to look, but the surface is choppy. I can't make out anything at this altitude," she answered. "You want me to use the thermal goggles, correct?"

"Our best bet," Bolan answered. Ten knots was just under twelve miles an hour. The enemy had at least a forty-five-second lead, which meant that he was running behind, left there by sheer speed. He did have a hope that maybe one of the enemy sub's mechanisms had been damaged by rifle fire or the proximity of his grenades, but that didn't seem likely. The hull around him and the glass were both thick and sturdy. He could make out the wire mesh sandwiched between panes of glass, proving that the cockpit was reinforced.

Even his mighty .44 Magnum pistol hadn't been enough at distance. The shell of the do-it-yourself sub was equally tough, probably a safeguard against a collision with regular river traffic. Each sub could carry millions of dollars in products, and losing one could cause an enormous dent in the FARC's budget, a setback that could threaten their operations. Bolan squinted through the darkness, then finally gave up.

He reached into his battle harness and pulled out a pair of ATN PVS7 night-vision goggles, slipping them over his head and turning them on. The infrared floodlight built into the unit hit the windscreen and went through, searching over the churning river surface. Currents were strong now, and Bolan had to hold on tight, or else his steering of the craft would be overridden by the flow of the river.

In the distance, his night-vision goggles picked up a small shape bobbing on the water. Infrared light bounced off the surface of the form, and the aerodynamic shape showed itself to be the canopy of the lead sub. Bolan grimaced as he tried to gauge the distance between himself and the enemy. A sudden surge of current suddenly struck his sub, and he had to crank the wheel to maintain his original course.

The torrent, however, was stubborn, wrestling with man and machine, trying to ram it up against the shoreline. Bolan could hear the belly of his sub scrape the riverbed. He pushed the throttle for all he had, knowing that he needed to get into deeper water. Slowly, inexorably, the sub pushed away from the riverbank, the incessant crunch and scratch of the keel on the bottom dissipating. Waves inundated one side of the canopy, producing a blind spot for Bolan.

There could be anything on the shore, or the Colombian rebels could be turning back. Bolan's night-vision floodlight had nothing; it couldn't push through the small wall of water slamming against his side.

"Mags?" Bolan asked.

"I'm looking," she answered. "I've got several objects moving in the river. *Infierno!*"

"Bodies picked up by the current?" Bolan asked.

"Sí," she answered.

He could hear the grimace in her voice. Bolan concentrated dead ahead, looking at the rolling, low waves. From a normal position of a boat floating on the surface, these waters would have been frightening, but they wouldn't have interfered with visibility. However, the top of the cockpit was a mere eighteen inches from the surface. Waves that rolled only two or three inches struck the front windscreen and splattered in his face.

Bolan spotted a thick black shape in the water. He recognized it as a tree branch, and he swerved the sub's wheel. At the speed he was moving, it was like trying to swim through mud. His arms bulged with the effort, and some part of him wondered if he would snap the rudder shaft.

The sub rocked as the hull scraped against the branch, and suddenly the canopy was tilted all the way to one side. Bolan had dipped himself below the surface. Water jetted through tiny fissures in the cockpit's design, but natural ballast and buoyancy righted the sub quickly enough. He glanced around, looking for landmarks, scanning to get his bearings.

Even as he did so, a corpse suddenly flashed against the windscreen, bones crunching as the lifeless torso was struck by the canopy. Bolan flinched from the impact, gritting his teeth as he realized that the body had more than enough mass to break through the glass. Fortunately, the sub builders had designed their craft well.

"I see you, McCormack!" Magdalena said via radio. "There's another cockpit like yours, but it keeps flashing in and out of sight."

"The waves are making it hard to see us," Bolan answered. "They're reflecting the illumination flood away from the craft."

"I noticed storm clouds on the horizon. That must be the cause of the surge in currents," Magdalena said.

"That explains much," Bolan replied.

"I see them!" Magdalena said. "You are closer to them."

"How much?" Bolan asked.

"Give it fifty meters," Magdalena returned.

"Which means they might as well be a mile ahead," Bolan grumbled.

That didn't mean the soldier was going to give up. He kept the throttle all out. He knew that there were objects in the river ahead of him, and by moving at such speed, in these turgid waters, there was going to be little margin for error when it came to avoiding rocks, tree trunks, even other ships. At least he had a glimpse of where the enemy was.

Another object crashed against the glass, and Bolan fought every instinct to swerve. He couldn't make out what it was that hit this time, so it could have been a log, or it could have been a living creature. There was fresh, bloody flesh in the water now, and that would provide a feast for countless Orinoco predators. There were anacondas, piranha and crocodiles, as well as smaller creatures. Bolan wouldn't put it past a jaguar or two to take a dip into the rapidly flowing river to grab a nice hunk of flesh.

The piranha weren't going to be a problem. They were small, and would be deflected by the hull and cockpit. Unfortunately, anacondas and crocodiles weighed in at hundreds of pounds, and possessed hides as tough as armor plating. If one of them crashed into the cockpit, Bolan could see that he'd be in for the fight of his life. He'd either have to swim against the current, or he'd be struggling against a reptilian superpredator in its element.

Bolan would prefer to drown if it came to that.

He looked around, cursing the blind spot produced by waves coming from the starboard of his submarine. He wished that he could do something like actually dip the cockpit under the surface, but the churning waters would make things just as hard to see beneath. Sediment and biomass were being swept along by the currents, leaving him blind, even with the full power of his goggles' infrared spotlight.

"McCormack! The sub's turned!" Magdalena shouted from above.

Bolan grimaced as he fought the steering, craning his neck to see above the lapping waves. He caught a flash of movement on the water, a brief glimpse as the spotlight caught the glass of the other sub. He steered toward it, and found himself following a long, curving arc, turning back on itself. The enemy could not have wanted to go out of this tributary, despite the choppy waters.

Bolan craned his neck once more, looking for movement on the surface when he spotted the enemy's cockpit, splitting the waves as it tore down his throat. Bolan turned back to straight and felt the hulls of the two FARC craft clang against each other, their bow bouncing against his aft. He checked his dash, looking at the systems. So far, the propeller screws seemed to be responding well. The glancing impact had done nothing to inhibit the movement of the smuggler sub.

Even so, that maneuver showed exactly how desperate the enemy was. He peered back over his shoulder, watching the canopy of the other ship disappear into the darkness, swallowed by waves. Bolan turned, pushing the sub as fast it would go, veering to an intercept course. He couldn't be certain if the enemy was going straight, but he did know that the best way to stay out of their path was to spin around and charge in their wake.

Waves sluiced around the front of the cockpit, and for another brief instant, he saw the Colombians come close, charging past. It was as if they were jousting, riding the backs of submerged beasts who were eager to knock heads against each other. Unlike a ram or a rhinoceros, the humans within each of the subs would be vulnerable to a collision. Bolan twisted his smuggler boat around, looping in a half figure eight and throttling toward the other ship.

Now his infrared flood was able to pierce the darkness. He could see the faces of the FARC submariners through their cockpit, and they, too, wore night-vision goggles. One of them reached up, throwing back a latch, wrestling with his folded AK-103.

Bolan grimaced as he knew that neither Winslow nor he had been able to damage the canopy of the submarines, but that was because they were shooting at a distance with bullets that were less than half the weight of those fired by the Kalashnikov. The other sub was barreling its way toward him, playing chicken. At a range of only twenty feet, the steel-cored 7.62 mm rounds would strike the armored glass hard enough to crack it. Enough bullets striking, say, a full magazine, would get through, hitting Bolan in his cockpit. The soldier swerved, swinging his sub wide from the other ship.

Instead of the close proximity pass, the FARC gunner had to track a low slung target in bobbing waves. Slugs plugged against the armored glass, and Bolan could see the spiderweb cracks formed by their impacts. Had he gotten closer to the enemy, those slugs would have hit with far more accuracy, and much more often, rather than skipping off the river surface or tracking wide.

Bolan throttled down his sub, forward momentum pushing him through the water until he struck the current. Working the rudder, he was spun. It was time to let the tributary of the mighty Orinoco assist him, not hinder him. The submarine turned, and he could now see the enemy's canopy. The FARC gunman was wrestling to seat the next magazine into his assault rifle.

Bolan pushed the engines to life, and with the current at his back, he was now a torpedo, angling right toward the enemy's sub canopy. The rifleman got his magazine in place, worked the bolt, but it was too late.

Suddenly, Bolan was far above the water, looking down as the FARC soldier was whipped down to the surface as his ship rolled over. The Colombian's arms were spread wide in shock, his rifle lost in the roiling current. Inside the canopy, however, Bolan's skull was assaulted by the scream and groan of metal grinding on metal. Hulls crushed against each other, and then suddenly gravity took over, and Bolan was cantilevered hard, nose down into the river.

The soldier was glad that he hadn't opened his own cockpit to engage the enemy in a gunfight. Even so, he could feel the spray of water tearing into the bulkhead beneath him. He'd ripped something below, but he had the advantage that he hadn't opened up the top. Nothing was blasting him in the face, not like the other submarine.

Bolan held on to the steering. There was no ballast or dive controls on this vessel, so he wasn't sure if he was able to steer upward. Fortunately, there was enough air inside the hull that it provided enough buoyancy to bring it popping back up to the surface. Unfortunately, the propeller screws were no longer responding. The other craft's hull had to have scraped them, and the weight of the two ships against each other had snapped them off or bent the shafts.

Whatever the diagnosis, the results were still the same. He was dead in the water, and at the mercy of the savage current.

"Mags, I'm adrift! My propellers are gone," Bolan called up.

"There's movement in the water near you," the pilot answered. "Oh, my God…"

Bolan didn't need to know what was happening. There was blood in the water, and now, there was living prey, splashing about. Perhaps it was the gunner, somehow having survived. Maybe it was the pilot of the other sub. It was even likely that both men survived. However the odds were cut, there were things in the river that knew they were living flesh.

A sudden surge broke the surface, and Bolan could see a torso locked between two sets of powerful crocodile jaws. The man between them was held still for only a brief moment, a terrified look on the victim of the two prehistoric predators, and then the powerful reptiles thrashed themselves around, barrel-thick bodies rolling in the water and in opposite directions. The torso was wrung out like a wet rag, tearing under the massive weight of at least two-tons of carnivore. Bolan turned and noticed a single arm was waving over the surface. He directed his infrared spotlight toward that thrashing limb and saw the deadly, two-foot thick coils of an anaconda wound around everything below the elbow. The arm suddenly bent, the joint snapping in the wrong direction as serpentine muscles squeezed. The arm disappeared beneath the turgid waves.

"Welcome to the feast," Bolan grimly stated as he realized that he was the last living human in these waters. He glanced into the hold and saw that the area was filling up with water. He pushed on the wheel, but it had been frozen solid. Obviously, the same damage that had wreaked havoc on the propellers had to have been laid on the rudder.

Something bounced against the cockpit, and the spiderweb patterns caused by rifle rounds striking the bullet-resistant glass started to grow, like an infection branching out along the outside glass. Bolan made out the side of a crocodile, and realized that he was solidly in their territory now.

That wouldn't last long as the submarine was filling fast. Even if the bulk of a crocodile wasn't pressed against the cockpit, jamming it shut, Bolan didn't find his chances too optimistic. It was bad enough that he was in the deadliest waters in the world, filled with reptiles and fish that flocked toward human flesh. The currents, however, were powerful. If they could bounce around the submarine, there was no way even a superb athlete like the Executioner could fight the rapids.

"McCormack! Look out!" Magdalena shouted.

There was nothing to steer, no way to propel the smuggler craft, but Bolan looked up at the doom that the pretty pilot warned him of. A tangle of trees that had toppled into the river as the shore had been washed away. Many were still stuck to the land, tendrils of roots anchored deep in the soil.

The sub came to a stop. Bolan had braced himself, but the force of the sub striking the copse of half-sunken trees was more than enough to bounce his head against the inside of the canopy. His forehead split open, blood pouring down and stinging his eyes. He gritted his teeth from the battering impact, but as far as he could tell, his out-of-control tumble through the river was over.

Tree trunks and roots had snagged the craft, catching him in a massive wooden mitt. He looked at the canopy and saw that there was no reptile pressed to the glass any longer. He threw it open, dragging himself out. Foamy white water tore at him, splashing him and knocking his breath away as he climbed. A wave crashed into his side, scissoring him against the edge of the cockpit hatch. The metal frame of the opening slammed hard across his waist, and he let out a gurgle, almost swallowing a gallon of water. He coughed and cleared his nose and mouth.

Bolan was hurting, but he couldn't allow himself to slow down or relax. He pushed his feet against the control panels, shoving himself farther out of the canopy. More waves swamped him, and suddenly Bolan slithered off the top of the submarine. He was in the river, and in the darkness, the thickness of the water around him, he was blind. He had no reference point, no way to tell where "up" was. He grabbed a hunk of bark and clawed himself toward it.

Bolan reached into his harness and pulled his knife,

jamming it into the trunk, using it as a handle. He pushed against it, providing himself with enough leverage to maneuver himself. Even as he did so, his head and neck sunk into the sediment at the bottom of the river.

Wrong way, Bolan told himself. Now he had a reference, and he twisted himself under the water, his fingers clawing at the sandy riverbed, searching for the trunk once more. He was about to push off the bottom when something snapped down hard on his right hand, its jaws closing with force.

Its taxonomical label was Brachyplatystoma filomentosum. The first word, Brachyplatystoma, meant "short, flat mouth," and indeed, the muzzle of the fish was blunt, yet strong, ideal for a bottom-feeding monster of an ambush predator. It was a juvenile, small for its species, only nine feet in length and had nestled in the wash beneath the trees, seeking shelter from the sudden flood pouring through this tributary. Its long, tentacle-like maxillary barbels felt movement, felt the touch of the Executioner's flesh, and its eternal quest to keep its belly full caused the nine-foot creature to surge, clamping its jaws shut.

Seized by the hand and yanked hard, Bolan twisted, somersaulted underwater. His boots now sunk into the riverbed, providing him with leverage as he tried to pull his hand free from the Goliath catfish's mouth. Even as he struggled, he realized that he wasn't in conflict with a crocodilian or a snake. He felt those barbels, those long, slimy whiskers that provided the monster, named Piraiba by the locals, with a form of tactile radar in complete darkness of murky, brackish water. With a powerful kick, Bolan tried to surge to the surface, but he was fighting against 330 pounds of bony-headed, sinewy ambush predator.

You have to be kidding me, Bolan thought as he felt his shoulder nearly wrenched out of its socket by the twisting and thrashing of a fish half as long as he was tall, and having a 100 pound weight advantage. Countless battles against man and machine, even conflicts with venomous cobras and the mightiest of living reptiles, and he was pushed to the edge of drowning, his lungs aching, feeling as if they were about to burst thanks to the stubborn, hungry jaws of a catfish.

This is South America, the Orinoco River, Bolan told himself, once again digging his boots into the sediment at the bottom of the river. He craned one hand back toward the trunk where he'd plunged his knife, fingers brushing the handle. Human beings drowned because these giant catfish thought that they were food, and once they drowned, that did become the case.

Bolan grasped the rubberized handle of his knife, clutching it tightly, twisting the point out of the trunk. Blood was roaring in his ears, and his chest spasmed, trying to force him to inhale. If Bolan did open his nose and mouth, though, seized under water as he was, he would fill his lungs with water and drown. The writhing catfish rolled over, and it spun the soldier with it, but now, the human was armed, and ready to fight back.

The soldier stabbed his knife toward his other hand, and the point of the blade struck the heavy, blunt skull of the catfish. Punching through water robbed energy, and when Bolan's knife struck the catfish in the head, the point deflected, but split the skin on the creature's head. Bolan yanked the knife back hard, running the steel edge along the river monster's skull, carving its head. The ugly mouth opened, the Piraiba breaking its engagement with the armed opponent. No amount of hunger or stubbornness could keep the predator latched on to his arm.

Bolan broke the surface after a single, mighty kick against the riverbed. Waves slashed past him, but this time the soldier reached out, grabbing the canopy of the sub. It was lodged firmly in the trees.

He had his anchor and gulped down life-giving oxygen.

Bolan reached toward his throat. His earpiece and mike weren't in place, dislodged by the water, by being driven under, or maybe just bounced loose from any one of several crashes he'd endured.

Bolan turned. His night-vision goggles were also gone, lost somewhere in the mayhem of waves, currents and impacts. It didn't matter. His eyes were adjusting to the darkness, and he could make out the outlines of the trees leading to the shore. He gathered all of his strength, coiled his legs beneath him and pushed off.

His big, strong hands wrapped around a root. It was solid, immobile, even with the soldier's 220 pounds plus of gear. He pulled hard, dragging himself closer to the shore. The currents battered at his legs, knocking his feet from beneath him on the loose mud that made what was left of the shore. He reeled himself up, crawling with every ounce of his strength.

Bolan hung himself over some of the roots, his feet still dangling in the river. Exhaustion had overwhelmed him.

He noticed that his microphone was dangling from

his collar. He felt around and touched his earpiece. He plugged it in.

"McCormack?" That was Winslow's voice.

"You're still watching the camp?" Bolan croaked.

"Until you say to come get your ass. Magdalena saw the submarine crash into the shore, and saw you go under," Winslow returned.

"*Hombre,* you scared me," Magdalena said.

Bolan looked at the river flowing past him.

"I'm not the frightening one here," Bolan said. He pulled himself up farther. He now had both feet on muddy land, but at least he was away from the river.

There was a saying about the Orinoco's sister river, the Amazon. Every five feet, there was something more than willing and capable of eating you.

Bolan, coughing to clear his throat, sucking down another life-giving breath, rested his bloody head against the root of an upturned tree.

The Orinoco was no less dangerous, Bolan discovered, where even the catfish could kill.

CHAPTER FOURTEEN

Emmanuel and Winslow worked together, looking over the camp, grabbing up contraband and tossing it into a pile that Emelda drenched with gasoline. Magdalena, on the other hand, was taking care of the laceration that Bolan had incurred on the crash of his submarine.

She used a length of heavy thread, meant for closing rips in tents, and a fishing needle to sew the cut shut. It wasn't going to be the prettiest of stitching jobs, but at least Bolan no longer had to worry about further tearing. The wound had been washed out with hydrogen peroxide and a splash of tequila. The combination burned like hell, but that was a good sign, the deaths of countless microorganisms that had infiltrated his cut spurred that pain. "This better be worth it, I'm using my good stuff on your head," Magdalena said.

"I'll make it up to you," Bolan promised, smiling.

The pilot returned his smile. She then pressed a compress to the still-puffy edges of the skin and pushed hard. Strips of tape were torn off, and now he had a bandage across his forehead. That hurt, but only for a moment.

She checked his eyes with a flashlight once again, making certain that he hadn't gotten a concussion from his ordeal.

"I'm good to go," Bolan told her.

Magdalena gave him some more water, and the soldier sipped it. He'd spent more than enough time sitting as one of the walking wounded.

The submarines had been easily scuttled thanks to the plastic explosives ripping out their hulls and shattering their engines. They were left utterly useless to the FARC's Eastern Blocs. There didn't seem to be any salvage for the ship that Bolan had taken, but just to make certain, Winslow had hiked back to the wreck and fixed strips of puttylike octogen explosives to rip the hull farther apart. The last of the four submarines was sunk in the cross-streams of tributaries leading down toward the Orinoco.

Bolan checked the pier, and realized that there had been moorings for six of the subs, two of which were missing. When they'd hit the jungle lab, they had been expecting a couple of the watercraft within a day or two. This left the Executioner with a couple of choices. He could abandon the expedition into Venezuela, or he could inform Villanueva on the coast to keep an eye out for the two smuggler subs and their cargoes.

Bolan took the obvious choice. Stopping the product in the pipeline could be done when he intercepted the cargo ship in Tumaco. However, as long as there was a printing press for the illicit money, it could keep churning out the fake notes. That had to be smashed, destroyed beyond all recognition and recovery.

The data that they had retrieved from the coke lab had given them the general location, but it had been Emelda and Emmanuel who had helped them home in on the waypoint for the smugglers, both up- and downriver. There was more information here. Bolan had been careful in his rampage against the FARC soldiers. He'd used mainly anti-personnel rounds, letting fragmentation and concussive pressure do the work of clearing out the enemy. This way, he wouldn't shoot through walls and smash any electronics equipment or burn files or maps.

Bolan and his companions had gathered four smartphones, a laptop and dozens of maps. Again, the FARC had been sparing, careful with their markings, being vague about revealing the location of other cells that were operating either within or outside Venezuela. Even so, Bolan was able to narrow down the identities of four major Colombian rebel installations. He marked this information on his rugged Combat Commander's Digital Assistant—CDA—and uploaded the whole of the map data back to Stony Man Farm.

With that, he took some time to sit with the others.

"I'm not sure I'll want to go back to Puerto Carreno," Emelda said as they shared a meal of MREs that Bolan had packed. Compared to restaurant dining, the food wasn't much, but to people who could afford only scraps, it was the feast of a lifetime. She was savoring each bite. Emmanuel was doing a good job on his package, as well. Emmanuel couldn't have been more than nineteen, and was obviously the older of the two.

Not by much, however.

Animated and vibrant, no longer hidden under caked-on makeup, Emelda's true age was visible. She was a mere seventeen, a situation that made Bolan feel sick to his stomach. His younger sister, Cindy, had been the same age as Emelda when the thugs at Triangle Industrial Finance—a mob front—pressed her into servitude as a prostitute. In Cindy's case, she had struggled to take care of a huge, gouging loan that was slowly bleeding the Bolan family dry. Mack Bolan didn't know what Emelda's circumstances were, but her reluctance to return to Puerto Carreno was a strong indication that this wasn't the life she'd expected for herself.

Emmanuel was quiet as they ate, and had been mostly silent except for a few yes or no answers, and the occasional *"aqui"* when he found something that might be of interest to Bolan and Winslow. The young man could talk, but he was taciturn, shut down by some trauma.

"How about we arrange something for them?" Bolan asked Winslow, speaking in Spanish for the convenience of the two Colombian youths.

The Secret Service agent was roused from his blank stare. He'd been watching Emelda in hypnotized silence, barely breaking his concentration to raise his sporkful of mashed potatoes to his mouth. "A job? Like in the city?"

"The city might be a little too dangerous," Bolan replied. He looked at Lupe Magdalena. "What about your office?"

Magdalena shrugged. "I've got room if they're willing to work and willing to learn."

"I don't know how to fly," Emmanuel muttered. "Medellín won't like us anyway. We're too brown."

"I'm a ways from Medellín," Magdalena replied. "And if anyone throws shit your way, I'll throw it back in their faces."

"What can we do at an airport?" Emelda asked.

"Clean. Fix things up. Take calls and make appointments," Magdalena said. "Until you want to learn how to pilot a plane."

"Didn't you have to go to a school?" Emelda questioned.

Magdalena shook her head. "No, I learned from my father. The plane belonged to him."

Emmanuel's eyes widened at the mention of a father. There was a hint of jealousy that flashed as he watched the pilot, but that quickly faded.

"What happened to your dad?" Bolan asked him.

Emmanuel flinched. "Colombia's violent."

The young Colombian looked at the ground, and he stabbed at the tray from the MRE, scraping up some burned chocolate cake stuck to the side of the package. He pushed it into his mouth.

Bolan rested a calming hand on the boy's shoulder. "I know how it feels."

Emmanuel looked up from his platter. "Your father died?"

Bolan nodded. "Father. Mother. Younger sister."

Emmanuel's lower lip quivered. "Does it ever stop hurting?"

"No," Bolan answered.

Emmanuel's spirits began to sink, but Bolan gave his shoulder a squeeze, drawing him back out from under the blanket of emotional gloom.

"But if you find something worth doing, if you find other people to help, to love, to care for, that old hurt becomes a glue. It becomes your anchor, making you cherish the living more. And in those still around, you can see echoes, elements of your lost family in them," Bolan said.

Emmanuel looked downriver toward the branching waterway, his gaze penetrating the rainforest all the way back to Puerto Carreno. "There's nothing worthwhile back there. Not how we are now."

"You have an invitation," Magdalena said. "And it's not pity. I don't think I could get help so cheap."

"How cheap?" Winslow asked. "I don't want them screwed over in this deal."

The American smiled, winking to Emelda.

"Room and board, and a steady paycheck, as much as I can afford," Magdalena answered. "And friendship."

Winslow looked to Emelda. "Good enough for you?"

The young woman nodded.

"Emmanuel?" Winslow asked.

The youth looked back at Bolan. "What about following in your footsteps? Being a soldier?"

Bolan shook his head. "Being a true soldier means that you fight for what you believe in. You don't believe in Colombia much. But you believe in your sister."

"You're telling me you'd rather work a wrench on an airplane than fight?" Emmanuel asked.

Bolan nodded. "I'm stuck in my job. It's a duty that I *must* serve because I've been built for it."

"You sound like a robot," Magdalena said. "And you felt like you were all man."

"No. I'm just trained, skilled. I'm used to this, but it's a life I'd never wish on anyone else. You take care of the family you have left...and maybe the extra family you're earning."

Emmanuel looked toward Magdalena. She smiled at him.

The pilot stepped around their campfire, then bent

over to whisper in Bolan's ear. The soldier had to suppress a smile at the comment. She walked off toward the trucks.

Winslow tilted his head regarding the exchange. "What's that about?"

Bolan tugged at his collar. "She said as long as she's got two new kids, she might as well have the fun associated with it. You won't mind a little babysitting?"

Winslow shook his head. "Better hurry. She's been set to rip your clothes off since we first met her."

Bolan rose and excused himself.

He could always write off the time with Lupe Magdalena as recuperation from the previous night's battle. He'd gathered information, and until the Farm ran some satellite surveillance, he could use the downtime.

Magdalena was in the back of one of the two still-operating trucks. Bolan had to push aside the mosquito netting, already thick and crawling with bugs. The dark haired, blue-eyed pilot had a grin on her face, her blouse partially unbuttoned, showing the line of her chest down to just above her navel. She wasn't wearing a bra, and the net fell behind him. They'd be protected from the hungry flies who would love nothing more than to chomp down on exposed flesh.

And as the pretty pilot demonstrated, the right to have a bite was reserved for the two lovers, as she took a nip of Bolan's neck before they fell together. And Winslow was right about her.

She was set for, and quite skilled at ripping off Bolan's clothing.

That was all right. The soldier had been in need of

some loving, and he returned the favor, voraciously yet gently.

After so many things looking to kill him, or eat him, he was glad to give of himself, and take some in the same measure.

AT SUNSET, THE Cessna pontoon plane rose from the surface of the river, climbing into the night sky. All five of the travelers agreed that the daytime was buggy enough, the forest alive with flies, ants and other hungry insects. Night, however, was an exercise in being drenched with bug repellent, wrapping oneself like a mummy, or being a living buffet for ten times that bloodthirsty number.

Inside of the Cessna, above the canopy and inside of a semipressurized cabin, the expedition was away from the swarming clouds of gnats and flies and were no longer in contact with a ground that would become a literal carpet of fire ants and beetles. Sunset was also when Stony Man Farm got in contact with the Executioner, pointing out that there was more than just a small force at one of the locations that Bolan had indicated on the confiscated maps. Going grid by grid, he read from the three-by-five-inch touch screen on his Combat CDA. The latest design had a graphics card in it that allowed for high-resolution image transfer, and the touch screen allowed for instant zoom and magnification with a simple gesture. A larger screen might have been easier to look at, but in truth, a larger screen would be easier to damage as it would no longer be able to be slipped within its armored case.

For better image quality, they had transferred the pictures to the largest of the cocaine workers' laptops, a seventeen-inch wide-screen monitor that had shown more than a little usage with pirated video games loaded on board. That kind of video display was ideal for Bolan and Winslow to see what was going on, and helped Magdalena navigate without the hassle of using a folding map, or having to rely on the rather spotty and unreliable GPS service to which she subscribed.

Her knowledge of the countryside and the rivers had been enough to get them headed in the right direction, but this far into Venezuela, they were working without a net. Magdalena had turned off her VOR radio so as not to provide a target for Venezuelan air force fighter jets. The Cessna was a fine, sturdy and reliable aircraft, but in the face of Sukhoi Su-30 multipurpose strike fighters, F-16 Fighting Falcons or even the more primitive Canadair CF-5s of the Venezuelan fleet, it would be like a duck flying into the talons of falcons.

Right now, the laptop was receiving real-time satellite reconnaissance of the national defense radar for the country, looking for areas of coverage. All of this information was being beamed from Stony Man Farm, Virginia, the Executioner's occasional home base. That intel was giving the Cessna a corridor to slip through with minimal exposure, keeping close to the Orinoco River and away from prying eyes that would, rightfully, see Bolan's expedition as an invasion of sovereign territory.

With the sensitivity of this operation, Bolan knew that he had to be careful, and that Magdalena was going to need all the help he could offer her. Even when they'd land on the river, there would still be the danger of naval "brown water" patrols that might encounter them. As such, he was working especially hard to keep the plane safe, looking for little inlets where the aircraft could be parked. There didn't seem to be any easy way for them to get the youngsters back to a safe city and have her return.

So, the group had to keep the Cessna as their mobile base, and try their hardest to stay off the radar. Literally.

"No chatter in regards to the locals spotting you," Barbara Price's voice came over his Combat CDA's earpiece.

"Good news," Bolan replied. He was still looking at the laptop screen, studying the camp. There were generators on hand for multiple pieces of heavy equipment, as well as what appeared to be a paper-processing plant. The Farm's crew had tried to correlate the building according to known machinery, and the best that they could come up with was the fiber-roll makers that churned out the basic materials for international money. "Paper money" was actually a blend of fibers, not wood pulp or cellulose, but cotton and linen. Creating that took a specific kind of machinery, and the shapes correlated.

All that was necessary was to mix the fibers in the proper amounts, and the base of the bank note, its makeup, was done. Extra things like metallic wire sensors or special inks would also be necessary, but if the counterfeiters were making their own paper, then it was likely that they had the technology to integrate the anti-duplication counters into their fake notes.

What concerned Bolan the most, however, about the intel that he'd received from the satellite imagery was that there was a small squadron of armored fighting vehicles on the scene. Their appearance was unmistakable—four V-100 amphibious armored cars, built in America by the Cadillac Gage company, and sent to Venezuela back when it was a friend of the United States.

The V-100 was an eleven-ton chunk of fighting, rolling force, protected by a quarter inch of Cad-alloy armored steel. Its turret mounted a 20 mm M-134 minigun and an FN-MAG 7.62 mm NATO light machine gun. That was a hell of a lot of firepower, and was more than sufficient to swat the Cessna out of the sky if Bolan tried to use it as before to get aerial intelligence. No, he was going to have to ground Magdalena; it was the best way to keep her, Emmanuel and Emelda out of the line of fire.

Those armored cars were beasts, deadly machines that would be able to turn any building in which Bolan hid to a sieve, high volumes of NATO lead tearing through even concrete. No place would prove to be cover. He started to regret using so many plastic explosives on the FARC submarines.

There was also an indication that there were close to two hundred armed personnel on the site. There were Tiuna jeeps, the local equivalent of the U.S. Humvee and regular transport trucks on the scene, as well. There was a dock, but it was empty. The satellites' downward-looking radar had been set to look for the smuggler submarines, but none was parked there.

This was going to be a tough situation. Two hundred people, with armored cars packing considerable firepower, all of them armed with AK-103 assault rifles, judging by the equipment carried by the FARC outpost just across the river from Colombia. The odds were going to be tough, and they wouldn't scatter here. The frontier outpost was too close to the border for the Venezuelans to send assistance, but an operation in the heart of their countryside, local military would come running fast and hard. There was a proper military installation not far down the road, only a mile and a half distant, to be exact. The sound of gunfire would mobilize troops and bring them running.

The Farm had provided intel on that facility, and there were eight Scorpion 90 FV101 light tanks, as well as more of the V-100 armored cars. Eight tanks, each of them packing, as their name indicated, a 90 mm long-barreled main gun, and storage for thirty-two shells for that powerful cannon. And 90 mm shells could pack a lot of high explosive.

"They're going to come down on us with the biggest fly swatter in the history of humankind," Winslow muttered, looking at the odds assembled against them.

"Which is why we've got to be smart and careful," Bolan returned.

"Smart and careful," Winslow repeated. "Taking on the Venezuelan army on their home turf is stupid and reckless. If we were smart and careful, we'd be working at the Department of Motor Vehicles."

Bolan grinned. "That's the spirit."

Winslow chuckled. "Sorry. I'm just trying to figure out how two men are going to take down those printing presses. You've got anything short of calling in a strike fighter to hammer this place with Maverick missiles?"

"A fighter would cause an international incident,"

Bolan said. "Especially if even one of the staff in that base is honest Venezuelan military."

"You're worrying about that?" Magdalena asked. "If anything…"

"If anything, the Venezuelan armed forces are predominately concerned with protecting their nation. Any involvement with the FARC is orders from above, or only grudging acceptance of orders," Bolan answered. "Sure, there could be a lot of them sympathizing with those rebels, but they haven't engaged in violence across the border."

"So, we act as sitting ducks when they shoot at us?" Winslow asked.

Bolan shook his head. "Far from that. We dodge, we duck, we retreat. You can shoot if you want, but ethically my hands are tied."

Winslow nodded. He didn't look happy.

"I've gotten this far with a rational mind only because I've set rules in stone for myself," Bolan explained. "Venezuela is not a shooting enemy of the U.S., so I'm loathe to open fire on them. A nation's military doesn't necessarily agree with the radical beliefs of their leadership. Even in the American military, while a soldier can't openly state disagreement with his commander-in-chief, I've heard enough criticism of war policy, for left- and right-wing presidents."

"I'm not interested in starting a war with Venezuela, either," Winslow agreed. "I just want to know how we're going to handle all of this."

"I've got an idea," Bolan stated, looking at the screen. "How are you at swimming?"

"In the Orinoco River basin?" Winslow asked. "Where

even a catfish can drown you, not to mention piranha, parasite fish that eat their way into your dick, anacondas and crocodiles?"

"You forgot electric eels and stingrays," Bolan added.

"You want me to swim in that," Winslow stated.

Bolan nodded.

"Oh, hell, you can only be devoured once," Winslow grumbled. "So what is the plan, McCormack?"

"We stealth in," Bolan said. "After that, it's all improvisation and quiet kills until we reach a spot to destroy the printing presses."

"And no plan for how to get out," Winslow added.

Bolan nodded again.

"Well, at least we have the first step," Winslow said dryly.

CHAPTER FIFTEEN

Diego Millagro was burning up the airwaves, calling his contacts across the border. So far, he knew that there had been incidents in Colombia, and one just across the river from Puerto Carreno. That one had been the last nail in the coffin for his confidence. Escapees from the Orinoco border camp had managed to reach communications, sending messages to Caracas and back to Millagro.

The Venezuelan was feeling the pressure now. He'd gotten a good chewing out from his handler back in the capital.

"Listen, Molinov was the one who was bringing in extra operatives to deal with this situation," Millagro said, talking to the man at the heart of the operation, Domingo Mentirosa.

Mentirosa's scowl could be felt, even through the signal his cell phone received. "We're right in the path of these bastards. Who the hell are they, Diego?"

Millagro sighed. "He showed up, and local law enforcement were told he was Special Agent Matthew McCormack."

"Special Agent," Mentirosa repeated. "Pretty special if the reports coming in are true."

"What? The Orinoco sub base?" Millagro asked.

The cell seemed to crackle with electric anger. "Yes.

We had dozens of people on the site, and while a lot of them survived and escaped, whatever was left behind was destroyed. We're talking a lot of product, vehicles and weapons that my people could be using in Colombia. And they tell me it was one man, maybe two who took the place down."

Millagro grimaced. "They're right. This McCormack went on a rampage and tore ass through Colombian cartel gunmen and a contingent of Slavic Mafia who were in Medellín to establish a presence. Then, for dessert, he annihilates ten gunmen sent to take out the guy who turned him on to them."

"Wait…he wiped out half of the sub base. That's twenty. Another six farther in on the river. And they found how many bodies at that hospital?" Mentirosa asked.

"Thirty-eight," Millagro answered.

Mentirosa cleared his throat. "Almost seventy-four gunmen? One man was responsible for all of that?"

"One man," Millagro reported. "Molinov said that McCormack might be just another alias for the American that they call the Soldier. And they're scared of him in Europe, too."

Mentirosa went silent for a moment.

"Sir?" Millagro asked.

"Sorry for snapping on you," Mentirosa returned. *"El Soldado."*

"Yes," Millagro answered, even though Mentirosa didn't ask a question. "Anything wrong?"

"No. Well, yes. We've got *him* down here, and he's making a beeline to our doorstep," Mentirosa said. "I'm going to have to get creative. We've got the plant locked down usually, and there's an army base close to us."

"That should be enough, shouldn't it?" Millagro asked.

"Should," Mentirosa repeated. "One man should not be able to wipe out seventy-four gunmen in the space of a few days."

Millagro nodded, but didn't say anything. The last thing he wanted to do was let a slip of his lip send Mentirosa back into his rage. Mentirosa wasn't Venezuelan. He was Cuban, and an old-school "spread *la Revoluccion*" Cuban. As a young man, barely sixteen, he'd gone to Angola with a team of advisers. He'd worked in Nicaragua with the Sandinista revolution and had waged bloody war on the *Contras* later. Mentirosa was not a gentle man, and given to rages that ended up with people dead, often in the hundreds. For him to show concern about the lethal ability of another was a sobering display of how terrifying the Soldier was.

McCormack was a menace, and that threat was making the Cuban's mind turn over, looking for any means, any advantage he could claim over the American coming to strike at their headquarters.

"Listen," Mentirosa said. "Molinov has people coming in from Malaysia, right?"

Millagro nodded. Molinov had been handpicked by Mentirosa to lead the operation in Colombia. There was a trust between him and the Russian, so if there was going to be a mistake, Millagro hoped that it would be Molinov that made it. Even so, if the Russian were the scapegoat, Millagro would end up decapitated himself.

"Make sure our latest shipment gets on the freighter," Mentirosa told him.

"Molinov is in Tumaco to take care of that."

Mentirosa was quiet for a moment. These pauses might have been only instants, but Millagro's own paranoia was running amok, dread turning instants into aeons, stretching out his anticipation of Mentirosa's response to the point of self-torture. Millagro punched himself in the thigh, sending a spike of pain through his leg.

"Then we've done everything we could possibly do to make sure that's all right," Mentirosa said. "Join Molinov, and bring everyone and everything you can. Everything. If it's a garbage bin on wheels, you bring it. If it's a broken spoon handle, you can still stab with it."

"Won't we be in the way of Molinov's imports?" Millagro asked.

"No," Mentirosa answered. "Maybe. I really do not give a fuck. We've been running light against McCormack for far too long. We need to pull out every last stop. The time for playing around is over."

"What about you, there?" Millagro asked.

Mentirosa paused again.

"I have a plan," the Cuban finally told him. "But I'm not going to lay it out on a cell phone."

"He does have a scary prescience," Millagro agreed.

Mentirosa snarled. "He's probably got access to the best electronic espionage the NSA could cobble together. Now, shut up and scramble your ass to Tumaco. I'll phone Molinov to tell him about your arrival, but if I forget, double-check and follow up."

Millagro cleared his throat. "Sure."

The call ended, and Millagro turned off his phone, pocketing it. He should have been on the phone immediately to Molinov, or sending out calls to one of his men, looking to pull in help, but he was still overwhelmed. There was an armed force coming in, and Molinov had taken Millagro's "chop" in order to gather all of the Western Bloc FARC members operating in Tumaco to work additional security on the transfer.

There was an army being assembled, all of them packing more firepower than the equivalent of a U.S. infantry platoon, and yet, Millagro couldn't fight off the creeping dread, the paranoia that McCormack, the Soldier, whatever the hell he called himself, would be prepared for all of that. Any defenses being set up now would only get slammed in the face by his onslaught, and this whole operation on the continent would crumble to pieces.

Millagro looked around his office, finally reaching down and pulling his pistol from its drawer. It was a heavy feeling in his hand, but he couldn't help but feel like it was nothing more than a fetish, a good-luck charm that possessed powers that had long since been drained. He'd thought that the counterfeiting wouldn't be something to inspire this kind of violence, but here was the evidence.

Almost eighty dead at the American's hand.

This was Molinov's fault. That bullheaded stupid Russian had to have his way, had to lure out the Colombian *federales* and the American agents in order to teach them a lesson in destruction. It wasn't just Molinov, though. The same bullshit happened at the U.S.

Embassy in Malaysia, local thugs hired to launch anti-tank artillery at United States government officials.

All Molinov's fault? No.

Millagro should have known better than to get involved with outside forces. The chances of wrecking Colombia's economy, crippling the nation with an influx of bad money, seemed like a quick, easy shortcut to the end of the problem of inept, weak, dying Bogotá.

Millagro got on the phone. It was time to call for more help. He needed everything he could to make sure his life wasn't thrown away in this effort to bring down Colombia.

That meant securing a special weapon or two.

THE FACILITY THAT allowed the Venezuelan FARC headquarters to receive and resupply their smuggling submarines was the target. Mack Bolan and Zachary Winslow had wrapped their assault rifles—long ago replacing the HK carbines with the folding stocked AK-103s, especially useful with the nearly endless supply of 7.62 mm ComBloc ammunition that they had captured. A bonus for this new load out was that both Winslow and Bolan could make use of the compact, but deadly GP-25 Kostyor 40 mm grenade launcher that had plentiful rounds for it.

Bolan's replacement of his HK M320 was no major loss as the GP-25 operated in a similar manner to the M203, and he'd been familiar with that model for years. The FARC had been supplied with plenty of VOG-25 grenades. As these launchers were actually caseless, they would be a touch quicker to reload, no longer having to eject an empty shell before feeding another into the mix. One of these 40 mm rounds could hit and produce a kill radius of six meters, thanks to the 48 grams of A-IX-1 high explosive in the warhead's core.

Unfortunately, that kind of firepower wouldn't be enough for them to fight their way to the printing presses for the counterfeit money. If they started out loud and violent, that would not only alert the two hundred armed personnel on the base, but it would also likely bring a squadron of light armor running, first the Commando armored cars already on the scene, and then Venezuelan National Army Scorpion 90 tanks and their LAV escorts, as well.

As much as Bolan didn't want to harm the grunts on the ground, it was that light armor and the firepower it could bring to bear that really made this situation touch and go. The 40 mm grenade launchers would do yeoman work against jeeps and the quarter inch of armor on the V-100 armored cars, not to mention groups of enemy troopers, but against the 12.7 mm of welded aluminum armor that encased an FV101 light tank, it would be like throwing jelly beans.

The two men had been in the water for about three hundred yards of swimming, having deflated and tucked their raft under a rock downriver. So far, the night had been kind to them, no lights flashing on the relatively calm surface of this tributary to accidentally splash them and give away their presence. Neither man was equipped with anything more complex than a snorkel and goggles as they moved along. Bolan was in his blacksuit, a formfitting high-tech wonder that kept him warm in the cold and cool in the torrid heat of jungles or deserts. The cloth didn't reflect light, and since he'd been alerted that he would be working with an American agent, he'd brought a spare along for Zach Winslow.

Bolan had also brought an extended, threaded 9 mm barrel for Winslow's SIG-Sauer P229, complete with a Gem-Tech suppressor. That, coupled with 147-grain ammunition, which only barely broke the speed of sound out of a five-inch barrel, and with a central post in the hollowpoint round to direct pressure to the cavity to open up the bullet's nose, made the P229 almost quiet. Even so, Bolan and Winslow knew better than to use their pistols unless it was an absolute last resort. It would take considerable distance for even a suppressed gunshot to be inaudible.

For the lethal work they needed, both men were equipped with fighting knives and other equipment.

Winslow had his blade, an Uzi Heavy Defender, a black piece of fearsome death forged from a solid bar of steel. The top was a lightly beveled full-length edge, broken at one point where the clip turned toward the spine, which helped with deep stabs, but the cutting edge was a fatbellied affair. Fiberglass grips made up the handle, and there was a large finger notch just above where the hilt would be, a way to gather more leverage on the knife and to act as a barrier between cutting one's fingers off on a violent thrust. The pommel had a loop ring, good for a lanyard, and there was a flat end that could be used as a single-slot screwdriver or as a means of smashing through someone's skull, making the knife dangerous up, down, forward and backward.

Bolan had his Emerson Combat Karambit, the brutal little hooked talon that could eviscerate an enemy with one swipe despite the blade being only two and a half inches long. It was an ancient Indonesian design, one likely inspired by the wicked beaks of raptors such as owls or eagles, and bore more than a striking resemblance to the deadly killing claws belonging to prehistoric therapods.

The soldier backed up this deadly little fighter with a longer, more conventional combat blade, the Ontario Spec Plus Marine Combat Knife. Resembling the classic World War II Ka-Bar fighting knife, but made with twenty-first-century handle materials and metallurgy, the knife was a foot long, seven inches of it being razor-sharp, black-oxide-coated steel.

The two Americans, with silenced pistols and folding AKs and their knives, were armed to the teeth, ready for a war in Medellín. Even with their grenade launchers, however, they were woefully undergunned should the enemy bring in armored vehicles.

Bolan and Winslow waited under the pier to regain their breath from the swim. They hadn't seen sentries on the dock, but they weren't going to make any sudden movements until they were certain that it was clear. There was light on the dock, but it wasn't much. The Venezuelans didn't want to do much to attract attention to the smuggler subs, and strong lighting would make the craft stick out at a distance, especially for spies in the area. Caracas was paranoid, nervous about their involvement with the FARC. Blatant displays would just confirm the rumors and provide probable cause for the Colombian military to make an incursion.

Bolan's Karambit knife slashed open the garbage bags quickly and quietly, barely making a rustle as he took out the rifles, magazines and grenade bandoliers.

One thing that they benefited from while wearing the blacksuits was that the fabric didn't absorb moisture, so when they got out, their heads, hands and feet were wet, but the rest of the material bled off water. They wouldn't be draining for minutes, and could get to work more quickly.

Their footwear and socks were in the garbage bags, too, so they didn't have to slosh along in wet boots, making noise as their soles squished, and avoiding jungle rot on their feet. It took only a few moments for the pair to maneuver into their load-bearing vests and holsters before they crept up the shore, using the support struts of the stairs to assist them in rising to the base. Poking up slowly, so as not to attract attention with their sudden movement, they scanned around, noticing that the whole of the docks were quiet and empty.

Bolan skittered up first, Winslow hot on his heels. As their vests' pouches were sealed and secured, neither man made a rattling sound as they rushed toward the gate and fence separating the dock from the rest of the facility. The guardhouse was darkened and empty, but any route that led directly into the camp was blocked by a rolling gate that was ten-feet tall.

"Can we climb it?" Winslow asked.

Bolan shook his head. He pointed to the warning signs on the fence, and the lack of vegetation and other normal ground clutter that got mixed up in normal chain link. "Electrified."

"Damn," Winslow muttered. "What now?"

"We find a way in," Bolan answered. "Quietly."

Winslow fell in behind the soldier. If anyone could penetrate a high-security installation like this, it would be the big American. He had the comfort, the grace, the moves of someone who'd been to this dance before, and he was comfortable with it. Even as they stalked the perimeter, something felt wrong, however. Off.

Like this was a sucker play.

"McCormack?" Winslow asked. "Are you…"

Bolan raised a fist, cutting the Secret Service agent off midsentence. He pointed for Winslow to move over to some bushes and go prone. The two men disappeared into shadow, and as soon as they were out of sight, Bolan shadowed the screen of his Combat CDA and looked at the map.

Winslow could make out Bolan's features in the light from the screen and could see the man wasn't happy.

"We've got movement from the other base," the soldier whispered. "They've called in support…and about the same time after sunset as when we first made our move on the Orinoco submarine base."

"Movement. Like…those Scorpions?" Winslow asked.

"And aircraft coming in," Bolan said. "Anything outside the fence is going to be an easy target. Maybe even inside."

"What kind of aircraft?" Winslow asked.

"Helicopters," Bolan returned. "Which means if they're going to be hunting us, they might be patrolling out far enough to catch a glimpse of the Cessna, Magdalena and the kids."

Winslow clenched his jaw. "Now what?"

Bolan glared at the electrical fence. "Too late for stealth. If we're going to be a target, let's make them work for it."

With that, the soldier brought out his AK-103, his finger going to the GP-25's trigger. "Hit the guardhouse and the gate."

Winslow quickly unslung the AK, made sure he had a shell in the breech, then aimed at the electrified fence. "We're really going in there, guns blazing."

"We've got no choice at this point," Bolan told him. He triggered the GP-25. The shell sailed toward the gate that they'd already left dozens of yards back. The 40 mm grenade spiraled in midflight, each revolution ticking down the fuze on the miniature missile. The shell landed and detonated with a clap of thunder. Winslow fired his shot immediately after he saw his partner launch. His grenade thundered a moment later, and not only was there the burst of smoke and fire that came from a normal 40 mm grenade detonation, but there were streaks of lightning leaping from the fence as concussive force and shrapnel severed the chain link.

Bolan had already reloaded and aimed at another section of fence, blasting it to pieces. Winslow wondered why the man would waste the shot, but then he realized that McCormack was practicing the art of misdirection. He didn't fire at a regular distance from their group. He was hammering the fence in multiple areas, giving the impression of more than one assault vector.

Winslow thumbed a shell home and fired well past the shattered guardhouse, dropping the next round ninety yards away. The miniature bomb struck the fence and he was rewarded with more sparks. Bolan tapped him on the shoulder, and the two men rushed to their feet, moving toward the chain-link weave.

Alarms were raised on the base, howls of sirens

screaming all around. The natural instinct of the defenders would be to move toward the positions that had been blasted. Those would be breeches in perimeter, where invaders could make their way in. In the meantime, the soldier slung his rifle and grabbed a section of fence, wrenching it upward. Winslow froze for a moment, expecting the man to be electrocuted, but he realized that McCormack's two initial grenades had done more than throw attention to the sides of their entrance. It had also broken the continuous circuit that kept the juice flowing.

Winslow threw himself prone, scrambling beneath the lifted fence. As soon as he was through, he reached back and grabbed the chain link, putting everything into holding up the flexible barrier so that Bolan could snake through. The soldier was on the other side in a flash, pulling his feet through then signaling for Winslow to drop the chain link. The fence rustled almost musically, but in comparison to the sounds of running men and Klaxons, it was the barest of whispers.

They were inside the base. Now, all they had to do was survive and take out the counterfeiters' printing presses.

All it would take was fighting or sneaking past hundreds of soldiers with armed jeeps.

CHAPTER SIXTEEN

Bolan knew that the enemy had found a pattern to his strikes, and that he'd stumbled right into their trap. According to the live satellite feed coming in from Stony Man Farm, all eight of the Scorpion 90 light tanks were tearing down the road at their top speed of 45 miles per hour, making it so that they would arrive in three minutes. Even so, he had been studying the map of the base, knew the layout from his hours of plotting and planning. There wasn't going to be a single step that he hadn't envisioned five times in five different modes of movement.

Forewarned was forearmed, and when it came to making an assault on an enemy camp, Bolan always brought in the biggest guns he could in terms of intel. The bit of fence that they'd penetrated was right off a gap between two buildings that shielded them left and right from view of the guards on hand who were rushing toward defensive positions around the grenade detonations. Bolan fed another shell into his launcher, angled the GP-25 straight up and fired. Winslow's eyes grew wide as the 40 mm shell shot up into the night. Bolan stuffed in another shell and shot it a moment later.

"Flare?" Winslow asked.

Bolan shook his head, then motioned for them to get moving. He had altered the trajectory of those shells only slightly. When they reached the apex of their arcs, gravity would bring them down hard, and the impact fuzes in both grenades would detonate. With the slight shifts in aim, he'd bring those two rounds down behind the fence, approximately in the areas where the defenders of this base would be assembling. A six-meter radius for each of the fragmentation grenades wouldn't do much to even the odds in terms of kills, but the roar of grenades landing in their midst would send sentries scattering and looking for cover.

They reached the end of the causeway between the two buildings and Bolan stopped their progress, looking left and right.

Sure enough, one of the V-100s had rolled to each of the fence explosions. Gunners manned the M-134 miniguns mounted on the armored cars' turrets. Just one of those brutal weapons would be more than sufficient to eviscerate a company of assaulting Marines and would be absolute overkill against Bolan and his ally. They stopped just perpendicular to where the two men had stopped.

Bolan pointed to the one on the right, feeding a fresh cartridge into his launcher. Winslow's eyes went wide, but he wasn't about to question his companion. He reloaded his GP-25 and took aim.

Before either man could fire, the two shells that Bolan had fired into the sky came down, striking the ground like the thunderbolts of an angry god. The shattering fragmentation grenades ignited a cacophony of screams and gunfire. All attention was locked firmly on the area beyond the fence right now, and the two V-100 gunners cut loose with their multibarreled

M-134s. Both of those weapons poured out lead at 3000 rounds per minute, and they sounded for all the world like chain saws as they unleashed their deadly streams.

Bolan tapped Winslow to signal for him to fire. The Executioner then took aim at the turret of a V-100 and punched a 40 mm grenade at it. The gunner was focused face forward, not expecting that their defenses had been penetrated and that they were flanked. Forty-eight grams of high explosive detonated with bone-smashing force, ripping the M-134 off its mountings after it pulverized the hapless turret gunner.

Winslow's round was a little low, striking his armored car in the side, just above the wheels and rocking the vehicle violently. The machine gunner in that turret was thrown left to right, and he had the controls of the chain saw–snarling minigun gripped tightly. What would have been only a minor bit of mayhem suddenly turned to madness as the M-134's six barrels swept across a dozen troops who had taken up position, expecting the mighty weapon to assist them, not hit them with a stream of death that ripped them to shreds at the tune of 3000 bullets per minute.

Bolan reloaded and popped another round almost straight up. Winslow opted to follow suit before his partner could say anything to stop him. Instead, he slapped the Secret Service agent on the shoulder, then pointed to the building where the printing presses were supposed to have been stored. Bolan was familiar with the trajectories of 40 mm grenades; he'd used them ever since he'd first been issued an M-16 back in the Army.

As such, he knew what he was doing with his GP-25 when he seemed to be firing upward without aiming.

Winslow didn't quite know. The two of them ran along toward the main building when Bolan's round landed, this time on the side where Winslow's grenade had merely shook the V-100 armored car. His shell landed close to the vehicle, and the explosion went off in concert with more screams. Winslow's shell came down right where they had been moments before. The two men had gotten ten yards, and as such, were safe from the shrapnel put out by the explosion, but both were buffeted and rattled by the overpressure wave shooting off the detonation.

That was a lucky accident, though. In the darkness, and with the madness of the presumed artillery strike, both Americans were spotted by one of the guards and waved toward a door.

"Get to cover, you idiots! They're shelling us!" the man shouted in Spanish.

Bolan charged on, picking up speed. He snaked one hand around and tugged out the Karambit knife surreptitiously. He hooked his index finger through the hole on the pommel so that the two-and-a-half-inch talon poked out from the bottom of his fist. In the doorway, he flashed up with his fist, raking the deadly point through the guard's throat, ripping it wide open. The South American's head yawned backward, carved to the neck bones, windpipe and arteries severed and spewing air and blood in fountains.

Winslow shoulder blocked the dying man, knocking him into the building as Bolan stopped, backtracked and slammed the door shut behind them.

There had been no one inside the double doors. They were made of glass, which meant if anyone were watching, they would see Bolan and Winslow with the corpse of one of their own.

Bolan did a quick check on the body. "No dog tags He's not in official Venezuelan military uniform."

"So, we're not hammering soldiers on the same side?" Winslow asked.

"If they're Venezuelan military, they aren't uniformed combatants. He's got all of the web gear and a VNA-issue Uzi submachine gun," Bolan explained. "So, I'm thinking that he's just an 'adviser.'"

"As in CIA?" Winslow asked.

Bolan frowned. "As in no accountability."

Winslow sighed. "Damn."

"That means that there is full government support for this operation," Bolan said. "And it also means that they're going to throw away grunts to keep this thing working."

"Lots of lives lost," Winslow agreed. "What now?"

"We move fast," Bolan replied. "Down the hall."

The two men rushed into the darkness. They knew that they would have only a few minutes until the cavalry arrived. Even if they did manage to wreck the presses, Bolan knew that escaping with their lives would be difficult, and they would have to disappear quickly, or else they'd lead the Venezuelan military vehicles and the FARC's allies right to Magdalena and the kids.

MENTIROSA WATCHED FROM afar, lowering his night-vision binoculars as the V-100 armored cars cut loose, their miniguns blazing bright green fire into the fuzzy darkness beyond. He was in a helicopter, and only by pure luck had the ground units and his chopper been on the move when the sudden staccato of distant grenades started, putting the printing facility on full alert, guards swarming to a position to watch the perimeter and contain the breeches in the electrified fence.

He was on the edge of his seat, headphones only barely canceling out the roar of the helicopter rotor and engines, the humid, sticky night ameliorated by the rush of wind through the open door. This was the last of the Bell 206 JetRangers in the Venezuelan army's inventory, and there were two Mil Mi-17 transport choppers flanking Mentirosa's ship. The Russian helicopters were packed with fifty troops apiece, and door gunners operated MAG-58 light machine guns. The second of the Russian birds also had hard points loaded with rocket pods and air-to-ground missiles.

Mentirosa had mobilized the Venezuelan military, and he figured that if he had to, he'd have the army slaughter everyone on base. They were only members of the FARC, and with the hundreds on base massacred, Caracas could use the "mistake" to show Bogotá that Venezuela wasn't fomenting rebellion and violence in neighboring Colombia. A mass destruction of their personnel would be the surest of signs of cooperation in fighting terrorism.

Mentirosa didn't care, personally, about the FARC. He was Cuban, *Direccion de Inteligencia.* The lives of non-Cuban Communists meant less to him than the lives of the ants he crushed while walking down a jungle trail. If they had to die so that DI's involvement in the operation was still concealed, then so be it. As such, Mentirosa was more concerned about his allies with him right now.

Colonel Joaquin Figueroa of *Direccion General de Inteligencia Militar,* DGIM for short, had assembled these particular commandos and vehicle drivers for the sake of engaging in a face-saving effort on the part of the Venezuelan government. DGIM Venezuela and DI Cuba had been working closely together with this from the inception, though, there were others higher up the food chain. Figueroa and Mentirosa were the highest-ranking operatives for this conspiracy in Venezuela, and Figueroa knew the dangers associated with a covert op intruding into this country.

If Venezuela were known to be linked to an attempt to destroy Colombia's economy, or to attack the financial stability of the United States, their standing in the world would turn around greatly. The discovery of Chinese yuan would also add to the pressure, as China was often loathe to act alongside U.S. interests in South America. However, with their own economy at stake, they wouldn't be afraid of putting actual teeth into a United Nations resolution, one that Russia would be forced to side with, lest their own efforts in this program be betrayed.

At least, that was what Mentirosa hoped would not happen. The only recourse that they had was to destroy all the evidence of compliance that they could. Figueroa was the man who had the most to lose in this instance, but Mentirosa also knew that if pressed, the colonel would turn around and point fingers at the Cuban influence.

Mentirosa was operating without a net of his own. He'd been given the go-ahead for this operation, and was allowed only the normal resources under his command. If anything happened, it would be just Mentirosa who would be left at fault, especially after the Party and his commanders had completely washed their hands of the affair. Naturally, his greatest asset was the ability to monitor, and thus bury, shipping manifests in his role as a counterespionage and counterterrorism officer. Mentirosa had been ordered to get illicit weapons and equipment out of Cuba and delivered to friendly forces on previous occasions; this had simply been one of the biggest operations he'd undertaken.

Even so, destroying the printing presses here in Venezuela would do a lot to cut off any chance of reprisal, burying the evidence. There was already tons—literally—of money in the system, ready for distribution. There was more being produced right now, but that would all be simply icing on the cake. Instead of total obliteration of the cash value of China and the United States, it would merely incur a gutting of their economic power.

Figueroa raised him on the radio headset. "It looks like we're running late."

"No, we're not. The intruders are just present on site. If they take pictures, it won't count," Mentirosa said. "We'll blow that shit to hell before they breech the perimeter!"

"Those Colombians are guests in our country," Figueroa replied. "If we shoot them…"

"Then don't miss the buildings. Even if you do miss, however, you can always point to the corpses and tell Bogotá that you're doing your part in fighting terrorism," Mentirosa snapped.

Figueroa disappeared from the line, but after a wait

of thirty seconds, one of the Mi-17s, the one with the wing weapon pods, suddenly flared to life. Rocket pods jetted flashes of flame out the back end, and in the dark, the only sign of the firing was the distant, fading sparks of their rear motors burning out after accelerating to top speed.

The SNEB Russian rocket pod vomited out its nineteen 68 mm artillery rockets, each of them carrying three pounds of high explosives in their warheads, at the building where they had set up the printing presses. In the distance, Mentirosa waited for those sizzling artillery rounds to strike home.

The result of the gunner emptying the pod was a sudden burst, a long string of pops and booms as the warheads struck and detonated against the side and roof of the building. Plumes of smoke and fire shot skyward under each hammering impact.

Mentirosa flicked to listening for the response from the base, and noted calls of alarm, cries for help as the Mi-17's assault terrified the FARC men on the ground. Rubble flew from the broken building, raining down heavily on the defenders.

After emptying, the rocket pod broke off the aircraft, jettisoned, making the Mi-17 rise a little, having suddenly lost the weight.

Mentirosa brought up his night-vision binoculars, looking toward the building. Smoke and fire blocked his view of the situation, though he noticed that the frame of the structure was no longer perfect and square.

They would have to hit that thing harder, but so far, the building was so wrecked that no sane person would take a step inside.

WINSLOW STOPPED AS the roar of gunfire behind them was cut by a new sound. Were there other FARC defenders who were turning their attention to the building that he and McCormack had just entered? Grenades had done incredible work in sowing confusion among the defenders of this facility.

The trouble was, the shrieks splitting the air were now confusing him. When they had arrived, they saw the printing presses, and the huge rolls of paper set up. The machines weren't in operation, but there were the makings of simply incredible amounts of illicit cash. One machine was set for U.S. currency, and they weren't simply making $100 bills; they also had it set up for simultaneous printing of twenties and fifties on the same sheets. McCormack was going to town with the digital camera installed in his combat CDA, and he was also taking backup pictures with another pocket-size, high-resolution device, as well.

Winslow simply kept watch on the entrance they'd come through, looking down the hall, watching as armed men and women moved back and forth, jeeps and their mounted machine guns maneuvering into position. With the sizzling snarls of incoming artillery rockets, he straightened, confused.

Instantly, he was body blocked, thrown to the ground barely in time as the roof, the whole building shuddered under an onslaught of high-powered impacts. Chunks of brick and masonry were blown to shreds, rubble crashing down from the roof. He could only see this out of the corner of his eye as McCormack had shielded him from the bulk of the avalanche caused by the impact of nearly twenty warheads, each packing pounds of high explosives in their nosecones.

"What the hell?" Winslow asked, dazed and surprised. He looked back to Bolan, who was rubbing his shoulder. "You hit?"

"Glancing blow by a rock," Bolan answered. "It'll leave another bruise, but I'll live."

"What's happening?"

Bolan looked at the machines, covered by a layer of rubble and wreckage. "If you're an optimist, they're doing our job for us."

"And what about if you're a realist?" Winslow asked.

"They're going to crush us in the wreckage and make it hard to trace this equipment back to its country of origin," Bolan said.

Winslow bristled at the thought. "Make it hard?"

"Not impossible," Bolan said. He patted one of his pouches on his harness. It was the same one that Winslow had seen him tuck the CDA into.

"What now?" Winslow asked.

"Whoever is on the way here is going to try to destroy all incriminating evidence on this base. That means they'll have some answers for me," Bolan said.

"You're going to stick around?" Winslow pressed.

"I'm not here to gather evidence on arrests," Bolan reminded his Secret Service partner. "I'm here to find what the food chain looks like, and where to get the next bite."

"Where should I go, then?" Winslow asked.

"Stay close, but get out of the line of fire," Bolan told him. "Things are going to get messy, but the folks already on the ground are going to feel a lot of heat, and not from us."

Winslow looked outside. "A few moments ago, we didn't mind dropping grenades on those assholes."

"I still don't, but now, they're going to be overwhelmed. I don't like bullies," Bolan replied.

The soldier did one last check, shrugging his shoulder, running through its range of motion to make certain he was not harboring a hairline fracture or a damaged rotator cuff. He was fine, ready to fight.

Winslow remained close to him. "So we're going up against the Venezuelans. You sure we're not going to be fighting regular troops?"

Bolan lead Winslow out of the building. With their weapons and the dust all over them, they resembled the locals on the scene. The FARC guards ran up to them, a couple pausing to see if the two Americans were all right, asking quick questions. Both Bolan and Winslow answered them in Spanish, dispelling any concerns of who they were. Jeeps were rolling around, and Bolan ran up to one.

"The Venezuelans just opened fire on us. They deliberately targeted the printing presses!" Bolan snapped in Spanish. "There's at least one helicopter up there! We need to move our people to cover before they tear us apart!"

The man riding shotgun in the jeep nodded, pulling out his radio. The driver pointed for Bolan to hop onto their machine gun.

"We knew this was too good to last," the driver snarled. "Think you can do some damage with that?"

Bolan climbed into the back, waving for Winslow to

join him. He patted the receiver of the M-2 Browning as it sat atop its heavy steel vehicle mount. "I think I can."

"Slaughter those traitors!" the driver snapped. Bolan held on to the handles of the .50-caliber machine gun, and the jeep accelerated from where it had been parked. Orders were being snapped left and right.

Even now, Bolan could make out the helicopters in the darkness. There were three of them, and judging by the shapes in the sky and the soldier's knowledge of the military aircraft in the Venezuelan army's inventory, there were two huge Mil Mi-17 transports and a smaller aircraft. At least one of them was packing heavy weaponry, and sure enough, the flash and sizzle of an air-to-ground missile being fired lit up the side of one of the machines.

Unguided rockets slashed into the ground in a line, aimed away from Bolan and the jeep, but that didn't mean the warheads hit the ground harmlessly. FARC defenders in the distance screamed, their cries of injury and death rising from the fading cacophony of detonations as the rocket pack emptied into the compound. Bolan swept the muzzle of the Browning toward where the Mil transport had illuminated itself with its fire, adjusted for the bird's speed and movement, then cut loose with the big Browning.

The roar of the heavy machine gun wasn't new to the soldier, he'd ripped into opponents before with the mighty fifty, but even without novelty, there was a jolt of excitement and power that rippled along his arms as he made the machine gun spit out its deadly message to the enemy aircraft. A .50-caliber round from the Browning was a massive piece of lead, zipping along at over two and a half times the speed of sound, and weighing an ounce and a half.

One shot was sufficient to punch a hole through all but the heaviest of armor plating. At 600 rounds per minute, the thunder Bolan unleashed was more than enough to rake the Mi-17 and leave it with dozens of holes in its hull. The helicopter flared upward, weaving off, its running lights aflame now that it had received damage. Bolan tracked the speeding bird and triggered another burst into the wounded craft. The vibration of the M-2 Browning was matched only by the violent puffs of pressure released when its .50-caliber slugs struck the atmosphere at supersonic speed.

Winslow, below Bolan, was closer to the muzzle, and he wrapped his hands around his ears as the concussive ripples rocked across his head, threatening to fracture his eardrums.

Bolan hoped that Winslow's stopgap measures were enough, because he needed to take out the armed enemy helicopter quickly. The Browning spit again and again, salvos of heavy slugs that slashed into the night sky.

Emboldened by Bolan's lead and his success, other FARC gunners with machine guns and rifles followed suit, spraying into the night sky, tracers from the machine guns lighting the path to whatever was in the air. Bolan doubted that all of this fire would prove effective to drive off all of the Venezuelan aircraft, but it would make them retreat.

Altitude was the best defense, the easiest cushion between the helicopters and the guns on the ground. Even so, the ship that Bolan had targeted was meandering, flames licking from a damaged engine and making it an easy target. One of the surviving V-100 armor cars cut loose with its M-134 minigun. The whipsaw of high-volume, high-velocity lead tore into the damaged ship, bits of its armor and hull disintegrating under the onslaught of 3000 rounds per minute.

During the several seconds of hell the minigun was working, a loud crack split the air.

The Mil Mi-17 broke down the center, the two halves spiraling away from each other after the punishing torrent of anti-aircraft fire. The segments burst into flame as they tumbled from the sky before crashing into the forest just beyond the fence. The landing and detonation of the shattered halves was spectacular and loud.

The FARC defenders let out a cry of victory as one of the enemy was swatted out of the air.

Bolan didn't allow himself that cheer of triumph, not when he knew that armor was already on the move. He looked toward the enemy base, and saw, somewhere along the road, the sudden flicker, like lightning crackling within the jungle.

"Move!" Bolan snapped to Winslow, grabbing him by the collar.

The two mean leaped out of the jeep; Winslow didn't need to be told twice. The ground shuddered as 90 mm shells smashed into it, tank rounds exploding amid the defenders of the printing operation. Their jeep had been untouched by the sudden rain of artillery shells, but fountains of smoke, fire and broken asphalt were blooming all around the base.

The Venezuelans had been hit, and they had lost some of their own.

Now, they were striking back with all the firepower that they could muster, and the FARC terrorists were paying the price for that vengeance in explosions and blood.

CHAPTER SEVENTEEN

Murder in the form of light tank fire and heavy machine-gun bullets rained from the column of vehicles rushing into action. Bolan and the FARC gunners had combined their fire in order to take down the lone, rocket-armed gunship that had been in the air, raking the base with warheads. Now, 90 mm cannons, 7.62 mm miniguns and .50-caliber Brownings took the place of the aerial assault, raking the entire compound with death and destruction. Even as the shells and bullets ripped down, Bolan and Winslow raced for cover, realizing that their brief alliance with the FARC had ended.

Bolan checked his load of grenades as he and Winslow huddled against a wall. A sweep of automatic fire raked the ground next to them, and the soldier grimaced, realizing that there was nothing on hand that would halt the advance of the Scorpion tanks that the Venezuelans were using. He looked around, seeing if there were troops who had scrambled for more impressive firepower.

Winslow pointed at a clot of bodies. "RPG rockets!"

Bolan followed the Secret Service agent's line of sight. "Good eyes."

He was about to stand when Winslow held up a hand. "I'll run for them. You provide some cover fire."

Winslow handed over his bandoleer of grenades. "You're a better shot with them than I am."

With that, the younger man was off.

Bolan couldn't do much in terms of taking down the advancing Scorpion-90s, but he could apply some damage to their support vehicles. He gauged the distance to the column, adjusted his aim and sailed a high-explosive grenade toward where he calculated a Venezuelan jeep would be. The 40 mm shell arced, reaching nearly its limit of 400 yards before dropping into the road.

A single detonation reverberated all the distance back to Bolan who was already reloading and taking aim again. His best tactic was to engage in rapid fire, even though he realized that his attack would only draw attention to his position. Even so, things were hectic enough that the enemy probably couldn't make out a single grenadier, not when he was using the wreckage of a wall to cover his muzzle-blast.

Machine-gun fire ripped up the ground around Bolan's position, and he ducked back, looking for Winslow. He worried that the Venezuelans were targeting the younger American, but in reality, the wave of bullets was targeted toward a V-100 armored car that had edged up closer to the soldier's position.

Apparently the FARC rebels were still under the assumption that Bolan was on their side, because the gunner in the armored car's turret fired up his M-134 minigun and ripped off a long, bellowing burst. Bolan grimaced and charged away from where he had hunkered down. As much as he appreciated the Colombian rebel support against the Venezuelan cleanup squad, the

V-100 was simply going to draw the fire of the Scorpion tanks.

Even so, things were heating up. Two jeeps were joining the V-100, so now there was a wall of fire coming from the three vehicles. Bolan didn't know who was getting hit right now, but so far, they were holding up well. He skidded to a prone position near Winslow who had loaded a single rocket into the RPG.

"You good with one of these, too?" Winslow asked.

Bolan nodded. The Secret Service agent handed over the portable rocket launcher and the Executioner shouldered it. He swept the horizon, scanning the road. The only way he could target specific vehicles was by the flash their muzzles made through the rapidly thinning forest. Machine-gun fire tore through the foliage between the road and the FARC installation, eroding their concealment, but it was only when he saw the bright flare of a Scorpion's gun go off that he could target it.

The RPG-7 had been loaded with the PG-7VR warhead, which had been designed specifically for enemy tanks with reactive armor, and thicker steel, than the Scorpions had. Bolan fired the 105 mm warhead at the tank's muzzle-flash, knowing that the crosswind would make up for the movement of the enemy armor. Even so, at over 350 yards, he'd have a one-in-five chance to make a solid hit, despite even his prodigious experience.

The 105 mm shell landed and detonated violently. Its explosion illuminated where it had impacted, and while Bolan had missed the Scorpion he was aiming for, a second of the tanks had rolled into the onrushing warhead. Intense heat and explosive force turned the internal cone of copper into a streaming lance of super-hot metal that punched through the Venezuelan tank's hull. The sheet temperature of that flaming lance made the insides of the tank inhospitable for the driver, whose flesh melted. The gunner crew screamed as fragments of burning metal and droplets of molten copper bounced around the interior of the tank, leaving massive injuries on them. Their pain ended when a droplet landed in the magazine for the tank.

The ammunition inside of the tank cooked off, ignited by the liquid copper, making the Scorpion-90 shudder as if it were suffering an epileptic seizure. The tank's treads locked up as the motor was smashed in the resulted conflagration of igniting gunpowder and bursting shells.

Even stopped, the tank could wreck vehicles, however, as was proved when it lurched to a sudden halt in front of the Venezuelan jeeps that were racing down to the scene of the conflict. The hood of the first jeep crumpled as the driver was unable to swerve in time. Metal folded, the driver and his second hurled through the windshield by the impact. The gunner in the back of the jeep was whirled around, clutching his fifty's controls as much for dear life now as for hammering the Colombian rebels downrange. His fifty raked another jeep that had managed to swerve out of the way, the quick burst of the Browning cutting the other driver in two.

Three vehicles were taken out with one hit, but fire still rained downhill from above.

Off to the west, Bolan heard the pop of more RPGs. The FARC terrorists were making use of what firepower that they could, and they slammed their rockets into the countryside. None of the men firing had the expertise that Bolan possessed, but by sheer volume of their fire, they peppered the column of Venezuelan vehicles with explosions that at least brought the enemy advance to a halt.

Bolan reloaded, looking back to see that the Scorpion's 90 mm tank gun had pulverized one of the jeeps that was backing up the V-100. The other two, however, weren't letting up with their machine guns. The M-134's barrels glowed like a sideways halo, muzzles rendered yellow-hot from the volume of lead running through them. The gunner laid off the trigger, letting the spinning barrels cool the overheated metal. The last thing that Bolan needed was for an M-134 to jam up when facing nearly impossible enemy odds.

Even as he thought in terms of enemies, he couldn't help but worry that some of the men in the mechanized cavalry attack might be just normal, day-to-day Venezuelan military men whose duty was the protection of their country. Yet, as those thoughts came forward, he realized that there was no way that a standard armored unit would be used to clean up collusion with FARC rebels operating inside Venezuela's borders. The chances that these were regular troops and not special operations who would be involved in acts of sabotage against Colombia was slim by sheer dint of the attack.

Bolan took aim and fired ahead of the Scorpion he had missed, gauging its speed and the curves of the road that he had memorized from Stony Man's aerial surveillance. He dropped his next four-pound warhead right in front of the Venezuelan tank, and when it burst, it tore up road and shattered one of the vehicle's treads. Winslow was spotting for the Executioner now, using his night-vision binoculars to watch the approaching column.

"They're dead in the water now," Winslow announced. "That tank's not rolling another foot."

"Stay in cover. Their guns are still working," Bolan warned.

As if to punctuate the soldier's point, the 90 mm cannon cut loose with another round. The section of wall that Bolan and Winslow had been using for cover, and that now partially shielded the FARC V-100, disappeared in a thunderclap as the shell struck home. By now, the M-134 had cooled enough, and its gunner turned it toward the enemy again. The blazing six barrels whirled and spit out flame in a deadly stream of lead.

Beside it, the jeep with its Browning and the driver and second's rifles were playing cleanup, firing as fast as they could. Bolan added to the mayhem, adding a third RPG shell to the mix. He had adjusted his aim for the stilled tank and punched this last round right into the turret. Heavy armor was no match for the HEAT round, which fired yet another lance of fluid metal through its shell. This time, the stream of liquid fire smashed into the Scorpion's magazine. Shells and propellant packets went off, the turret literally flying off the body of the tank atop a pillar of fire and force. That explosion shook the ground so hard that Bolan could feel the blast through his boots.

Even so, he didn't have the time nor the inclination to celebrate this victory. Two tanks down, as far as he could tell, was not going to stop the enemy advance.

Gunfire rattled above them, the pop of rifles almost

swallowed up by the thudding of rotor blades. The helicopters had swung back over the compound, and now they were doing what they could to support the mechanized column. Bolan let the RPG launcher drop to the side and he swung up his AK-103. The helicopter above him was close enough to be tagged by the rifle, and the Executioner shouldered his weapon, slamming a salvo of 7.62 mm lead into its belly.

Even as he did so, he knew it was too late for more of the FARC defenders. The second jeep was empty of gunmen, the hail of rifle fire from above having cleaned them out brutally. Winslow swung up his weapon, but he put his finger on his GP-25's trigger and pulled it. The under-barrel grenade launcher bellowed, tossing a round straight up at the helicopter.

"Please don't..." were all that Winslow could get out before there was a bright flash and a crack of thunder from above. The 40 mm Russian shell hit and shook the Mi-17. It wasn't enough to damage the flight mechanism, but it did knock two riflemen off the ramp of the hovering bird, their screams stretching 150 yards to the ground before they ended with ugly, wet crunching sounds.

The helicopter struggled to get higher, and Bolan scanned above for the third of the choppers. A V-100 downrange swung its M-134 upward and opened up on the staggered bird, sweeping it with autofire, but the Mi-17 had its own door gunners, and they were returning fire with Brownings and MAG-58s in side ports.

The V-100 easily shrugged off the MAG-58 rounds, but the .50-caliber rounds struck its armored shell and punched right through, tearing into the hapless FARC crew within. The gunner scrambled out of his turret, but he was picked off before he could run twenty feet. Bolan grimaced as he watched the poor Colombian rebel blasted to a pulp.

Again, this was a case of one enemy eliminating another, but gunning down fleeing, unarmed foes was not in the Executioner's bag of tricks. He took aim with his GP-25 launcher and triggered it. Bolan realized that it was a shot in the dark, but the 40 mm shell exploded, rocking the side of the Russian helicopter. The bird's armor held, saving the men inside, but the pilot was still fighting to get the helo out of the firefight.

There were too many guns on the ground that could hurt them.

"Follow me," Bolan said to Winslow. He let his rifle hang on its sling and fed the fallen RPG launcher another rocket. He shouldered the weapon, scanning for another enemy vehicle up above, but the dueling machine guns of the FARC and the mechanized cavalry had whittled down those willing to fight to very few. Bolan spotted a Scorpion that was trying to push its way past the trashed hulk of the first tank taken out by an anti-tank rocket. He pulled the trigger on the rocket launcher, then dropped it.

Winslow paused to watch the detonation of the shell in the distance. His jaw hung slack as yet another heavy rocket smashed through armor, causing massive damage inside. This time, the flame and explosion came off the engine and the fuel in the back, not that it made much difference in crippling the tank. However, only the driver had been able to climb out of the machine, escaping as the turret gunner crawled halfway into the open, then died, engulfed by burning fuel.

"Come on!" Bolan called to Winslow.

The Secret Service agent ran, and found that they were headed toward the V-100 that had been hammered by the helicopter's port guns. Bolan crawled up into the turret, then dropped down, popping open the side door for Winslow to get in. The pair quickly tugged at the bodies stuck in the driver's seat and riding shotgun. Gore dripped on the chairs, blood oozing from single wounds punched through each of the men.

"We're going to use this to clean up the armored column?" Winslow asked.

"No. I want that last helicopter," Bolan answered. "Can you drive?"

"I'll do it," Winslow replied. He started the engine and put the vehicle into gear. As it was a regular wheeled car, he didn't have to worry about working the tracks as on a tank. Bolan was on the gun.

Winslow was glad to be back on the hunt, though he wasn't certain just how the hell they were going to deal with a helicopter from the ground. It turned out that they could give chase. With Bolan barking orders, they seemed to be tearing across the compound toward a section of downed fence. The soldier ripped it asunder with the M-134, short, concise bursts that shredded chain link, sparks flying as the last of the electricity flowed through the dying connection.

"What about the rest of the Venezuelans or the Colombians?" Winslow asked, keeping up a steady speed, about 40 miles an hour if he had his kilometers to miles conversion right.

"They can deal with each other. The presses took several direct hits from the Scorpion tanks, making sure that nothing could be found on Venezuelan soil connecting them to the counterfeiting plot," Bolan said. "You heard the booming of those guns."

"Yeah. I was wondering why we weren't completely flattened," Winslow mused.

"Targeting the machinery," Bolan said curtly. "Keep going straight."

Winslow had pulled on a helmet with night-vision goggles. The batteries were still working, which was a relief. He wouldn't want to speed down a jungle road without a means of seeing things.

Bolan cut loose again with the minigun. The weapon roared, making the whole armored car vibrate inside. That was a lot of horsepower plowing through six barrels.

"You have enough ammunition for that?" Winslow asked.

"Two more cassettes," Bolan answered. "Two thousand rounds."

"That thing eats up ammo fast, though," Winslow warned.

"Yeah, with my trigger finger," Bolan said. "There's a fork ahead. Go right!"

"Got it!" Winslow returned. He accelerated and followed the soldier's direction. He couldn't see the sky, nor the target that his partner was tracking, but he wouldn't have to. All he had to do was keep the armored car on the road and not crack it up.

Meanwhile, Bolan swept the sky. He'd made out the Venezuelan bird by its silhouette, a Bell JetRanger, which was either the only one in the army's inventory, or from an outside source, which cemented Bolan's belief that the soldiers sent after them weren't ordinary troops pressed into service to support terrorists. He also doubted that regular troops would open fire so brutally and off the bat.

The JetRanger was a swift aircraft, and the V-100 on its best day wouldn't be able to keep up with one in full flight, but Bolan had hammered it with the M-134, doing damage to it. He didn't want to blow it out of the sky, as there would likely be men on board who would know more about the extent of the counterfeiting conspiracy. He needed them alive for answers.

The pilot of the JetRanger was good. Despite the damage wrought on the aircraft, he was keeping it aloft, looking for a safe place to touch down. The pilot was using the momentum of the rotors to autorotate to safety, the engines billowing smoke from bullet holes, which meant that the machine was losing power rapidly.

Bolan kept tabs on the copter out of the corner of his eye, swiveling the turret to see if anyone was in pursuit. Sure enough, he could see the muzzle-flashes of machine guns in the distance. It had to be the last of the quartet of Scorpion tanks that were on the road, judging by the fact that one of the guns was lower than the top-mounted gun, which was easily ten feet in the air, higher than it would have been on a jeep. Bolan depressed the trigger on the minigun and swept the tank with a brutal rain of 7.62 mm lead. His rounds sparked against the relatively heavy armor of the Scorpion.

Even though the burst did little to affect the pursuing tank, Bolan had confirmed who was on his tail. There were still other vehicles out there, he could hear them now that the helicopter was running quiet in autorotation. Bolan spotted one jeep burst into the open, visible by its headlights.

The soldier brought down the symbolic ax on the enemy vehicle before its gunner could acquire the V-100 as a target. The fifty mounted on the jeep would tear through the armored car's hull, killing both Winslow and him. Rather than risk the life of his ally, he cut loose with a blistering burst at 3000 rounds per minute. It was less than a second, between forty and forty-five rounds slashing across the vehicle. The jeep's hood blew off as high-speed rounds blew up the engine. The vibration of the spinning gun let the mount drift upward to sweep toward the windshield and vaporize the driver and one of the machine gunner's legs.

Stricken violently, the jeep slewed sideways, skidding out of control then tumbling down the riverbank, crashing through foliage before ending up in the Orinoco with a loud splash. Another machine gunner opened up, and Bolan was relieved that it was only a 7.62 mm machine gun, not quite able to tear through the armor of the V-100. Still, that was a reminder that the enemy was far from done with this chase.

Bolan had detached the GP-25 from beneath the barrel of Winslow's launcher to make it more maneuverable with him in the turret for the minigun. The GP-25 had a conventional pistol grip, which made it easier to use independently, but he had still run a length of paracord through an attachment loop, making an improvised sling with tension that could steady the launcher like a rifle stock with no additional bulk.

The actions had taken only seconds while Winslow cleared the driver's seat of a corpse and started the armored car. However, the action would prove more than worthwhile. Bolan triggered the grenade launcher, and he knew that though the 40 mm bomb wouldn't have the power to penetrate the half inch of armor on the tank, it would still make the men wary of getting too close.

Bolan's shell struck the turret hard, and the soldier was rewarded with a sudden explosion of smoke, far larger than what would have been from the grenade he had used. Bolan had been counting on the tank to have its standard equipment, including the quad-barrel smoke launcher that was usually on the turret. The rupture of those smoke canisters engulfed the machine in a choking chemical cloud as it barreled along the road.

The Scorpion swerved to a halt, the men on board not knowing what was going on. Had they been set on fire?

It was a moment of confusion, but it had bought the V-100 another few hundred feet of lead on the tank. He didn't know why the enemy hadn't decided to use their 90 mm cannon, but so far, it was a blessing. Even so, he quickly reloaded the GP-25 with another 40 mm shell. The Browning on the jeep behind the tank was going to be a major threat once it got around the obstruction in the road. Bolan triggered the launcher, striking the tank in the side. As the grenade hit and detonated, the second of the Venezuelan jeeps had pulled up parallel to the tank, looking to pass the stalled vehicle. The shrapnel from the grenade bounced off the half-inch armor and into the exposed driver, obliterating his left arm and the left side of his face. Crippled and half blind, the driver lost control of the speeding vehicle.

It skidded, swerved, toppled and rolled over, crushing everyone inside of the jeep and the mounted machine gun. It was grim work, but the Executioner was being pressed hard.

The crew of the Scorpion realized that their smoke dispensers had been blown up, the thick cloud clinging to the hull of the tank. The gunner was at work, spinning the turret around to track the V-100 armored car.

They were finally going to bring that 90 mm cannon into action.

"Winslow! Get off-road now!" Bolan yelled.

The Secret Service agent yanked on the wheel, and suddenly they were crashing through saplings and low foliage. Bolan had to duck into the cabin of the armored car to prevent being brained by low-hanging branches. The turret's steel, however, proved stronger than a human skull, protecting the M-134, at least for now. Even as they crashed into the woods, the road behind them vomited a flash of fire and thunder from where the 90 mm shell struck.

The cannon would take a moment to reload, but now machine-gun fire sliced into the woods. "Back to the road!"

Winslow grumbled something that sounded like "make up your mind," but the armored car wove between trees and back onto the dirt road along the river. Streams of autofire slashed into the forest, but now the V-100 was back on the road, which had kinked to the left, and they were out of sight.

That wouldn't last long. Obviously the Venezuelans would know this area and its roads. All it would take would be some rough guessing, and they could drop cannon rounds on the road ahead.

"There's the helicopter!" Winslow announced.

Bolan gave the man a clap on the shoulder. "Time to go EVA!"

Before Winslow could ask what the soldier meant, Bolan opened the door and was outside.

EVA—extravehicular activity, which meant, in plain English, leaving the vehicle and continuing on foot.

CHAPTER EIGHTEEN

Mentirosa couldn't help himself, and despite his Communist and atheist indoctrination by the Party and the military, he crossed himself like a good Cuban Catholic. The JetRanger's pilot had brought down the helicopter in one piece. From the sound of guns and explosions on the road, however, there was little reason for him to relax. Trouble was still on the way.

Mentirosa was still on the radio with Figueroa, the Venezuelan military intelligence officer who had been working with him to watch the FARC base, their operations and the progress and safety of the presses. Figueroa had done well, directing artillery to finish off the building when the rocket pods on the Mi-17 failed to work. Even so, he was surprised at how vehemently the Colombians were reacting to the Venezuelans' sudden attack.

It was almost as if they were expecting betrayal, or they had been tipped off.

Mentirosa's thoughts immediately turned to McCormack. He'd been chasing the counterfeiting operation from Medellín back to Venezuela. Somehow he realized that the best way to deal with a Venezuelan cleanup crew was to rally the FARC into defending themselves.

Figueroa complained that he'd lost three tanks and a half-dozen jeeps in this battle. The DGIM colonel had also lost a helicopter, and there were wounded on board his Mil transport from where .50-caliber rounds punched through the bird.

"Come pick me up now!" Mentirosa said into the radio.

"You got yourself into this," Figueroa answered. "Get yourself out of it!"

"Damn it, Joaquin!" the Cuban snapped.

"I'm already going to have to explain how the FARC commandeered so much equipment and did this kind of damage to my forces."

"I can't be captured!" Mentirosa responded.

"Sure you can!" Figueroa said, before his radio cut out with a loud snap.

Mentirosa grimaced. He looked toward the others on his bird. The pilot, the copilot and the two others were also Cubans, part of DI's counterterror operations crew, just like him. "Break out the weapons. We're going to have to punch our way to freedom."

"I heard that," the pilot returned. He already had pulled a machine pistol from beneath his seat. He made certain the magazine was seated, then checked the chamber. The copilot was doing likewise. Mentirosa's bodyguards, however, were already armed.

That's when the armored car veered into the clearing next to the helicopter, its wheels kicking up dust.

"Someone coming to our aid?" a bodyguard asked, but keeping the muzzle of his weapon trained on the newcomer.

"Let's not risk it," the other guard said. "Get on the other side of the bird. I'll cover us!"

Mentirosa wasn't interested in taking more risks than

he had to. He followed the instructions of his protector and leaped out of the cabin of the chopper.

Mentirosa took a moment to draw his CZ-75 from its holster under his jacket when he heard the sudden chatter of the guard's PM-70 submachine gun. The bodyguards and the pilots had brought with them the PM-70 compact machine pistols for the sake of familiarity and the relative efficiency of the weapons. Looking akin to an Uzi or the newer Heckler & Koch MP-7, the PM-70s could be carried under a jacket as concealed as a pistol, yet be fully controllable thanks to a folding forward grip and a collapsing stock that halved the length of the weapon when closed. Firing 9 mm Parabellum rounds at 650 rounds per minute, it wasn't an M-134 minigun, but it was still a devastating weapon in close combat.

Anyone foolish enough to take on his men would learn the error of their ways as their entrails were pouring out of entrance and exit wounds.

Or so Mentirosa thought. The sputter of the pistol-caliber automatic weapons was answered not with rifle fire, but the throaty roar of a hand cannon.

The American was here!

MACK BOLAN LEFT the grenade launcher and his AK-103 behind. He needed precision to take a prisoner, and he also needed speed and agility. The assault rifle was simply too much to haul with him, especially since the men on the helicopter were making a break into the woods.

Bolan was out of the V-100, his .44 Magnum Desert Eagle in hand. Even as he set foot on the ground, he spotted one of the men in the chopper with a compact automatic weapon in his hands. The gunner cut loose, and Bolan lunged sideways as a stream of auto-fire slammed into the side of the armored car, bullets plinking and flattening against the steel of the truck. Bolan hit a shoulder roll, coming up with the mighty .44 pistol clutched in both hands, its front sight locked on to the gunman in the helicopter.

The Executioner slammed two heavy 240-grain hollowpoint rounds into the sub gunner's chest, bowling him backward in his perch before he could adjust his aim and track the American. The twin .44 slugs had struck home, smashing ribs and lungs alike, fragments of one bullet and splinters of bone severing the man's aorta to quickly shut him. Bolan continued his advance toward the helicopter, running broken-field style in order to keep an enemy from acquiring a good target on him.

Winslow dropped from the V-100, his rifle at the ready. He was kneeling, crouched to present a low, small target, and he had on night-vision goggles, so he could see into the forest.

"I'll cover you," Winslow said over his hands-free communicator. "Rifle's on single shot so I don't tear up the wrong target."

"Thanks," Bolan whispered, moving around the nose of the helicopter, the Desert Eagle's muzzle leading the way. He trod forward on silent feet, the grass making little sound as he stepped through it. He could make out movement through the cockpit windows of the JetRanger, and brought up the .44 Magnum pistol. He wanted answers, but the guy here was alone, still holding the line drawn by the first sub gunner.

Bolan fired, slamming a slug through the cockpit

glass. The bullet struck the man behind, spinning him around as the windshield deflected a center mass shot into a shoulder hit. Even though it wasn't a heart hit, the enemy gunman's shoulder joint was turned from bone, muscle and sinew into a gory pulp of rubbery wreckage. The man collapsed to the ground, and Bolan moved closer, kicking the machine pistol from his hands.

The man looked up, bleary eyed and in shock. It was no wonder. The bone was pulverized, as well as clusters of nerves and sheets of muscle. Taking a moment for mercy, Bolan kicked him in the temple, knocking him out.

"We've got wounded. Front of the chopper. I'm heading into the forest," Bolan told Winslow.

"On it," Winslow answered.

Bolan knew that things were going to get noisier now. The need for stealth was rapidly going out the window. About the only saving grace was that there was no sign of the Scorpion tank still in pursuit. It either turned around, or was stalled by damage to its tracks. They also didn't open fire, but the way that the men in this copter were running, it didn't seem like they were expecting a rescue. A quick glance to the sky showed Bolan that the other transport had broken off.

The men in the JetRanger were on their own, and their numbers had dwindled. Bolan could follow their trail in the darkness of the forest, three men, and they were moving all out. The soldier settled into a ground-eating jog, careful not to go so fast that he would miss obstructions in the path, but not so slow that the enemy would escape, or find a position to entrench themselves.

The Executioner's sharp ears detected movement up

ahead, and he slowed to a crouch, finding the cover of a trunk. Three silhouettes were visible in the darkness beneath the forest canopy. He could make out one of them pulling off a helmet. Probably one of the air crew for the downed JetRanger. Bolan mentally marked him as a target who could be dropped if things became hostile.

He also noticed another man, also carrying a machine pistol like the ones used by the bodyguards. He pegged this one as helicopter crew, as well. The third shape had to be the man who everyone was gathered around, the man the two bodyguards had died protecting. Bolan edged closer to them as they settled in to spring a trap.

Too bad for the trio that they were dealing with Mack Bolan, the Executioner, who cut his teeth fighting in jungles before becoming a hunter of human savages and parasites. Even as he flanked the ambush, he noted that the third man, the one he'd pegged as his primary target, was armed with only a pistol. The "boss" didn't feel the need to arm himself with much, at least until he found himself being stalked through the forest like wild game. Bolan focused on him, skirting one of the air crew as he slithered through the shadows.

Bolan closed on the last of the group, the guy armed with a pistol. He was still backing away from the ambush, seemingly as if he were ready to let his two flunkies do his work, letting distance be his shield and cushion. The Executioner fought off the urge to smile as he crept closer. The man was so intent on avoiding the pursuit behind him that he walked backward, not keeping an eye on where he was going.

With a sudden flash of movement, Bolan snaked his

arm under the man's throat, scissoring his throat into a vise. The soldier jammed his other fist under his prey's jaw, applying direct pressure to the carotid artery, putting the final touch on a sleeper hold. With the blood supply suddenly slowed to his brain, Mentirosa's brief and sudden thrashing grew quickly, inexorably weaker until finally, within a few moments, Bolan held a limp rag doll in his arms. He lowered the body to the ground softly, checking his pulse.

Despite the choke hold and the lack of consciousness, he was all right. Bolan rolled him onto his stomach so he wouldn't vomit and choke himself to death upon awakening, the inevitable result of being rendered unconscious. With his prisoner secured, the Executioner rose, drawing the Desert Eagle once more.

"Gentlemen?" Bolan spoke, his weapon leveled at the pair.

The two Cuban pilots turned, momentarily confused as they gazed at the tall figure in the shadows. They couldn't quite make out the man's features, adding to their bewilderment, but they did realize that the mystery man who'd addressed them was taller than their charge Mentirosa.

One of the pilots brought up his machine pistol, tracking its muzzle toward the Executioner, but Bolan had his Desert Eagle drawn and ready. He pivoted and hammered off a single brutal .44 Magnum slug at that gunman. The fat slug caught the man on the point of his chin, splitting his mandible apart in explosive fashion before the deformed hollowpoint round tumbled, turning from a compact bullet into a spinning propeller tearing through flesh and tissue.

Even as it spiraled through the man's throat, it stayed on a relatively direct path, the flower petals of the flattened bullet steering it into neck bones before the mass of lead was stopped. The chunk of lead and copper decelerated from 1600 feet per second to zero, dumping all of its energy into a blow that snapped his target's neck, severing his spine.

The other gunman realized that he was not facing a friendly, and was spurred to fire his weapon at the lone killer who had all but decapitated his partner. The copilot pulled the trigger on his PM-70, ripping off a salvo of 9 mm slugs that he would walk into the Executioner. It would have been a good plan against a slower opponent, but Bolan twisted, pushing himself straight toward his enemy and pulling the trigger again.

Bolan punched his next two .44 Magnum slugs into the sub gunner, both rounds striking the Cuban in the breastbone, shattering it to pieces, bone, flattened lead and shredded copper flying into the heart, lungs and aorta behind the sheet where his ribs met in the middle. The two hollowpoint rounds came apart on contact with solid bone, detonating ribs into splinters that shot off in their own paths of tissue destruction. The dual slugs ripped a channel, one of them missing the Cuban's spine, but the other struck a vertebra and split it in two.

In the meantime, back toward the entry wounds, fragments of copper jacket torn off by explosive expansion sank into heart muscle, shredding into ventricles while splintered bone fragments sliced through bronchial tissue in the lungs. Within an instant, the copilot's chest was a wreck barely resembling a healthy man's internal organs. Lungs deflated and blood jetted straight out of the wounds torn in the heart.

Broken spine, lacerated heart and demolished lungs all combined to kill the target three times over with only two bullets. The Cuban let out a grunt, bloody froth spurting through his lips before he toppled, face-first to the forest floor.

Bolan dumped his spent magazine, feeding it a fresh one and scanning the area for more potential opponents.

There was no one still standing, save for Winslow and himself.

"Come here. We've got a prisoner to take back to the plane," Bolan said.

"On my way," Winslow said. "I just follow the sound of the Magnums?"

Bolan retrieved a glow stick from his pouch and broke it. "I'll leave a candle burning for you."

"I see you," Winslow answered.

With that, Bolan relaxed. No more helicopters, no more grunts of tank or jeep engines. The Venezuelans had suffered heavy losses in their conflict with him and the FARC rebels. The DGIM had been involved in this operation, and in the end, they decided to cut their losses and their ties to the man Bolan had tracked and left unconscious.

Answers would come soon.

MILLAGRO FIRED UP his tenth cigarette in a row, having only moments ago stubbed out the last one. The room was thick with smoke, and it hung, stagnant, choking in the confined, claustrophobic quarters. Sweat glistened on Millagro's forehead, droplets reflecting the light of the bare lightbulb that struggled to push the shadows away. His stomach twisted, and he'd been grinding his teeth for so many days straight that just biting into something felt like a demon had stabbed railroad spikes into his gums. He was going slowly mad, sustaining himself on a diet of coffee and nicotine with occasional splashes of liquor that did little for the quickly growing ulcers boiling inside his hungry stomach.

It had been two days since he'd last heard from Mentirosa, two days since the man had told him to gather up all the firepower he possibly could and bring it to bear in Tumaco. In another six hours, the freighter was due to leave the port, and cargo was being hauled on board as fast as crews could get it done.

Molinov opened the door, waving in front of his face to clear some room for oxygen, his face twisted in disgust at the conditions in the cramped office. Millagro glared at him through red-rimmed eyes, accusing eyes that wanted nothing more than to see the Russian's face turn purple, tongue lolling out between lips. Millagro didn't care who throttled the burly European, he just wanted to see Molinov choke.

"Was it something I said?" Molinov asked, sneering. "If anything, I should be chewing you..."

"Just shut up," Millagro snapped. "What the living hell am I supposed to do? You're off with your little specialist team, and what are you doing?"

"Making damned sure that this freighter gets out of port without a single hitch," Molinov said. "We're close. Once we're done, we can disappear into the woodwork."

"*You* can disappear," Millagro corrected. "Me, I'm stuck. I go back to Venezuela, I'm going to have to answer to DGIM for how badly I exposed them to danger. Do you know how many of our operatives died?"

"No," Molinov returned. "Neither do you. DGIM isn't speaking to either of us. I have an excuse. I'm not one of their members. What about you?"

"That's right. What about me?" Millagro asked. He took out his pistol, a 9 mm SIGSauer P226, held it in his hand, his knuckles white as they stretched over the handle. He kept his finger out of the trigger guard, however. The SIG was a simple pistol, no safety lever, only the stiffness of its initial double-action trigger preventing an unintentional discharge. He was tempted to put a bullet right into the Russian's belly, but he knew that it was his nerves betraying him.

"Listen, we shouldn't be at each other's throat," Molinov said. "You've got as many FARC on hand as you possibly could. I've got some cartel friends, and I've got my security team. No one is going to make it onto this boat. No one is going to damage our cargo. We're hours away from being home free."

"McCormack took out a Cuban officer on Venezuelan soil. I don't know if he killed my man, or if he captured him. Mentirosa was the one who told me to bring in all the manpower and all the guns that I could," Millagro answered. "Who's to say he didn't talk."

"McCormack is an American. He doesn't torture," Molinov returned. "And that's one thing about the Soldier. He has his standards. He's allegedly stood up, and put down, agents who have murdered and tortured."

"Allegedly," Millagro snapped. He finally stood and went to the door, leaving the office for the first time in eighteen hours. Fresh air nearly made him drunk and dizzy as he inhaled it. Molinov rested a beefy paw on the Venezuelan's shoulder.

"We're ready. There is nothing that the Soldier can attempt that would bring us down," Molinov told him. "He'd have to be a god of thunder to penetrate our defenses."

Millagro looked at him out of the corner of his eye. "You have six people brought in from Malaysia. Six people."

Molinov nodded. "And there's hundreds of your people on the scene here already."

Millagro repeated the term *hundreds*. "There were hundreds at the presses. And tanks."

"One man. Maybe two," Molinov said. "He can't deal with all of this."

"So you say," Millagro said. "But he charged up river, destroyed four of our submarines, killed dozens and then had my contact with Caracas cut off cold. That's far more than any man could have done. Any normal man."

"You've been watching too many movies," Molinov returned. "We've been attributing magical abilities to one man, but he's got no super-soldier serum running through his veins. He's got blood. Blood we can spill."

Millagro's eyes were stinging. He'd have thought that they would have been burning, even after hours in a smoke-filled room, but the fresh air seemed to be returning some sensation to his senses. Tears were leaking from the corners of his eyes. He rubbed one, then took another puff on his cigarette. He glared at Molinov.

"We're ready for an army to try to take us," the Russian reassured him. "We're fine."

Millagro turned his head slowly toward one of the containers being lifted from the dock. He went over the manifest in his mind, correlating the numbers with the list. This was a container packed with U.S. currency, hundreds, fifties and twenties, wall to wall, enough to duplicate the gross national product of an entire South American nation. Flooding the international market with these would be more than enough to crush the United States economy for decades, ruining its standing in the financial community.

He took a deep breath. The container was one of twelve. Six for U.S. dollars. Six for Chinese yuan.

It was like loading a dozen nuclear missiles, except these missiles had the capacity to spread their destruction to all the corners of the world, throwing millions of people into slavery and despair, spread rioting and starvation.

These were the weapons that would make the world tremble, and leave one economy as a stable superpower. After all of these years, these decades, the plan that gutted the KGB's coffers, a master stroke that would have eviscerated capitalism and brought nations to their knees, would come and bear fruit.

Russia, for all the knocks it had taken over the years, would once again be a force to be reckoned with, while China and the United States, her greatest competition, would be rendered toothless and crippled.

"This could work," Millagro whispered to himself.

Molinov smiled. "Now you are seeing things my..."

A loud crack split the air. The container, lifted by a crane, suddenly snapped loose from its mooring, dropping sixty feet in an instant. The moment it struck the ground, the metal walls of the container burst open, counterfeit bills flying like green-tinted snow on the docks.

Millagro's neck hairs rose.

"He's here!"

CHAPTER NINETEEN

The bursting cable and the dramatic results of its crash into the concrete dock was a flashy opening, but it had been one that Mack Bolan had spent the past twenty-four hours working on. His eyes ached from the contact lenses he wore, changing his piercing blue gaze into a dark, smoldering brown. His well-worn tan and jet-black hair already made him a good semblance for a European-descent Colombian with the blue eyes. With darker eyes, he could have been mestizo, a mix of European and Native American blood, far more common out of the larger cities of Medellín and Bogotá.

The crane's suspension cables had been one way in which Bolan could sabotage the transfer of counterfeit money. All it had taken was a little bit of work earlier in the day. The hook had been raised and lowered enough times, dockworkers guiding it into the harnesses to lift the containers and bring them on board. Bolan had been among those groups, in fact being on it yesterday, climbing partway up to make sure that a bulge in the wound steel cables wasn't a weakening of the cable.

Bolan waited for the crane to dispense the cable low enough, then inserted a half kilogram stick of plastic explosive in there. He wound a steel sleeve around the cable as a stopgap repair, and that sleeve provided cover for Bolan to also place a small radio detonator on the cable, hidden from view. The sleeve squeezed the puttylike explosives until it was permeated along a large section of the powerful line.

The soldier would bide his time, but he thanked Miguel Villanueva and the local Tumaco dockworkers for letting him slip into the position of repair crew. Hours later, Bolan was back on the docks in a change of clothes, cleanly shaved, his hair trimmed short after it had grown out for a week in the jungle. Again, he had on the contact lenses that changed the hue of his eyes.

Armed guards were around the freighter, all of them grim and eagle-eyed. They looked at him every so often, but Mack Bolan was a master of role camouflage. Not only did he look like a local, he *felt* like a local. The spices of local food was on his breath and sweat. His style of clothing and walk were copied from the dockworkers. He didn't act or appear armed, despite having a .357 Magnum Ruger in one pocket and the brutal Karambit hook knife on a neck sheath.

They didn't notice that the tall rangy dockworker also had a toolbox, and he was inspecting containers. Well, they noticed his inspections, but he was merely looking at the tags, and the counterfeiters had gone the extra mile to make sure that all the seals and stickers were one hundred percent legit, so that the containers wouldn't be opened. That didn't matter much to Bolan. He bent, checked off a box on his clipboard then moved on, no one noticing as he palmed a SLAM munition, a device the size and appearance of a nineties-era MP3 player, slipping it into tiny vent holes where an adhesive backing would anchor it against all but the most violent of shakes.

The SLAM—short for Selective Lightweight Attack Munition—was a marvel of combat technology, a one-kilogram mine that could be used to cripple even a tank with its armor-piercing copper-penetrating charge, a jet of liquid metal that could slice through 40 mm of steel as if it were butter. It could also be used to sabotage, and the mines were all set on a twenty-four-hour active cycle. If the soldier didn't need to detonate them before then, the tiny mines would render themselves inert and sterile.

The shaped charge could blow the legs off humans walking along a trail, smash a hole in the side of a bunker, or as stated, could punch through a tank's armor. The copper lance of superheated metal had one more advantage that Bolan could see. Metal that hot increased the heat in an area. It could reach temperatures far beyond the ignition temperature of rags, let alone conventional paper.

Now, hidden in the shadows on the deck of the freighter, Bolan removed his contacts. He would need his vision clear and eyes comfortable for the upcoming mayhem. He unzipped his coverall, as well, exposing the blacksuit beneath, as well as the chest straps of his combat harness. Across Bolan's shoulders was his shoulder holster for the Beretta 93R machine pistol. Around his waist was a web belt with an attached holster for his .44 Magnum Desert Eagle. His suspenders had pouches attached, dozens of pockets set aside for spare ammunition for the pistols, small munitions up to two more of the high-tech SLAMs. What wasn't a bullet or a bomb was either a tool or a melee weapon, often both. Even the compact folding pliers he carried sported a four-inch blade that was razor-sharp and strong enough to stab through a phone book with a strong enough thrust.

But now, Bolan peeled out of the coveralls, confident that the sudden crash of the container had drawn every lick of attention off him. He was right, having spent plenty of time devising and pulling off diversions. Nothing quite seized the imagination of even armed professionals like the sound of ten tons of steel crashing into concrete. Bolan thumbed the detonator again, and the crumpled container, full of stacks of illicit money, burst into flame as a spear of liquid metal punched through. The temperatures involved created a thunder clap that vented out the ruptures in the steel sides, the bent walls forming horns that released a clarion call of devastation into the air.

Bolan changed the channel. He had up to twenty frequencies plugged into the detonator, and he intended to do as much as he could to sow mayhem among the defenders.

Mentirosa may have nominally been a Communist operative of Cuba's DI, one of the last of the hard-core Soviet–era espionage agencies, but having seen his men destroyed and the Venezuelan military trampled thanks to the Executioner's machinations had given him pause. Bolan made an offer for his life. Information about the kind of security set up in Tumaco, or a slow death.

"You're an American. You're *el Soldado!* You don't torture," the Cuban had snapped.

"Who said I would be the one killing you?" Bolan had growled.

With that, the Executioner had pointed to the Orinoco River tributary, hundreds of yards away from Lupe Magdalena's Cessna. "I'll leave you in the water with a bloody, but harmless cut. Once a drop gets in the water, the beasts of the river will be lining up for a taste of you."

"Beasts," Mentirosa repeated. "What do you mean?"

"Crocodiles. Anacondas. Piranha Tiger fish. Catfish."

"Catfish?" Mentirosa questioned.

"Catfish that grow to a hundred and eighty to two hundred pounds, and don't mind eating humans whole. I doubt you'll get to the deep water with them, though. The crocodiles will twist you apart like taffy long before that."

Mentirosa looked at the river.

"I've barely survived a couple of encounters in those waters, and you saw what I did to an armored column. What do you think a novice like you can survive?" Bolan asked. He pulled the knife on his folding pliers, pulling on the Cuban's hand.

"Wait!" Mentirosa shouted.

"I don't have much patience," Bolan returned.

The Cuban talked. He told the soldier everything that he needed, making the next forty-eight hours much easier for Bolan. In return for that information, he left the man with a knife and a compass.

"If you contact Tumaco, I'll find you again," Bolan warned. "And then I'll drop your ass into the Amazon. They have bull sharks there."

Mentirosa got the message. Bolan didn't expect to hear from this particular Cuban operative for a while, at least not for a couple of years.

With the explosions and the fire, the soldier now introduced that level of terror into the enemy group. He set off some explosives that were planted under the fuel tank of a forklift at the rear of the ship's deck. The compact little lifter detonated, blowing up in spectacular fashion.

Guns were coming out now, men screaming, looking for trouble.

The Executioner could have remained in the shadows, detonating charges with safety and anonymity, but he needed to send a message to the conspirators. The FARC Western Bloc members in Tumaco were already violent, dangerous people who showed no qualms about murdering soldiers and civilians alike in their reign of terror. These savages deserved all the fear and pain that he was ready to unleash upon them.

Already, a squad of armed riflemen was heading toward the site of the explosion on the stern of the freighter. Bolan, tucked into the shadows, waited for them to pass, then lurched out into the open, suppressed Beretta up and spitting its 9 mm death messages in 3-round bursts. Slugs ripping out at a rate of 1100 rounds per minute had little chance to rise and spread under recoil, so when the Beretta whispered, all of its rounds hit the same target within inches of one another. Two riflemen collapsed instantly before one of the others skidded to a halt, realizing that the group was under attack.

He'd turned halfway when Bolan cut a burst across his neck, smashing vertebrae, clavicle and shoulder joints with the next trio of rounds. Spine crushed by a 9 mm slug, the rifleman let out a strangled cry before slithering over the railing of the freighter, dropping to the dock below. The fall was forty feet, and when he struck the ground, headfirst, his skull exploded like a rotten tomato.

The gunners on deck reacted to the death sputter of their friend, but the Executioner was in full-on assault mode. Outnumbered and outgunned, he needed to be ruthless, and he continued hammering off 3-round bursts, pausing only to swap magazines after the sixth flesh-ripping blast of slugs was launched. Bolan fed the hungry Beretta an extended 33-round magazine and continued his butcher's work, leaving eight gunmen lifeless on the deck of the freighter before he was finished.

"They know someone's on the ship now, Striker," Miguel Villanueva told him over the radio. In the forty-eight hours of preparation for this final blowout, Bolan and the Colombian top cop worked together to get the frequencies of local security for the ship, tapping into the FARC's communications and picking up heavily encrypted traffic that could come only from Molinov's spoiler force. They had come from across the Pacific, and had been sent running simply because they realized that the Soldier had brought his attention to this operation.

Whoever they were, they had to be skilled and well armed, possibly a Russian mafia version of the KGB's wet work squads back at the end of the cold war. Bolan could figure out who they were, and what their likely strategies would be. He'd worry about them once he ran across them. Right now, he had his hands full in dealing with the FARC gunners who were more than enough to overwhelm even the bravest of fighting men.

Bolan paused, scooping up an assault rifle, another AK-103, and spare magazine pouches off the dead. So laden, the Executioner was ready to unleash devastation on a much wider scale. He turned the channel on his detonator, pressed the fire button, and an empty, idle container that had been surreptitiously loaded with gasoline suddenly spewed an enormous fireball. The effect was brilliant, turning night into day and sending a dozen men to the ground, flames licking at their limbs and clothes as they rolled, trying to douse their burns. More were running in fear from the sudden eruption of fire.

If the FARC chose to run, they'd meet up with a perimeter of Villanueva's *federales* who were poised to pick up the leftovers of this attack. Those who wanted to live would. The luckiest would scurry into the shadows, riddled with terror, while others would rot in Colombian prisons. It was all a calculated response to the Western Bloc's prior activities.

Bolan didn't care how the terrorists—kidnappers, murderers and drug dealers most of them—ended up. Alive or dead, he was here to send them to their judgments. He sincerely hoped most of them would put up a fight, but he was all right with being a recurring nightmare, a post-traumatic-stress-disorder symptom to these so-called "freedom fighters." They claimed to be fighting for social justice and economic equality, but in truth, they were nothing more than common criminals looking for an easy buck.

Putting bullets into the heads of reporters, court stenographers and bailiffs was a far cry from "fighting the power."

The gangway shuddered as dozens of pairs of feet started trampling their way up it. Bolan plucked a grenade off his harness, armed the bomb and rolled it toward the top of the plank, taking cover behind a steel-walled container. The minibomb's fuse counted down as the footsteps drew closer, but finally it detonated, eliciting a storm of screams, bodies flipped over the support ropes on the gangplank.

Some men fell into the brackish waters of the Tumaco bay, others bounced off steel and concrete, bones crushed by gravity. Those who were closest to the grenade's explosion were pelted, perforated with steel ball bearings from an MGU-50G anti-terrorist grenade. The tiny explosive was packed with hundreds of ball bearings, insuring a small five-meter kill radius as those little pellets struck with the power of an omnidirectional shotgun blast. Injuries would spread out for another ten meters, but the disruption of the gangplank tossed bodies around.

It was a crushing blow to anyone who was on the docks, watching a force of their fellows devastated by the burst of a single grenade. There was movement on the deck, however. Bolan moved to the cover of another container, spotting crew members on the freighter, packing rifles, shotguns and submachine pistols rushing to repel the lone boarder. Bolan snapped the AK-103 to his shoulder and ripped off ten short bursts, emptying the 30-round magazine. He'd downed six of the enemy and calmly reloaded the spent weapon.

"Now?" Winslow asked on the other end of the LASH radio.

"Give them hell," Bolan replied.

Winslow was situated on the arm of the crane that had been loading containers onto the ship. He'd gotten up there with a change of shift crew of otherwise innocent dockworkers, and stayed behind, setting up a sniper's nest well out of sight. As soon as Bolan gave the word, the Secret Service agent poked out from his invisible position and let fly with the first shot from his rifle.

It was the HK 416, converted to its sniper configuration with a change of barrel and magazines. Now chambered for 7.62 mm NATO, Winslow could drop a precision bullet through an enemy's skull at out to 800 meters. Winslow's first muffled shot exploded the face of a Western Bloc trooper shouting orders. The semiautomatic mechanism of the rifle fed another round into the breech, and Winslow triggered a second shot, bringing down the man who had been standing close to the squad leader, the bullet piercing his rib cage and emptying blood and guts onto the dock at his feet.

Suddenly confronted with bullets raining down on them, those on the dock were showing less willingness to stick with this fight.

Bolan changed the channels on his detonator again and hit the fire button. One of the containers on the freighter burst open under the force of a SLAM going off, flaming yuan notes fluttering through the air like burning snowflakes.

That was a morale killer on the deck as a squad of men attempting to flank the Executioner were suddenly cut off by flames. The burning money illuminated a clutch of them and Bolan cut into them with the AK-103. ComBloc rounds tore into three of the gunners, swatting them from existence with their internal organs ruptured by the passage of .30-caliber bullets.

That's when the first of the response team tried his hand at taking down the Executioner. Something powerful thundered from the superstructure of the freighter. A bullet slammed through the steel of a shipment container, leaving a half-inch hole in its wake, the slug coming within a yard of blowing Bolan's torso into flying hamburger.

The Russians had a high-powered anti-materiel rifle on hand, and were going to use it to bring down the wraith in black. Whatever optics the enemy had, it was obviously good enough to nearly tag Bolan through a steel container, the contents having disrupted the path of the heavy .50-caliber or 12.7 mm bullet to save his life. The Executioner rushed between cover, knowing that if he stood in one place for too long, the enemy sniper would track him down easily, just by his muzzle-flash.

To deal with the crew of the freighter, Bolan plucked out another MGU-50G grenade and tossed it toward a knot of them. The riflemen saw the deadly little ball hurled in their direction and tried to scramble to safety. The grenade burst in midair, and thousands of pellets ripped loose in a storm of flesh-piercing hell. Four more men were down, but there were supposedly dozens. The gangplank rumbled again with the advance of more gunners.

"I'm trying to pick them off the walkway," Winslow said in his radio.

"Never mind that, I've got a sniper getting too close to hitting me. I'll deal with the grunts, you take down that fifty," Bolan returned.

He lurched into the open, his rifle tracking the end of the plank. Western Bloc rebels rushed into a stream of 7.62 mm Soviet rounds, steel-cored slugs piercing one body and tearing into the one behind him. Corpses were piling up on the deck, or otherwise tumbling backward. Bolan advanced, firing his rifle, knowing that the muzzle-flash would attract the attention of the sniper who was after him.

Bolan reloaded before he reached the railing and saw that bodies were being shoved over the gangway's ropes, hurled to the water below. The throng of fighters stopped cold as they saw the Executioner standing before them at the top, surprised at his brazen appearance.

The Executioner didn't give the Colombian terrorists an instant to recover, holding down the trigger on the AK-103. The steel-cored rounds cut through body after body, and when one bullet ran out of energy, another having gone through one fewer torso came along and hit the next man who thought he had a shield of human flesh in front of him. The grisly slaughter on the choke point was simply a one-sided massacre.

A .50-caliber round slammed into the deck next to Bolan's feet, but that was immediately followed by a quick apology from Winslow.

"I hit him. He just got off a final shot as he died," Winslow explained.

Bolan looked up to the crane arm and raised a thumbs-up.

So far, so good.

Still, even at his best estimates, five highly trained commandos were out there looking to complete a mission that they had trained for years to accomplish. Given the high-powered sniper rifle he'd already encountered, that meant the others were utilizing equally cutting-edge weaponry and tactics, which would give even the Executioner a run for his money. Winslow's actions may have drawn attention to him, though it didn't seem as if gunfire coming from the dock was aimed at the crane. Rather, the gunmen down below were firing at the freighter, sweeping the railing and trying to get a bead on the man who had rained slaughter on their allies who had tried to rush him on the gangplank.

Bolan turned toward the superstructure once more and spotted a flicker of movement only moments before he dived to the deck. A buzz saw of firepower cut loose. The enemy was close, because he could still hear the gunfire despite the suppressor on the machine pistol, and the weapon had to have been a special-caliber PDW, because bullets punched into containers rather than ricocheting off them.

Bolan slithered behind a bulkhead, drawing his legs in behind him just as the floor he'd left exploded with sparks, slender midrange bullets destroying themselves on the heavy steel of the deck. The soldier affected a low crouch and raced toward the other side of a stack of containers, knowing that the enemy would be expecting him to go in that direction.

Bolan plucked yet another grenade from his harness and lobbed it up and over toward the superstructure. This one wasn't a ball-bearing filled bomb, but a flash-bang grenade. The device went off, producing a blaze of light and sound that elicited a scream of pain from whoever was on the other side.

The dark shadow of an enemy gunman had been utilizing night vision in concert with his high-tech PDW submachine gun. With the sudden blaze of the flash-bang, he was left blind, brilliant balls of fire hanging in his vision and making it difficult to see.

Bolan charged to the last position he'd registered for the gunman and saw a figure in a blacksuit, much like his own, scrambling for a doorway. The Executioner ripped the Desert Eagle from its fast-draw holster, snapped off the safety and chased the shadowy foe through the portal with a pair of .44 Magnum slugs. One bullet struck a metal wall, another elicited a pained grunt.

Bolan pushed toward the portal, head swiveling as he anticipated more crew to try to protect the ship as he went after the lone commando.

There was a rustle of fabric as something rushed from the darkness, striking the soldier in the stomach. Bolan's reflexes had instructed him to go limp, but even so, the sudden kick from the shadows still folded him, knocking the breath from his lungs.

Suddenly, the Executioner was face to mask with a slender, swift-moving brawler whose clawed fingers snagged his battle harness. A head butt lashed forward, and Bolan saw stars from the sudden impact.

The doomsday numbers were stacking against the soldier as he toppled to the ground, a hundred and seventy-five pounds of tight-muscled opponent hanging on to him like glue.

CHAPTER TWENTY

Bolan recognized a close-quarters combatant just from the opening salvo. The kick had been meant to put him off balance, possibly take the fight out of him. Two strong hands kept him from squirming too far, and that head butt had scrambled the Executioner's concentration.

If it was hand-to-hand combat that this guy wanted, then Mack Bolan was willing to accommodate him. He wound both arms around his foe's, creating a snarl of limbs that formed a barrier between the pair. There wouldn't be any more head butts until Bolan wanted one. Using his weight advantage, he rolled, pulling the enemy wrestler to the ground with all the force he could muster.

The dark-clad combatant snapped a knee up, but Bolan had brought his thighs tightly together to protect his ground. Unfortunately, this guy brought the knee in sideways, striking the American soldier on his hip. An inch higher, and it would have been the equivalent of a kidney punch, but even so, a spike of pain lanced up and down Bolan's side. The enemy had hit him in the same spot where the crocodile's tail had struck him nights before. The old bruise and battered bones groaned in protest from the renewed assault.

Bolan disentangled one arm from his foe's, then

lunged forward, his fingers spearing toward the slit in the man's mask. Whether he was trying to be a ninja, or simply trying to blend in with the shadows, Bolan's foe had little of his face exposed, but he'd neglected eye protection. The Executioner's fingertips brushed one eyeball as the man recoiled from the eye gouge, and his face scrunched shut in discomfort. Even a light touch on the eye's surface could cause discomfort, and Bolan felt something snag on his middle-finger nail as the man pulled back.

The enemy wrestler extended a knife hand toward Bolan's throat, his rigid fingers looking to collapse his windpipe with a deadly lunge. The Executioner twisted, putting all of his weight into the enemy's still-trapped arm. There was a sickly crunch and pop as his opponent's shoulder dislocated, eliciting more reaction from the enemy fighter. Bolan pulled his knees up to his chest, then kicked out, his boots striking his foe in the stomach. He felt his shoulder harness pulled hard, a finger snapping as the wrestler was dislodged.

Bolan rolled across the deck, scooping up the fallen Desert Eagle and aiming at the enemy. This hand-to-hand fighter was good. With spiderlike quickness, he brought his legs under him and was leaping away from the Executioner's gunfire. He didn't know how long the melee lasted, but there seemed to be plenty of gunfire going on.

Sirens filled the air, meaning that Villanueva had held off the Colombian police and soldiers as long as he could. There was a war on the docks, and the Tumaco law wanted in on it. They sensed the blood of their enemies in the water, and owed the Western Bloc of the FARC for dozens of deaths over recent years.

Bolan recovered his balance, got to his feet and caught motion out of the corner of his eye.

The soldier was lucky that the PDW gunner he'd winged was only able to use one hand on the weapon, because the start of the burst was wide and high. Bolan was once again on the ground, but this time he was facing the gunner. He pulled the trigger on the .44 Magnum pistol, spearing three more slugs into the darkness. There was yet another grunt.

The Executioner got to his feet again when he heard the soft padding of footsteps on the deck. He whirled, bringing the butt of his heavy pistol up to chin level on the masked foe. Jawbone popped like a lightbulb as three pounds of steel handgun met the point of the brawler's chin.

Thrown back, the swift, agile wrestler struggled to regain his footing when Bolan snapped a hard kick between the man's splayed legs. Testicles were driven into his crotch, bursting under the force of the stomp. This sapped the fight from the hand-to-hand brawler. Bolan swung his foot again, this time bringing down his heel in an ax-kick that was rewarded with the sound of crunching pelvic bone.

A dislocated shoulder might not have done the job, but no one was going to walk around on a fractured pelvis. Even so, Bolan dumped the nearly empty magazine from his Desert Eagle, reloaded, and triggered a skull-crushing bullet into the mauled, fallen foe. There was no reason to let a man suffer needlessly.

Now with a pronounced limp, Bolan swept into the

entrance where the injured PDW gunner had retreated. The gunman was slumped on the floor, sitting in a puddle of his own blood. The man was wearing body armor, but Bolan had fed the Desert Eagle with tungsten-cored rounds topped in Teflon. The chemical coating kept the dense steel from destroying the handgun as it was cycled and fired down the barrel, and that tungsten core met Kevlar and punched right through, even with the presence of a trauma plate. The high-density slugs had churned up the PDW gunner's intestines, and he finally bled out.

Bolan kicked the PDW away from the gunner's lifeless hands. "Winslow?" Bolan rasped. His mad minute of fighting with the two foes had left his voice hoarse. More than a little of it was pain from the head butt and the aggravating kick to his hip.

"I'd love to talk now, but the guys on the docks seem to have figured out that I'm up on the crane," Winslow answered.

Bolan pulled out his detonator and turned the switch to the master fire. He triggered it, and the remaining ten containers suddenly erupted, blowing apart as SLAMs went off within. Elsewhere, another six hidden charges also went off, Claymore mines left around the warehouse where the counterfeit cash was stored and the enemy had their offices. When he'd peered over the railing and down the gangplank, Bolan had noted that groups of men were heading toward the warehouse, presumably to pick up bigger, more dangerous weaponry, or at least to seek cover.

The half-dozen Claymores erupted, spitting a sheet of death across scores of Western Bloc and cartel muscle who had been brought in to supplement the smuggling operation. The roar of the explosions faded into cries of pain and dismay. Suffering was sprawled across the docks, and Bolan wasn't proud of his work. He and Winslow were outnumbered, and the soldier was loathe to allow Colombian law enforcement to bear the brunt of their murderous counterparts in the underworld. He'd spent a day setting up traps and familiarizing himself with the terrain to take any advantage he could get over a larger, deadlier force. Right now, he'd struck an army, and left it bleeding and reeling.

"Okay, I think I have time to talk now," Winslow said in the wake of the Claymore and container detonations.

"Scan the deck. Are there any more ninjas or gunmen in hiding?" Bolan asked. Three of the containers had already been on deck, and the soldier had blown one of them. The other two had gone up, and burning counterfeit cash lit up the deck of the freighter.

"I've got no movement down there," Winslow responded. "Where are you?"

"Rather not say," Bolan answered. He was recovering his breath. He looked down hallways and up a stairwell, knowing that even as he hunted, he was likely being stalked himself. So far, he'd taken down what could have been half of Molinov's mysterious specialists.

"So where should I go?" Winslow asked.

"Parachute off the crane and into the drink. You've done your job well enough," Bolan responded.

"That's bullshit. I've only tagged about fifteen. Twenty tops," Winslow argued.

Bolan grimaced. "This isn't a competition. You've gone above and beyond the call of avenging your friends. If you stay up there, someone will remember your position and might just fire a rocket at..."

"Jumping!" Winslow shouted. Out of a porthole, Bolan saw the streak of a rocket sail from the docks and toward the crane arm. The soldier scanned for any sign of his younger partner, even as the arm erupted with a brilliant yellow explosion.

He sent a prayer after the Secret Service agent and looked back to track the trail of the shoulder-fired missile. It was from the stern of the ship, and the Executioner wondered just what the hell was being thrown at him now. A rocket flared, sizzling its way toward the superstructure. Bolan turned and slid down a stairwell, gliding along the handrails. The rocket shooter had to have figured Bolan's position from the bellow of his Desert Eagle, because the grenade struck the doorway he'd entered moments ago.

The thunder of the detonation reverberated off the metal bulkheads, pounding at Bolan's brains even as he rolled at the bottom of the steps. He dragged himself through a portal, watching flaming debris bounce down the steps he'd just been in seconds before.

"Winslow?" Bolan whispered into his hands-free radio.

"Safe," came the response. "Well, as safe as a piñata in the dark."

"Hit the water and swim," Bolan replied.

"Will do," Winslow answered. Though he'd been equipped for a base jump off the crane, he still wouldn't disconnect his parachute harness and drop to the waves below from too high of an altitude. A matter of ten feet would mean the difference between being drenched, or hitting the Pacific Ocean hard enough to shatter his legs.

Bolan got back to his feet. A goon with a rocket launcher. He figured Molinov's strategy. Six specialists with various weapons, or unarmed combat, would be brought in to engage the Executioner with their chosen means of battle. So far, he'd survived three of them, one thanks to Winslow's position on the crane, the other two from pure skill and dogged determination.

Working against a foe who lobbed high explosives across hundreds of feet of deck, however, was going to be interesting. Bolan would handle that when he got there.

He looked up. The bridge of the freighter was on the decks above. Bolan had the advantage of knowing the layout of the ship, thanks to Stony Man Farm's computer records. With their help, he would be able to navigate within the hallways of the boat. He picked a route to take him to the next stairwell over, then moved out.

The bridge would be a good place to keep an eye on things from above, perhaps get a hold of that big f.50-caliber rifle, and give the enemy rocketeer something to consider.

That all depended on if there were more guards still in place on the ship, or if they had been routed or killed in the firefights on deck.

There also would be at least two more enemy specialists out there, possibly between him and the bridge.

Wiping his brow, he realized that something had lacerated his forehead. Bolan paused and wound a strap of cloth around the injury, taping it into place. He grimaced, realizing that this battle was taking more out of him than he'd counted on. The emplaced explosives, the preparation, it had all gone a long way toward evening the odds against the Western Bloc and the rest of Millagro and Molinov's minions, but the soldier knew that this, like most other battles, was hardly going to be a walk in the park.

One foot in front of the other, Bolan began his trek up the stairs to the bridge.

The Executioner was glad for the coated soles of his boots. While they did little to reduce the destructive force of one of his kicks, they went a long way to minimizing sound as he walked on metal. It was that quiet that gave him an advantage as he heard a footfall above. Bolan drew the Beretta 93R, thankful for its suppressor. In the close quarters inside the ship, it wouldn't wreck his hearing like the Desert Eagle. The hallways were echo chambers, and high-volume sound could almost knock a man out.

He aimed at the shadows on the stairwell above, looking for movement. One step, two steps. Risking a quick peek, then turning the corner. Whoever his opponent was, things weren't going to go easy. Fighting up stairs was a difficult thing. The enemy could have much more cover, and had all the time in the world.

Bolan, on the other hand, had to work his way up, trying to remain quiet.

That's when he saw the ugly black pipe poking over a railing. Bolan adjusted his aim to where its owner would be and triggered the Beretta. Instead of a flurry of grunts, he heard the impacts of hollowpoint rounds on metal and the sudden swish of a mop handle tumbling down from where it had been tied to the rail. Bolan cursed the ruse and ducked back swiftly.

The crash of a shotgun roared in the confines of the stairwell, the roar slamming down on him with nearly the same force that its discharge of buckshot would have carried. Blinking away the rattle his brain had taken, Bolan exited onto a deck, firing a burst to entice his opponent to follow.

Fifth opponent. Shot gunner.

Molinov had been playing too many video games, or he had simply picked some of the deadliest men he could find in their areas of expertise. In the confines of a ship, a man with a shotgun would be a terror. Shot would ricochet off metal bulkheads, bouncing behind cover and nailing the Executioner. He wasn't sure what kind of a weapon had been fired, but it must have been more than a mere 12-gauge. Either a 12-gauge 3-inch Magnum, or a 10-gauge from the sound of it.

Keeping to the shadows, he saw there was movement in the gangway off the stairs. He leveled his Beretta at the figure, but held his fire. The shadow was indistinct, and it moved oddly.

Rather than give away his position, Bolan pulled out a partially spent magazine, stripped a bullet from it and threw the round toward the doorway. Again, that mighty weapon discharged, and the Executioner saw a huge muzzle-flash, tearing through a windbreaker that had been waved over the doorway.

He heard the sound of a shotgun action breaking, empty shells hitting the deck.

The enemy gunman had a double-barreled 10-gauge, and whoever he was, he was strong enough to shoot two barrels simultaneously. At ranges out to twenty-five yards, that kind of firepower could cut a single man in two, especially with the right buckshot loads. Bolan knew that he was vulnerable to that. Even if he had been wearing body armor, a cannon like that would still crush bones, stray pellets tearing through his thighs or tearing through his face. Nothing, short of head-to-toe bomb-squad armor, could protect against a blast like that.

"Clever." The taunt came from the stairwell.

Bolan felt in his harness. He had one MGU-50G grenade left. He plucked it from its pocket and pulled the pin, counting down the fuse.

"Come on out. Let us see who is faster on the draw," the shotgunner said.

"Pull," Bolan growled, lobbing the miniature bomb down the hall. It bounced once, twice, through the doorway into the stairwell.

Bolan tucked himself behind the bulkhead even as the grenade detonated. The shotgunner pulled both triggers on his weapon, perhaps in an effort to shoot the bouncing grenade away from him, but the roar turned to an odd rain of metal on metal, ball bearings bouncing and landing on steps, flowing down.

Bolan peered around his cover and saw a mangled heap slide down the steps and into the open. A quick confirmation by flashlight showed Bolan that there was no way that this specialist was going to reload, or do anything else ever again. The grenade's shrapnel had torn him to shreds, leaving him a bloody lump of oozing muscle and partially stripped bone.

With a breath, Bolan advanced to the stairwell, climbing over the corpse.

Four down.

And Bolan wasn't certain if Millagro or Molinov were here on the freighter, or somewhere else.

Up. That was the only way to go.

MOLINOV CLUTCHED HIS bleeding gut. Millagro's patience had finally reached its end, and the Venezuelan snapped, putting two 9 mm bullets into the man's stomach. The Russian had thrown himself back into the office, kicking the door shut before more gunfire could chase him, and he reached the doorway into the warehouse beyond. His legs were rubbery, weak, and he could barely take two steps without a stumble.

Millagro's pistol barked again and again, the doorknob jerking as the wood was perforated with each shot.

Molinov knew that he was in a bad way. His strength was ebbing, and he had one pissed-off South American on his tail. Molinov had a revolver tucked into his pocket, but both of his hands were slippery, blood slicked. He didn't think that he could grip the .357 Magnum gun, let alone aim and pull the trigger. He staggered along, letting gravity help him slide down the steps, grimacing and grunting as he bounced over each stair.

Western Bloc gunmen were rushing in and out, grabbing firepower and more ammunition. They were all primed and ready for a battle, but when they saw the bleeding Russian, they measured him up.

I'm harmless, Molinov projected. He stumbled, bouncing off a crate and toppling to the floor.

The Colombian terrorists ignored the fallen Russian. He'd been shot, his worth had been diminished. They preferred to let him die while they threw themselves into battle against the enemy who had been hounding them these many years.

El Soldado was out there, a one-man war who had come to Colombia time and time again, acting as a tool of the devilish United States, a champion of the capitalism that they hated vehemently. To combat him would be an honor, to defeat him would bring them honor once the revolution was complete.

Let the bleeding Russian expire out of the way. They had battle to engage in.

Molinov blinked. Once. Twice.

His eyes snapped open, and his mouth was dry. Had he blacked out? Passed out from pain or blood loss? If so, for how long? There was the roar of dozens of rifles outside the warehouse. Gunmen were blazing away at the freighter.

What was going on? How was the battle going?

Molinov dragged himself to his feet, stumbled a couple of steps toward the windows.

That's when the world shook to pieces, six Claymore mines detonating in rapid progression. The purpose of the Claymore mine was not to focus destruction into one point, as with the shaped nose charges of the anti-tank rockets. Its purpose was to spread out pain and force, splaying wide with shrapnel and ball bearings in fans of destruction and devastation, .25-caliber pellets hurtling on the brink of a shock wave with all the speed and force of high explosives pushing them.

One Claymore produced a wall of death that could bring down a small patrol in the jungle. Six of them, expertly placed by the Executioner, had proved to be such an assembly that where had once been the unending cacophony of seventy rifles was now complete silence.

Molinov looked out over the devastation wrought by the single-chained detonation. Mangled corpses were strewed about the dock, severed limbs quivering, an occasional figure gathering enough strength to crawl a few inches before expiring.

Tumaco had become ground zero for the hand of death, and it had slapped down the Western Bloc forces of the FARC. How many were dead out there?

"All of them," Molinov answered himself. His hands were numb, tingly. He was close to the end of his life. The blood was draining from his limbs, the body diverting it to the torso, which hemorrhaged through its stomach.

He grimaced, looking down at the wound.

"There you are," Millagro said from behind him.

Molinov didn't bother turning. "I'm tired. Get it over with."

"Get what over with?" Millagro asked.

"Put the bullet in my head. I'm tired and I want to go to sleep," the Russian explained.

A strong hand grabbed him by the shoulder and whirled him. Angry eyes met Molinov's.

"No. You're not going to get an easy end. You don't deserve that you incompetent fuck!" Millagro snarled.

Molinov smirked. "Deserve? We both deserve the fires of hell, *amigo*."

Millagro shoved him back against the window, then looked past him.

"Dios mio," Millagro whispered.

"Prayer at this point," Molinov muttered with a chuckle.

"Did you see this?" the Venezuelan asked him.

"Who couldn't see it?" Molinov replied.

Millagro sneered. "You think this a joke?"

"The ultimate cosmic joke on the two of us. We played with fire, we took our fight to the United States and drew the wrath of her greatest defender," Molinov replied.

"Shut up," Millagro snarled. "You had all these perfect plans of how to deal with him. We're not even sure your specialists are still in action."

Explosions thundered in the distance. Molinov knew the sound of RPG shells striking their target.

"One of them is still out there fighting," the Russian answered. "But I doubt that he is going to be successful."

Millagro glared at him. He prodded Molinov in the belly with his foot. Blood pumped from the oozing wound, and the Russian's face paled, his teeth peeled from his lips in a grisly grimace. "Then I'll finish it."

Molinov coughed. Trickles of blood ran over his bottom lip. "Be my guest, idiot."

Millagro looked at the Russian, then raised the muzzle of his pistol to his face. "You do not deserve this."

Molinov broke into a cough, a long, wet, hacking spasm accompanied by sprays of gore from nose, mouth, gut wounds. The Russian toppled over, curling up into a ball. Blood puddled beneath him, spreading quickly.

Finally, the spasm ended.

The quick, clean death Molinov wanted hadn't been there for him.

Millagro wondered if anyone would get what he wanted this night.

CHAPTER TWENTY-ONE

Bolan reached the bridge's level, recovering much of his breath. He was still alive, he was still walking and he'd even managed to lose most of his limp. The ragged pain was draining from him. Maybe this was simply adrenaline, a second shot of energy kicking through his body.

The Executioner had been pushed to the edge like this before, and once this battle was done, he would sleep for hours, and awaken with aches that would hopefully disappear in a few days. His ears rang from the high-decibel thunder he'd released, and had been on the receiving end of over the past...fifteen minutes. It had been fifteen minutes since he blew that first container off the crane cable, starting the chaos and mayhem that had followed. As he entered the bridge, he looked out to see flames illuminating a terrain full of carnage.

Once more, Bolan realized, he had brought war to his enemies, and the results were horrifying. What he saw couldn't have been the work of one man, it was the result of a rampage by a living force of nature that struck out with violent wrath, crushing any and all in its path. Bolan drew his assessment back in.

It only looked that way. This was the efforts of planning, technology, the Executioner's experience. He'd brought every trick, every surprise, all of his weapons to this boat, and the freighter, the dock, were a testament of what one man could do with good tactics, good stealth and a nerve that made iron seem flimsy.

"Impressive work," a voice said behind him. Bolan turned and saw a man carrying a heavy .50-caliber sniper. It was a design that he couldn't place, and one he didn't really care to.

The man looked at the rifle in his hands, then shrugged. "This?"

Bolan nodded.

The man set down the rifle. "I got tired of my idiot partner firing goddamned missiles at the part of the boat I was in."

"Self-preservation," Bolan replied. He faced the new-comer, looked him over.

The man had a pair of pistols, one on each leg in a thigh holster. They were tactical holsters, not cowboy, but the butts of the two weapons poked up, each within a flicker of movement of his hands.

"Fast-draw artist," Bolan said. "The sixth member of this…anti-me group."

The gunslinger smirked. "Yeah. You have a hell of a reputation for a man with no name."

"Good or bad," Bolan answered. "Not ugly."

"All right, Clint. I don't need a name. I just know what you are."

"The end of people like you," Bolan said.

"Defiant," the gunslinger added. "Why do this? Why take on groups who throw this much at you? It can't be for fun. You look like hammered shit right now."

"Not fun. Duty," Bolan told him.

The gunslinger looked him over. "They call you the Soldier. But you're in no man's army."

"No. I have my own agenda. That doesn't always match national security."

The gunslinger took a few steps. He always remained square shouldered to Bolan. "You can tell what kind of a fighter I am. And, from this, I can tell what you are."

"What's that?" Bolan asked.

"A generalist. Someone who tries to think his fights through," the gunslinger said. "I was wondering why you went at this in a relatively sloppy manner. You could have hung back and destroyed this ship at leisure. You had the bombs on board."

Bolan nodded.

"But then, Millagro brought in the Western Bloc of the FARC. Those guys are crazy as a bag full of cats. They've killed plenty of folks in this town," the gunslinger added. "No. Blowing up the freighter wouldn't stop them."

Bolan didn't react to that assessment.

The gunslinger continued. "No. You wanted this to be a statement. This would be your treatise on violence in Colombia. It goes to show. You took on local cartel gunmen, terrorists, even hit a base inside Venezuela. And yet, you knew that your actions should be remembered, even if the enemy didn't know your name."

"Right," Bolan said. "Who I am is unimportant. The survivors, if any, have to learn to fear."

"Yeah, these crazy bastards got a little too uppity," the gunslinger agreed.

"Molinov brought you in. From where?" Bolan asked.

"Not important, like you said," the gunslinger responded. He squinted. "Desert Eagle. Unusual gun for a professional. A .50?"

"It's .44 Magnum," Bolan answered.

"Roll your own ammo for it?" the gunslinger asked.

Bolan nodded. "Me. Or close friends."

The gunslinger nodded in returned. "Same here. Course, mine is a little more mundane."

Bolan decided to let the man continue to talk.

"Matched pair of polymer frame hi-cap .45s," the gunslinger returned. "Polymer and fiberglass. The triggers are light, the firing pins are made of titanium and they're both ported with weighted guide rods. Full powered +P .45 ammo that kicks less than a .22 auto, and I've got thirty shots before I have to reload."

Bolan shrugged.

"A .44 Magnum and…is that a Beretta?"

Bolan lifted his arm. "Yes."

The gunslinger's eyes narrowed. "Naw."

"What?"

The gunslinger smirked. "You didn't once use a .44 Automag, did you? Had a Brigadier?"

"I've gone through my share of changes in equipment," Bolan answered.

The gunslinger took a step back, grinning.

"I know you, now. Why didn't you try sniping our guy?" he asked. "You used to do that in the old days. What was it that they called you?"

"I had more business to take care of," Bolan told him. "You know, I'd love to stay here all night, but I'd like to get to Molinov and Millagro."

The gunslinger nodded. He thumbed the straps off the twin custom .45s.

Bolan didn't have to do anything for his Desert Eagle.

"A fast draw against you. Goddamn!" the gunslinger said. "You could knock me over with a..."

Bolan lunged, ignoring his handgun and pulling out the talon-hooked Karambit knife. In one smooth movement, be brought the short edge up, his other hand clutching the fast-draw artist's shirt lapel.

As soon as the movement was over, the gunslinger staggered backward. His throat was opened from ear to ear, and his eyes were wide.

"No...fuh..."

"No fair?" Bolan asked.

The gunslinger didn't have even the strength to nod. Instead, he collapsed to his knees, crashing face-first to the floor.

Bolan sighed. "Fighting fair is for honorable men. You're working for a gangster."

The Executioner realized he was talking to a corpse, one he'd throated with one wicked slash of the Karambit. The blow had gone deep, despite a two-and-a-half-inch blade, the point having scraped bone in a nearly decapitating slash.

"Thanks for taking out your last buddy," Bolan told him.

He wiped off the hooked blade on the corpse's sleeve before rising.

Bolan heard panting from the stairwell, then snapped the blade back into its neck sheath. He transitioned to the Desert Eagle. The newcomer had not to have been in good physical condition, because his steps were slowing, breaths coming raggedly. The Executioner won-

dered if the gunslinger had lied about shooting the
rocket man, that he had sprinted across the length of
the freighter to come and attack him.

No. The fifty had been fired recently. He could still
smell the powder in the ports, and the gunman seemed
entirely too honest, too willing to protect his life and
secure his role as the man who brought down Bolan.

This was someone else.

The Executioner grabbed a fistful of collar and
hauled the corpse of the fast-draw artist up to its feet,
then pushed it, walking it into the doorway at the top
of the stairs.

The sudden appearance of the shadow did exactly
what Bolan wanted. A flurry of gunshots resounded in
the stairwell, and the lifeless body jerked under multiple impacts, rounds exiting its back and plunking into
the ceiling. Bolan had let go as soon as he heard the
first shot, the body leaning into the side of the doorjamb, thanks to gravity and the mechanics of the human
body. Even so, Bolan noticed that he had a fresh warm
rip in the sleeve of his blacksuit, the skin beneath blis-
tered by the graze.

A minor inconvenience, but if Bolan hadn't with-
drawn his hand, or had held the gunslinger up at a
slightly different angle, the 9 mm bullet would have
smashed his wrist into uselessness.

The shooting stopped, and Bolan could hear the
click of a magazine being released, its shell bouncing
on the stairs. He pushed through the doorway, lowering the Desert Eagle's muzzle and firing off two shots.
In the echo chamber of the stairwell, the Magnum pistol's twin issue was nearly as bad as the heavy shotgun

used on Bolan. He'd equalized the pressure in his ears before, but loud was still loud.

Down below, the enemy gunman let out a cry of fear as the bullets came close, but the Executioner's rounds had missed, not by much, but they only scared, not killed.

"Molinov?" Bolan called out.

Gunshots snapped upward, ringing off the ceiling to Bolan's left. Ricocheting rounds lost energy after fighting gravity and striking steel. *"Hijo de puta!"*

"Millagro," Bolan stated. "Mentirosa told me about you."

"What?" Millagro called weakly from down below.

"DGIM for Venezuela, working under Colonel Figueroa," Bolan spoke up. "Just a cog in the machine, a captain looking for the fast track to a promotion by involving himself in an economic attack on Colombia, right?"

"Shut up!" Millagro snapped.

"That's you," Bolan said. He moved slowly on the stairs, keeping well back, blending into the shadows. In the echoing stairwell, his voice rebounded, coming from odd directions with each step taken. It helped that Bolan was speaking directly, aiming his voice at walls that would reflect sound, bounce his words, obfuscate his position.

Another bullet. This one went right to a corner that Bolan had just talked into.

His ploy was working.

"You think you know so much?" Millagro asked. "You think you're so damned tough?"

"I'm not tough," Bolan replied. "Your people just sucked that much."

The curse he shouted was accompanied by a flurry of gunshots, five bullets stabbing into the flight of stairs above. Bolan had managed to close the distance with the Venezuelan *agent provocateur* silently, easing down one step at a time. He could make out the shadowy movement below. Millagro was on the retreat, snapping glances over his shoulder, his head twitching as he sought out the advancing Executioner.

"You're a fraud, McCormack!" Millagro spit. "You have everyone scared, and yet, I've shot at you, and you've shot at me, and I'm still alive! Where's this one-man army everyone says about the Soldier? One little screw head like me shouldn't be that tough that you have to take baby steps to come after me!"

"I'm feeling lazy."

Millagro punched a bullet to where Bolan bounced his echo.

"Speaking of lazy, I don't have to go far to kill Molinov, do I?" Bolan asked.

Millagro rolled out a long string of curses. Another magazine shell bounced on the floor. "The Russian? He's dead! He died slow, coughing up blood, curled up like a dying bug!"

"You sound proud of that," Bolan offered.

"He's the fuckup. Tries all these plans to draw your attention away from us. And you keep coming. You roll right over our hit squads. You crash along the river. You invade my home country and murder my people!" Millagro snarled. "All because he couldn't take you down!"

"Others have tried. It hasn't worked before. And

you... You sure as hell aren't going to succeed where they all failed," Bolan taunted.

Millagro was out of the stairwell now. Bolan had seen him dart through a gangway. He was where the dead PDW specialist had bled out. Metal clattered on metal, plastic scuffed on plastic. The Venezuelan picked up the corpse's submachine gun, because obviously, a handgun just couldn't cut it. Millagro allowed a chuckle to escape his lips.

"Come and get me, McCormack," Millagro taunted. "What have you got?"

"Your life," Bolan responded. "Your destiny. Your judgment."

The PDW barked. It was suppressed, but the supersonic projectiles whipped out, cracking the sound barrier as they left the barrel, pinging against metal. A ricochet struck the stair's rail, bounced up, sliced across Bolan's shoulder. It cut the skin, drew blood, burned. Bolan winced at the graze.

"Judgment?" Millagro repeated. "You're not a judge!"

"No. I'm just executing your sentence," Bolan returned.

More autofire, then Bolan climbed two steps as more of the supersonic projectiles entered the stairwell, bouncing off steel, rocketing from surface to surface. One of the bullets came to an abrupt halt in the wall right where he had been a moment ago.

"How are you going to do that, just hiding?" Millagro asked.

"Come in here and I'll show you," Bolan offered.

"I saw the mess you made of that other bastard,"

Millagro barked. "What did you do? Throw a grenade at him?"

The Executioner had used up his munitions in battle already. Corpses everywhere were laden with shrapnel from his grenades and the mines he'd laid as traps or hurled at them. Even so, Bolan wasn't going to give his enemy a status update on his equipment.

"Now you're quiet. What's wrong?" Millagro asked.

The sound of plastic scuffing plastic sounded again. The Venezuelan reloaded the PDW, the clear plastic box settled into its sleeve on the top of the weapon, ready to unleash another fifty rounds that bridged the gap between pistol and rifle. They weren't large bullets, but they had a significant powder charge behind them, and their velocity made up for what little mass they carried.

Bolan had used the compact weapon plenty of times before, cutting enemies in two easily, maneuvering it in the tightest of quarters. Millagro had Bolan outgunned, but there was no way the soldier would be outfought. This battle was one of wills. Millagro kept going for kill shots, while Bolan conserved his ammunition, took his time, waited for the Venezuelan to make a mistake.

The evidence for a breakdown was already clear in the man's voice. Millagro was on the edge, more nervous than confident, even with fifty-one rounds on tap for his weapon. This was a war that was being won on the mental level.

"McCormack?" Millagro called.

Bolan's breathing slowed. He was a shadow pressed to the wall, Desert Eagle leveled at the doorway to the stairwell. A quiet, deadly calm entered the superstructure of the ship. Even though there were sirens outside on the dock, here in the stairwell, silence ruled.

The soldier was now a hollow void, and nature and curiosity both abhorred a vacuum. Footsteps sounded, closing with the portal. Millagro's patience had given out. He needed to know why the American had grown quiet, he needed to see if the man was wounded, or just what trap was being set for him. It was inevitable. Humans needed answers, needed to open doors that should remain closed, touch the stove to see if it was still hot.

The muzzle of the SMG poked through the doorway, sweeping left, right. Up. Down. It moved, Millagro peering, trying to see around corners, look at blind spots, figure out just what the hell his enemy was trying to do.

"McCormack!" he bellowed. "Goddamn you, McCormack! Where are you?"

Bolan had been answering him every other time, responding with a taunt, but now, his silence was the greatest taunt. Millagro leaned through the doorway, his head an easy target only two feet from the muzzle of the Desert Eagle.

"McCor..." Millagro shouted again, but he turned his head, looking down the .44 Magnum barrel. His words trailed off.

The Executioner pulled the trigger, and a 240-grain hollowpoint round struck the Venezuelan between his eyes. The back of his skull burst apart as the heavy slug exited, blowing brains all over the wall.

"McCormack?"

This time his name was being called over the hands-free radio. It was Villanueva's voice.

"How is Winslow?" Bolan asked.

"Fine. The harbor patrol fished him out of the water," Villanueva answered. "You?"

"I could use an aspirin, some bandages and maybe a nap," Bolan told him.

"You've earned it," Villanueva replied.

Bolan stepped over Millagro's corpse, then looked at the "specialist" brought in from Malaysia. "I might have earned a rest, but this is just the first steps of this mission. These guys brought in a strike force from across the Pacific."

"What are they going to do without the counterfeit money?" Villanueva asked.

Bolan frowned. "That's what I have to figure out."

He thumbed the safety back on his Desert Eagle, then pushed the weapon back into its holster.

"What about you?" Villanueva asked.

"There will be plenty of time to rest when I'm dead," Bolan told him.

This skirmish in the Executioner's War Everlasting was far from being over. He had an ocean to cross to look for more of the conspirators, to figure out what this power play was.

* * * * *

Don't miss the action-packed conclusion of BLOOD MONEY.
Look for SuperBolan #161
EXPLOSIVE DEMAND in October 2013.

TAKE 'EM FREE
2 action-packed novels
plus a mystery bonus

NO RISK
NO OBLIGATION
TO BUY

GE13

JAMES AXLER

DEATH LANDS®

Motherlode

JAMES AXLER
DEATH LANDS
Motherlode

A struggle for survival
at the end of the line...

Seeds of Sustainability

Desperately short of supplies, Ryan Cawdor and his crew approach the prosperous-looking ville of Amity Springs. Hired to retrieve a stolen relic, the band is quickly caught in a power struggle between two strong-willed lady barons. Each covets the predark goods buried in Amity's backyard. But they are not alone in their zealous desire. All that stands between a mother lode of buried bounty and the destructive power of unchecked greed are grim warriors determined to survive another day in the Deathlands....

Available November wherever books and ebooks are sold.

AleX Archer
SUNKEN PYRAMID

**At the bottom of a Wisconsin lake
lies a deep secret....**

Determined to investigate her friend's death—and find out why
another is the prime suspect—archaeologist and TV host
Annja Creed starts gathering
the pieces of an erratic
puzzle. At the center of it all
is an ancient pyramid at the
bottom of a Wisconsin lake...a
discovery that could completely
rewrite Mesoamerican
history. But with each puzzle
piece uncovered the mystery
becomes more dangerous. And
what Annja knows can—and
will—kill her....

*Available November wherever
books and ebooks are sold.*

An ancient Mayan temple at the bottom of a lake leads to murder...

ROGUE Angel
AleX Archer
SUNKEN PYRAMID

GOLD EAGLE ®

GRA45